DAY STRIPPER

A MYSTERY

JENNY Scholten

New Victoria Publishers
Norwich, Vermont

Published by New Victoria Publishers Inc., PO Box 27 Norwich, Vt. 05055
A Feminist Literary and Cultural Organization founded in 1976.

Cover Art by Jack Pabis

Printed and bound in Canada
1   2   3   4   5   2003   2004   2002   2001
2000

Library of Congress Cataloging-in-Publication Data

Scholten, Jenny, 1968-
    Day stripper / Jenny Scholten
        p.   cm.
    ISBN 1-892281-10-4
        1. Stripteasers--Fiction.   2.Labor unions--Fiction. 3. San Francisco(Calif.)--Fiction. -- I. Title.

PS3569.C52547 D39 2000
813' .6--dc21

                                                    00-039432

To Pablo

Chapter One

I don't normally chase customers out of Naughtyland. In the two years I've worked as a stripper, I've learned to tolerate catcalls, wandering hands, the breast fetish and the mommy complex. Besides, I depend on these men for my income and the majority of them are well behaved. It doesn't pay to be impolite in return. The few who are bounced certainly are never followed, at a run, down Jones Street.

But this guy had not only batted my breasts around like tetherballs, he'd also extracted my small wad of earnings from my bra, where I kept the twenties I charged for each lapdance close to my heart and safe. Nobody fools around with my money. For me it wasn't just green paper, it was independence, it was freedom and it wasn't easy to come by. I'd removed myself from the polite society of those who did their jobs in clothing in order to earn a wage that I could live on in San Francisco. This guy wasn't getting away with my hard-earned hundred.

My ankles turned painfully as my four-inch heels pummeled concrete. Running in high heels wasn't all that much harder than dancing in them. They slowed me down, but I didn't want to kick them off and risk slicing bare feet on a shattered crack vial, then bathing the cuts in a fetid yellow puddle.

As the evening fog pressed smells of urine and Chinese take-out into the Tenderloin, my lungs were shredding and I was losing sight of the mudflap of yellow hair that marked my lanky quarry like an enemy flag. He had too big of a lead. I grabbed my breasts to keep them inside a bikini top made of a pair of triangles no bigger than quilt pieces and sped up. Nights are cold year-round by the Bay and it was only late April. Chill bumps popped up on my skin as I pushed past onlookers who didn't have the courtesy to move, or maybe wanted a free feel. I was half a block behind my target when he stopped and looked back at me from the corner of Market Street.

When I got close enough to see the round white outline of a snuff tin in the back pocket of Yellow Hair's boot-cut jeans, I jumped and tackled him. It was like wrestling a wiry Gumby. I went for his hair and his crotch. In an instant my former customer had slithered out of my grasp and wrenched one of my arms behind my back. He torqued the arm and I gracelessly fell. He released my wrist and jumped between a cable car and an electric bus that moved as slowly as a bride-to-be and her escort down Market Street.

Powered by electricity, San Francisco's bus system runs without noise. Antennas connect the fleet to a grid of thick cables that sag like old clotheslines above the city's streets. I watched the buses' umbilical progress smelling the acrid cloud of Brut the man's flight had left behind. By the time the buses passed, Yellow Hair and my hundred dollars had vanished.

"Shit."

"He'll come back to you, baby." Our momentary tussle had attracted an onlooking crowd of homeless people and patrons of a nearby Wendy's. Other words of encouragement followed. An elderly gent who appeared to be wearing his laundry pile beneath several blankets gave friendly advice. "Put something on. It's cold out."

I stood and brushed unidentified grit off my backside. A young man poked me in the shoulder with the straw that stuck out of his yellow soft drink cup. "You looking for a date?" he said. He shoved twenty or so French fries into his smile, then examined the four inadequate black triangles of my bikini.

I smiled back, minus the foodstuff. "I don't know. You see, I haven't had the opportunity to see you in your underwear."

I left him with his pants tangled around his knees so he couldn't follow.

I walked back to Naughtyland at a slower pace. The street atmosphere of San Francisco's Tenderloin district varies from block to block, depending on what is on offer nearby, but most local citizens consider all of the neighborhood's blocks sleazy. Although it divides the Financial District from City Hall, the Tenderloin isn't listed in any guidebook. Tourists headed from the Powell and Market cable car turnaround to UN Plaza walk through a community as uncharted as Conrad's Congo. It's the part of the city where the restaurants are all fluorescent-lit and ethnic, the residents pass the time on the sidewalks, and the groceries are sold in convenience stores alongside liquor and Lotto. It's the neighborhood forgotten until someone remembers they need to score a hooker, or some cocaine. It's the place to go for stolen electronics. It's the place to see a live nude girl. These neighborhoods seem inevitably to teem across a city's flat bottomlands. Perhaps shame runs downhill.

Live Nude Girls. The words pumped over Naughtyland's door, alternating blue, then red. The neon sputtered the words, flickering like a mosquito zapper. The colors rang off the club's plate glass lobby windows. Red, then blue highlighted the spiderweb cracks made by a bullet aimed low. A boyfriend of one of the dancers had taken a revenge shot the year before. I opened the door into the dark theater lobby.

"Aisling. Where've you been?" Lance's voice startled me. The sign's glare prevented me from seeing into the lobby from the street. Lance had started working at Naughtyland about a month before, and his new-guy enthusiasm for his bouncer job didn't seem to be faked for the boss's benefit. He stood leaning against the plate glass. I should have known he'd be lurking in the lobby somewhere, positioned so that no one could approach him from behind.

"I've been doing your job. Bouncing, that is. Where were you? That guy got away with my hundred dollars."

Lance moved the thin beam of his penlight from a catalog of military supplies to each of my eyes. He held the small flashlight in his fist, forearm braced, as though he were delivering an uppercut. I focused on the shiny rectangle of his polished brass belt buckle while my pupils tooled down from the interrogation lighting. Lance believed in camouflage. For his night job in Sin City his uniform was black, from cloth epaulettes down to the boots he deliberately scuffed to cut the glare. Only the brown curl that began at his widow's peak dared to step out of formation by refusing to obey pomade.

"You're about to miss your set. Give me forty and I don't tell Mose Junior about your close call." Satisfied that I was blinded and therefore temporarily neutralized, Lance returned to looking at his military supply catalog. He shone his penlight onto glossy photographs of the kind of knives meant to be carried between the teeth.

"I think I'll make it in time, thanks." Inside the club, Bruce Springsteen was rasping at a decibel level certain to hasten deafness. "Dancing in the Dark" was Cameron's second song of three. I knew her set by heart; it never varied. I had at least five minutes. "You're giving yourself away, you know. That buckle could be seen miles behind enemy lines."

"Shut it. I can still fine you. Don't know why people pay to see you." Lance had the kind of smile in which only the bottom teeth show.

7

"Here I am getting it for free."

I pushed through the black curtain that divided the lobby from the club's interior. My eyes had to readjust to the stage area's psychedelic lighting scheme. Disco balls pixilated the spotlights and spun galaxies of colored dots across the floor, walls, stage and the ten or so customers. Naughtyland's interior was small, so the ten men felt like a crowd. Lone, slouched figures seemed frozen to the round plastic tables. Onstage, Cameron teased the hem of her miniskirt upward. The customer's faces followed her like flowers turning toward the sun. A few bolder sorts had chosen to sip their nonalcoholic beers while leaning against the runway, baseball caps turned backward, their faces, at lucky moments, only three inches from some part of a live nude girl. The stage poked their chests like a stuck-out tongue.

Before I discovered stripping, I worked a variety of jobs. Though I wasn't aware of it when I filled out the applications, all of my previous jobs turned out to be in the sex industry. I was a restaurant hostess, barely decent in the off-the-shoulder hacienda dress they gave me as a uniform, until I discovered that the male host, though he wore a more demure outfit, was paid more money. I was a photographer's assistant, until he tried to feel me up in the darkroom. As a waitress, I actually had my ass pinched, an event with unfortunate timing that caused me to drench the pincher and his slice of strawberry pie with three large iced teas. I was fired for that one. Sexual harassment was clearly going to be part of any workplace and, since that was the case, I was blunt enough to appreciate it being the entire point of my workplace. I now received generous compensation for specializing in it. My momma impressed upon me, mostly by example, the importance of not being dependent on someone else for money. As a professional sex object, my financial independence was assured. Unless, of course, I continued to give private dances to pickpockets.

The dressing room was in chaos. The small room's smell of sweat, tobacco smoke and floral perfumes had thickened to the saturation point, threatening to drip in the humid air. Women leaned into the dance-school-sized mirror to rub in lipstick. Others sat against their reflections talking on cell phones. Jeans, boots, padded uplift bras and glittery spike heels drifted up to the row of gray lockers and made dangerous piles all over the pitted red rug. A countertop along the back wall slowly melted under smoking curling irons that forged new elements from spills of make-up and polyester thong underwear. A coffee urn dripped an expanding caramel puddle into the mess.

I opened my locker. It was identical to the one I had in high school except for a stenciled "Aisling" across the front. A leopard-print bra and panty set fell into a lacy embrace at my feet.

My stripper name is what my first husband, who was Irish, wanted to name the daughter he wanted us to have and raise on a bog somewhere in the moonscape of Connemara. He would dig peat for a living and I would bake soda bread. We'd have locals over for Guinness at the trailer and entertain them with my exotic dialect of the American South, which resurfaces when I'm drunk. But a few days before his Resident Alien status had come through Conor went back to Ireland alone. There were many things about America he'd never understood: bagels, four-lane highways, casual adultery. From my point of view, it had been a casual marriage. He'd needed a green card; I'd needed financial aid for Ohio State. Conor never understood my point of view, either. He's no doubt better off in the cozy little green quilted land where divorce is barely legal and things are slow and perfect and happy. Aisling is pronounced Ashling.

The smell of Liz Taylor's Passion suddenly elbowed away the competition. I looked up to find Jossie, my best friend at work, gesturing in disgust at my leopard-print panties. "I would ask you how long it's been since you've washed those," she said, "but I won't because we've got real troubles here. You know Peaches?" Jossie grabbed my elbow. Tall and thin, she was deceptively strong with the kind of stiletto-shaped body created to part sheaths of stretch-knit.

"You've got troubles? Some asshole just stole a hundred bucks off me." I ripped off my black bikini bottoms by untying the loopy bows on each side and was reaching to untie the top when my arm was immobilized. "Let go. I'm onstage in like two minutes."

"A hundred dollars? You'll earn it back. Come with me. You've got to see this." Jossie pulled the string at my neck and the two black triangles slithered toward my waist.

"Did you hear me? I just lost a hun. I'm trying to change. I'm on next."

"Baby, this is bigger than money. Come on." She grabbed my elbow to steer me toward the crowd at the mirror.

I let myself be steered, because Jossie is almost impossible to resist and because her remark had left me temporarily dumbfounded. At Naughtyland, nothing was "bigger than money." Money was as overvalued to strippers as Parisian francs or London pounds to tourists.

Regular United States twenties were as mysterious and romantic as a foreign currency, inflated by the things we'd done to earn them. No dancer ever talked about money light-heartedly. Jossie normally considered getting money stolen the gravest of tragedies.

Peaches was a petite dancer with a gush of straight black hair and clear apricot skin that needed no concealer. Like most of the dancers at Naughtyland and many of the other clubs in town, she was Asian American. We found her applying mascara, her face three inches from the wall-to-wall mirror. When she pulled back and held herself still, unblinking, to let the tar she'd brushed on her lashes harden into unsmudgeable crust, I saw her face. Peaches' left eye was swollen and blackening within its now visible encirclement of bone. Where her pink dusting of blusher should have gone, the skin grew taut over purple swells. Her face looked like the ground side of a cider apple. Jossie looked grimly into the mirror for my reaction.

"Are you okay?" I asked Peaches, after a moment of shock. Rumors flew around Naughtyland; about Peaches the latest whisper was that her boyfriend beat her. I ignored the gossip, but maybe this time the whisperers had been right. Lots of women in my profession have trouble with their boyfriends. They have to lie about where they work, or put up with a bad attitude from the guy who hates the fact that his girlfriend takes off her panties in public but sure likes the money that such activity brings home. Boy trouble was a common dressing room complaint.

Jossie had heard the rumors about Peaches, maybe had started them. "Can you wait and inquisition her later? She has to go onstage in thirty minutes. She's got to be presentable in half an hour, unless she's going to do the battered housewife act, so lend me your pancake. You two are about the same color."

My friend was wrong about our complexions. I'm of white trash descent. I wordlessly retrieved my compact from my locker and handed it to Jossie. Peaches' face looked bad, but she seemed angry rather than pained. She stood impatiently while Jossie dusted M.A.C. Ivory-Peach powder over her cheeks. Peaches was new to the club, had been working there about three weeks and I didn't know her well. She was friendly, quiet, and she kept her distance. From me at least. It was impossible for anyone to keep her distance from Jossie.

"This isn't thick enough, you got liquid?"

"Of course not. That stuff clogs your pores."

Jossie glared at me, annoyed, "Who else is pale as Casper...

Plantagena." She strutted off to find a more powerful bruise-disguiser.

"Boy trouble?" I asked Peaches, after Jossie was out of range.

"No. I've heard the rumors about me, too. Don't believe the hype."

"I usually don't. When did this happen?"

"Last night."

"After work?"

"Obviously."

"Who did this to you?"

Peaches examined her face in the mirror, running her fingers delicately over her jaw stippled with four bruises where blood vessels had exploded under the impact of knuckles. She didn't seemed worried about the bruises, her swelling features or the fact that she was expected to perform in full drag in thirty minutes. Instead she had the focused yet distant expression that my roommate Hugh got when he was working on cryptography, one of his hobbies. Like she was thinking how to maximize the points of her Scrabble word. Or determining which customer to approach for a lapdance by factoring in his race, age, net worth, attitude, nationality and willingness to spend money on a small-busted Asian girl and whether he was worth her time.

After a moment she shook her head, then winced at the pain of the movement. "Long story."

"I've got one minute."

"I'm okay, stop staring. I only came in to avoid the fine. I'm going to do my show and go home. Aren't you on now? Wasn't that Cameron's last song?"

"Yeah."

"Ziggy Stardust" was beginning to fade out. I still had a pair of short-shorts to negotiate before I could take the stage. Peaches twisted a tube of lipstick and ran a half moon of bright red across her swollen bottom lip.

"Go on. You'll get fined." We were charged fifty dollars for getting to the stage late or missing our set. We were charged one hundred and fifty dollars by management if we didn't show up for a shift we'd been scheduled for. One hundred for the stage fee, fifty more for missing our set. It was an effective solution to absenteeism. She insisted, "Look, I'll be fine. After tonight, this will all be over with. Go on."

Jossie's red sequin-clad figure reappeared in the mirror at the end of the row of lockers and I ran to finish getting into drag.

I was struggling into the skin-tight pair of Levi's cut short as a bitten nail that I always began my show with when I heard the first notes of Lyle Lovett's "She Makes Me Feel Good." Shit. My song. I grabbed a pair of pliers out of my locker and used them to haul up the over-taxed zipper. An old trick I'd learned from Momma. I did my second windsprint of the night to the tall red-velveteen curtain that was our entrance to the stage.

I enjoy dancing. We dance several sets each night, depending on the number of women that show up to work. At least I enjoy the first two songs out of the requisite three, before I get bored with the pain of my tensed thighs, the country music I always danced to and the sweat that finally breaks under the hot lights.

Red lighting is a constant backdrop. Bright varicolored lights scurry through it. Onstage, a dancer's retinas are left so confused that all she can see is her own body in the wall-to-wall mirrors with disembodied heads staring at it.

Since I am more interesting to me than the disembodied heads, I often look at myself while I dance. I am almost six feet tall with the help of high-heeled black cowboy boots. My breasts are just big enough to sag. Wavy dark brown hair, highlighted in red, falls past my shoulder blades. I wear the requisite strata of liners and shadows in shades dark-er than my green eyes. More powder creates the illusion of cheekbones in a round face. I don't consider my face prettier than average or my body especially well-proportioned, nevertheless, dollar bills are always anted up for me.

For my sets I wear cowboy-themed clothes. Aisling is a country girl, and in the niche market I work in, it is better to keep one's image con-sistent. That night I chose my small red suede vest so my breasts popped out through the fringe. My ass, which is bigger than fashion magazines approve of, fell far below the cutoffs. For a little pizzazz, I strapped a silver plastic gun around my hips with a black leather hol-ster. It was a squirt gun and when I noticed audience members' eyes glazing over, I would give it to lucky customers to spray me with. They always aimed it at my tits.

After my three-song performance I landed a customer, a polite if heated Malaysian businessman dressed in a Western suit and turban. We went to one of the cubicles. These are a few square feet of the floor curtained off with the ubiquitous black drapery to provide the illusion of privacy. One chair is within; it's a shade lighter than pitch black inside. I'm never sure whether the darkness is to disguise the beauty flaws of us women or to absolve the shame of the men. About twenty such cubi-cles rim the walls of the club. It can be tricky to find an unoccupied one, rather like looking for an empty stall in a ladies room, with similarly embarrassing consequences. Customers happily pay more to have lap-dances inside a cubicle. It's a lot less humiliating for dancer and customer alike when these ungainly events take place without an audience.

I straddled this man. Grabbing his turban for stability, I ground my panties on top of his crotch. My thighs burned with the pain of supporting my entire weight. Joints cracked from the impossible spatial configurations my gyrations demanded between inner thigh, spine and buttocks. I was sure I was doing permanent damage to my lower half and no workman's compensation would be forthcoming. The song was "What's Love Got To Do With It?" and I was sweaty after one minute of it. After paying to be sat on for five more songs, my customer loosened up.

"I have three wives." He spoke in halting English.

"Really?" Great, a talker. I hated talkers.

"Yes, I am a lucky man, no?"

"Oh, yes. Where are your wives now?"

"Can you show me the pussy?"

"No." That wasn't part of the repertoire in the cubicles.

"Show me, show me the pussy. I want to see how to please the woman. My wives, she don't let me see nothing." He grabbed my ass.

"Time's up." I probably should have explained about the clitoris as a favor to the three wives, but screw it, I thought, I wasn't getting paid for sex education.

I clambered off the Malaysian. "So quick?" he protested.

"Thank you." I smiled sweetly and opened the curtain for him, letting in the slightly less dim light of the main floor of the club. He reshuffled his pants.

As he left, not bothering to wave, I noticed that Jossie was gesturing me over to her table. Two tables near the entrance were reserved for dancers, but every shift that she worked, the one to the right was the exclusive territory of Jossie. The other thirty or so dancers never complained. Jossie sat alone. Her legs were crossed in such a way that one, light brown and perfect, lay exposed by the slit of her dress. My friend worked as a hostess, which meant she sat with men and conversed with them over soft drinks they bought her at twenty dollars each. She kept ten. I'd far rather dance naked for customers than have to chat with them and didn't envy her her job. I slipped into the other plastic chair at her table.

13

"Buy you a drink?" I said. The City of San Francisco had proclaimed that naked girls and alcohol don't mix, so the only beer served at Naughtyland was the nonalcoholic brand O'Doul's. A good many customers seemed to get drunk off it anyway.

"Got one." She had three, actually, soft drinks in skinny glasses with red straws arranged in an arc in front of her, the ice in various stages of melt diluting the caramel color. "How'd I do, baby?" Jossie indicated the stage with a lift of her freshest Diet Coke. Peaches was up there, hooking a leg around the pole, holding poses for long seconds, her movements bearing no relationship to the beat of her music, "LA Woman," by The Doors. "Can't even tell, right? I loaned her your leather bikini to cheer her up. It looks better on her."

"Thanks."

"Well, you're the one who leaves your locker open for all the world to paw through your cheesy underwear."

"People like to borrow my shoes. She looks good."

Jossie had done an expert job on the dancer's face. It was now a uniform, though aggressively beige hue and giant red seventies-style sunglasses concealed its entire upper half. My leather bikini was the sickroom pink of those peppermint lozenges favored by old ladies. The pastel color lent the battered stripper some innocence. Colored lights spun over her skin giving it the appearance of a neon leopard's. Peaches looked like the caricature of womanhood that Naughtyland's customers expect.

"Baby, you do have that shoe fetish. Know my secret? Don't skimp on the base. Liquid. I don't care if it is the consistency of crude oil. You've got to slap it on there and don't be shy about it."

"Well, she looks uniform. Congratulations." I'd have appreciated Peaches' artificial color more if I'd known what she'd look like the next time I'd see her.

But I only wondered who punched her?

I felt expensive cloth brush my bare arm. "Would you excuse us, baby?"

"Sure." I stood. A man in a suit was waiting to take my place. His belly was headed south, the light shirtfront a punch through the dark wings of his sportcoat. His leather shoes were both wide and widely-stanced. That's all I noticed about him. Jossie had many such visitors, men as expensive as she was. The shine of this one's gold watch winked out as my friend slid her manicured hand slowly down his wrist.

I went looking for another lapdance.

The dressing room smelled of sweat even more pungently at the end of the shift. By two in the morning my hair had humidified into sticky crinkles and the pancake was no longer able to muscle away the bags under my eyes. Wearily, I pulled my night's earnings out of my Wonderbra and tossed it into my locker. I'd removed the garment's push-up pads in order to have a place to store my tips. Wonderbras are a boon to dancers in more ways than one. What other kind has a built-in wallet?

Jossie joined me at my locker as I was stepping into my hip-hugger stretch pants. My engineer boots were low heels, so Jossie towered over me by six inches, ten if the measurement included her sprayed upsweep. She was dressed for her cab ride home in a sheath minidress. The strap of a silver evening purse divided her deltoids from her collarbone. Jossie didn't look much different in real life.

Clothes were as comforting as a goose down quilt after seven hours in the grip of thong panties and underwire bras. Jossie and I compared notes about the shift, who'd done well, who'd done poorly, who'd gotten frustrated and left early. Jossie kept tabs on everybody, and at the end of a shift she could tell you exactly how much money every dancer had made, if one was rude enough to be interested.

"Peaches left after her set," she said, watching me dress. Going home after one set was permissible. As long as you danced once and paid your fee, you could abandon the field to the other strippers. "Where'd you get that bra? One of your mother's cast-offs?"

"I know it's frumpy but I've got to be comfortable." It was white cotton and loose enough to fasten in front, then spin around.

"Not like you'll be showing it to anyone later, I guess."

"What's your take on Peaches' bruises?"

"Aren't they the work of her man?"

"Come on," I pulled my shirt out of my locker, causing a high-heel avalanche. "That's the old story. She denies it. You can come up with something more melodramatic than that."

"I've got an idea, baby, but you wouldn't believe it."

"I wouldn't? Why not? Is my imagination as frumpy as my bra?"

"She's not what she seems, dig?"

"No I don't dig. What does she seem like?"

"I'm saying you wouldn't believe me, but I would stay away from her business."

"Your cab's here," Lance parted the curtained doorway that divided the dressing room from Naughtyland's main floor. The house lights were on in the club, and it was suddenly obvious how dirty the place was. The black curtains were hemmed in crud, the plastic tables stained from spills. Oily smears blemished the silver pole onstage and the mirrors behind it. Lance had been speaking to Jossie. For some reason, he was always polite to her. I suspected he had a crush.

"Gotta go, baby. Can't keep my date waiting."

"Your date?"

She leaned across me to check her make-up in the tiny mirror I'd affixed to the inside of my locker door. "One of my regulars. Grady, he came in earlier tonight. When Peaches was onstage. Gold watch?"

I shook my head. "I met about a hundred men tonight. Sorry."

"Well he was one of the richest you'll ever meet." Jossie was already sweeping toward an exit. As she passed by Lance she raked his grease-trained platoon of curls with a manicured hand. He watched her with an open look so odd on him that it took me a moment to register the expression as a slight smile. Dog-like, he rolled his head to follow her touch. I turned away in disgust.

"And you, the boss wants to see you." Lance said.

"Who me?"

"Yeah, you." He yelled it to the curtains, which he'd let fall shut behind him after following Jossie out.

Our boss never wanted to see any of us, unless it was time to pay him his nightly cut. He literally didn't want to see us. He was terrified of a sexual harassment lawsuit resulting from an inadvertent glimpse of a bare breast.

"Shit." I began with the bottom button of my clingy black rayon shirt. The shirt gapped slightly over my chest and I thought of all the things my momma would find wrong with it: too dark for my complexion, breast pocket adds bulk where you don't need it, really should fix that bust gap with a hidden safety pin. What could Mose Junior want with me? My leather jacket weighed me down like a drunk's hug.

Chapter Two

"What do you mean I'm laid off?" I was standing on the worn wall-to-wall carpeting in front of the wobbly metal desk in Mose Junior's office. The bass line of the Black Sabbath tune that played downstairs for the benefit of the bouncers, who were supposedly cleaning the place, vibrated my engineer boots.

Naughtyland's manager's office is upstairs, small and furnished only with a desk and a metal filing cabinet. One drawer was labeled Human Resources, the other Payroll. The wood-paneled walls were decorated with posters of naked women. The room did have one small window, facing the alley. Judging by the oppressiveness of the air, which smelled like decades of Italian sausage subs and Marlboros, that window hadn't been opened in years.

Mose Junior leaned his greyhound-thin frame backward in his desk chair. His clothes were always too large for him. The navy suit of supple cloth that he wore draped backwards with his tilt, leaving behind the outlines of his long bones.

"What can I do. I hear you chase a customer. This is not good for business. You see the pre, predict—"

"Predicament."

"—The situation you put me in." Mose Junior's skull was the prominent feature of his thin face. He looked at me with brown eyes set far back behind fleshless cheekbones. I thought of flashlights, sturdy round exoskeletons with small bulbs deep within.

"That guy stole one hundred dollars from me."

"I'm sorry."

"I've got bills to pay."

The flashlights blinked and looked away. My boss picked up a cigarette with a long-boned hand made paler by the contrast with his sleeve. "Sit down," he said.

"Where?" His was the only chair.

"On the desk, here." He cleared away a stack of porn magazines, all with the banner headline "Naughtyland's Peoria!" inked across Peoria's bare chest on their covers, to make room for me. "I am sorry for your bills. But no chasing away business! Let the bouncers do their jobs." He held a lighter to the Marlboro, his face fluttering like a tent in a sandstorm with the effort to ignite it.

So Lance had ratted on me. It figured. Since I am female and haven't undergone Special Ops training, the bouncer probably considered me underqualified to chase someone down the street.

Mose Junior ran a hand through his thick pile of slicked-back black hair, his body's only luxury. He dragged on his cigarette more often than I breathed. He turned the flashlights on me. "Okay. I go easy on you so you don't have to be waitress for two dollars an hour. You can come back in two weeks."

"Two weeks?"

"Here, you have a paycheck." He handed me the document, made out to Audrey Lily and signed with the usual indecipherable scribble. My real name is Aubrey Lyle. Naughtyland's management team, which was Mose Junior and his father, also named Moses, wasn't detail-oriented. I was always amazed when my bank accepted these things. "You can pay Lance downstairs."

Dancers got paid minimum wage in a check to make us official employees. Of course we had to pay back the amount of our check, in cash, straight into the till. Payment was just a formality so we wouldn't have independent contractor status. Moses Senior had explained it to me once. "Mosey is afraid that as independent contractors, you girls would sue us every time you trip on stage. You Americans, you always want to sue." The senior Moses always referred to his son as "Mosey," though Mose Junior was in his thirties and had two families of his own. One set of wife and kids remained in the old country.

"Thanks a lot," I said.

"What can I do?" My boss held up his hands. His sleeve fell below an expensive watch, cinched to its tightest but still dripping crookedly from his bony wrist. "I'll be happy for you to come back in two weeks."

"I can't believe this." I stuck the wad of gum I'd been chewing onto the neatly trimmed bush of one of the poster girls as I left his office.

Fuming, I stomped down the stairs and back through the club, which now reverberated with a deafening version of "Back in Black" by AC/DC. This fit my mood nicely. I felt like banging my head against the wall. I considered not turning in the cash equivalent of my paycheck on the way out, but that would have gotten me fired for good.

Lance was wiping the counter of Naughtyland's 'full bar.' This was a two-foot-long piece of plastic, positioned beside the curtained-off front door of the club. It supported a cash register and a few glasses. Tucked underneath the counter was a refrigerator short enough to be shut with a knee. I wasn't used to seeing Lance under lighting. Illuminated, his shirt gained an inflated look that suggested he was wearing a bulletproof vest.

I flipped through my wallet for the sixty-one seventy that would cover the check Mose Junior had given me. Minimum wage really does not add up.

"Hear you're outta here." He carefully counted my money.

"Gee, Lance, how did you hear that? I didn't even know myself until five minutes ago."

"One less snail track on stage." The cash drawer rang open and my money disappeared into it.

"That's pretty, Lance. Your smooth talking must get you a lot of girlfriends."

The aviator sunglasses, clipped into his breast pocket, heaved. Perhaps his protective vest restricted lung volume; he didn't manage to get a retort out before I left.

Little did I know what work I'd eventually find when I moved from Ohio to San Francisco after my graduation and divorce two years before. There was nowhere further away to go. Tilt the United States, my momma says, and everything loose rolls to California. The money I'd saved to support my first months in the big city lasted one week. I spent that week in pantihose and my Divorce Dress listening to temp agency secretaries tell me to keep trying. I lived on just-add-water pancake mix for a second week of trying. I realized that just-add-water pancake mix would continue to be a major part of my diet even if I actually got work from the temp agencies. San Francisco was oppressively expensive. But Ohio had been just plain oppressive and I was determined to stay. The want ads for exotic dancers were enthusiastic: Make Three Hundred a Day! Co-eds Welcome!

Even with my newfound lucrative career, I didn't make enough money to live alone. When I got to my apartment in the Lower Haight, my roommates were situated boy-girl-boy-girl on the living room couch, watching a television movie, faces glowing blue. Vivian and Zan were a couple. They'd been dating for longer than anyone could remember, but Viv lived in fear of what she called lesbian merger and made conscious, anxious efforts to differentiate the two of them. She had recently gotten a razor cut and dyed what was left of her hair black.

Vivian watched television as intensely as she undertook all activities. Her face rebroadcast every nuance of the actors. Zan sat patting her lips with her index and middle fingers to simulate smoking which she had just given up. Like me, Zan was from 'back east', though only as far back as Colorado. She sang in a guitar band, had a low-maintenance wardrobe, and studied psychology, disappointed that in California this discipline mostly involved crystals and chakras. She wore her long blonde hair in two wispy braids that hung halfway down her back.

Sitting between the couple, pulling hard on Zan's braids to help combat the pain of her nicotine-withdrawal headache, was Geoffrey, who often positioned himself between the girlfriends to prevent any public displays of affection. He felt those were distasteful, unless the party had achieved alcohol blackout. Geoffrey considered our living room public, which was accurate enough considering the high volume of houseguests that used it as their bedroom. He had the pale complexion of one who spends his time indoors and golden brown hair that was beginning to recede, but these flaws were more than made up for by enviable bone structure and his eyes, huge, responsive and the color of a New England sky. They devastated men and women alike. Geoffrey was a construction-paper artist. Above the couch where my roommates sat hung a series of five silhouettes, each one of our profiles done in bold colors and cut out by Geoffrey's blunt green-handled Lefty scissors.

Our current houseguests, Peter and Rainbow, stretched out on the floor between the couch and the television, with their dog Yohimbe panting on the floor between them. These two shared one wardrobe of overalls and tie-dyed shirts as well as hair care advice, which had resulted in matching heads of dreadlocks. Vivian was no doubt appalled by their sameness, Geoffrey by their hair. They'd come from the north somewhere with their pregnant German Shepherd. It was unclear to me exactly whose houseguests they were. Everyone mumbled greetings as I made for the couch, trying not to break sightlines.

I sat next to Hugh, my fourth and final rent-paying roommate, a bibliophile whose thick black-framed glasses reflected two miniature convex images of the television screen. Hugh was handsome, but he'd never know it, unlike Geoffrey, the accomplished flirt. Hugh's eyes were the color of Coca-Cola, with sand-colored lashes, but they were hidden behind his glasses. An adorable flop of straight blond hair from his bowl cut skimmed the top of the frames.

"Is that Marilyn Monroe?" I asked him, trying to make sense of the small blue movements in his lenses.

"Stop it," he complained. After Hugh's expensive private liberal-arts college education he had left Connecticut, two or three years before. He worked three days a week pricing books for a thrift store. His room in the apartment was stacked floor to ceiling with books he had taken home from the job. He had read them all. My tabby cat, Hodge, was on his lap, asleep.

Hugh dumped the cat into my lap. Hodge startled awake and reflexively sunk his claws through my rayon pants into my thigh. I flinched then rubbed his ears to make him purr.

"*Some Like it Hot*, Marilyn Monroe. How was work?" Hugh said.

"I got laid off. Any food left?" We shared food. My roommates were vegetarians.

"Laid off? Is there an excess of labor in your..." Hugh hesitated, pushed up his glasses. Jack Lemmon was adjusting his bosom in the two lenses. "...profession at the moment?"

"Not exactly." I sighed. "I'm going to see what's in the kitchen."

"Then you were, technically speaking, suspended." Hugh, following me, spoke quietly until the swinging door into the kitchen flapped shut behind him. "The term 'laid off' implies termination through no fault of your own, usually due to company downsizing."

Our kitchen was narrow and long and filled with a rectangular Formica table as well as a bulky refrigerator and a huge World War Two-era stove. The two of us barely fit in there standing, so I sat at the table. Hugh filled a bowl for me from the Crock-Pot.

"The Moses are definitely not into downsizing. Every dancer on each shift is a hundred dollars profit for them. What is it?" Hugh had placed a full bowl in front of me. The food looked like porridge and smelled sour. But maybe that was the odor from the cracking porcelain sink full of dirty dishes, or the ominous scrap of kitchen sponge.

"Kimchee and brown rice. Like it?"

I didn't. I was suspicious of anything from the Crock-Pot, which was always filled with bubbling vegetarian goo.

"It's not like Momma used to make." Her staples were soup beans and cornbread. My parents were Kentuckians who had migrated north to Dayton, Ohio. Most of our suburban neighbors of their generation had given up whatever down-home dishes had sustained their unassimilated childhoods, but poor Momma wasn't a very adaptable cook. She never got the hang of Midwestern aspics and casseroles. I nibbled at the pickled cabbage.

"What happened at work?" Hugh sat. The Formica table was

paired with two disintegrating chairs.

I added ketchup, mustard and sugar to the mixture in my bowl. Better. "Mose Junior informed me that I can't come in for two weeks because I chased away a customer."

Hugh gave a rare smile. "That doesn't sound like you."

"Right. No, I literally chased him away."

"What'd he do?"

"Stole a hundred dollars from me."

"You're kidding."

"Nope." I described for Hugh the amusing spectacle of myself chasing Yellow Hair through the Tenderloin in my heels and two-piece. "I caught up to him, but he weaseled away." I went to the refrigerator to get a Coke.

Hugh was quiet until I rejoined him at the table. I noticed his face was flushed.

"Can you believe that?" I took a final bite of mustard-smeared kimchee and pushed the half-full bowl away.

Hugh took a breath. "Why would he take your money?"

"Why not? He thought he could get away with it. We're alone in these private booths with customers, Hugh. They think they can get away with lots of stuff."

Hugh didn't laugh. He coughed, reddening further.

"But most of them are appreciative and polite. It's not usually a problem. Want some of this Coke?" I turned the can around.

Hugh pulled my bowl over to him to finish off my meal, and I left him to it. I wanted to call Momma. I had to break the news to her that the weekly check I sent wouldn't be there this week or the next. It was early morning, Eastern Time, and my mother's latest drug combination would have perked her right out of bed. I helped her with money because she worked in a beauty shop and her third husband was too cheap to pay her medical bills. Perhaps his job as an insurance salesman didn't pay enough.

The insurance salesman answered.

"Is Darylynn there?" I asked. Our only telephone was in the living room and my roommates, beside me on the long couch, couldn't suppress giggles. They found my mother's name so funny that they uttered it whenever they had the excuse. Californians didn't get the down-home tradition of the American South, where children may be named, logically, after both their parents. Darylynn was a Yankee misinterpretation. Momma had been christened Darylleann.

I heard the click of her manicure against the mouthpiece first. "Well,

I thought you'd forgotten your old momma. Hon, it's Aubrey! Haven't heard from you in a long time."

"We talked last Sunday like usual, Momma."

"Eb says hi. He's been planting his beans and carrots and lettuce, haven't you hon? He stays out there till dark sweating. Great big garden this year, right hon? I thought he'd kill himself with that manual rototiller, I made him rent a riding one down at the Rent-'n-Save. What else did you put up in your garden, hon? Oh he's got some okra planted for me, you know I just love it rolled in cornmeal and fried up. And he's got azaleas planted all the way along the back for a border. Tomorrow he'll put in two rows of beets. I'll be celebrating my birthday next month, can you believe I'll be forty?"

Her pause for breath was my opportunity to break in. "No, because you'll be forty-eight."

"Eb is planning a big party. Aren't you, hon? He's inviting everyone from his office, the Bernses from next door and the people we play hearts with. Right hon?" Momma must have waved the receiver in his direction, because I heard a grunt. "He says yes. Isn't he sweet? Hon, fetch me a Pepsi, would you? Yes, diet. Yes, I know what Doctor Hillman says about my kidneys, go on, now. Now, Aubrey, you wouldn't tell her real age on your old momma, would you? He thinks I'm younger."

"He's sixty or seventy, isn't he? What difference could your age possibly make?"

"Forty-eight is practically fifty. I'm still a size ten. When I married your father, I was a six. Of course after you have a baby—"

"So he thinks you had me when you were fifteen?"

"Why not? His momma had a baby when she was fifteen, it happens all the time down in the hills. Here he comes now with my Pepsi. Thank you, honey, I was just telling Aubrey about your little momma." Momma recounted for me again the troubled history and complicated genealogy of my second step-family, saving her spicy judgmental commentary for when Eb left the room to fetch her cigarettes, an ashtray, lemon wedges and more ice. Like her own and the families of Momma's previous husbands, Eb's claimed kin in coal towns and hollers all over southeastern Kentucky. My own father, Momma's first husband, had left that area at a young age to live with an aunt in Dayton, Ohio. Only ten, Early Lyle was already scarred by the violent lifestyle of his coal mining father and uncles. He revisited the violence on the Kentucky girl he eventually married, until I belatedly came of an age and fought back for her. She had gotten hooked on Valium before that could happen. Mercifully, Momma's subsequent husbands, a custodian she'd met during one of her hospital stays and, after he'd died, his life insurance agent, were passive if incredibly dull men.

"Have you been listening to your old mom? There's a car I want only a thousand dollars. It's an eighty-six Nissan with only seventy-five thousand miles. You know what a junker my Buick is. I barely trust it to run me over to the doctor's for my check-up. I have to go more often now, you know, and the insurance is killing me. I just need to think of how to come up with one thousand dollars. AT&T's going to pay me one hundred dollars to switch back to them, so that's something. Well, here's Eb telling me it's time for our bacon and eggs. He keeps me so well-fed I'll be busting out of my, did I tell you I can get into some of my old size eights?"

I hung up feeling depressed, then realized I'd forgotten to tell Momma about my financial straits. Zan would tell me that I was in denial. She'd also tell me that depression masks anger, but at least when you're depressed no one fires you for showing it.

Some Like it Hot was over and Geoffrey, Hugh and I were on the couch watching *Gentlemen Prefer Blondes* when the phone rang again. I was half-asleep, slumped into one of the four permanent indentations that together made our green couch resemble an eviscerated pea pod. Jarred awake by the shrill ring, I reached for the phone.

"Baby, it's me," Jossie's voice frizzed from a poor connection.

"What time is it?" I fought off television-induced stupor. My stomach was experiencing the acid lather generated by nighttime phone calls that could only signify deadly emergencies.

"Three-thirty. Were you asleep, baby? Listen, this is important. You don't know what I went through to get to use the phone." A bass line in her background suggested arguments, frustration, fury. It beat like a melodyless equivalent of a heavy metal song, syncopated with an occasional leaden clang.

"Where are you? What's going on?" I used the tone you'd expect. The phone had also woken Hugh, who blinked nervously beside me. Geoffrey was draped across two of the couch's ass slots, mouth open, eyes shut, snoring lightly.

"You're my one phone call," Jossie said. "I'm in jail."

Chapter Three

"Can you hold on, baby?" I listened to Jossie tell someone to back off, if he wanted some of this he could get in line and she didn't care how crowded it was getting in this pen and she didn't care who he was friends with on the inside. Her voice echoed oddly. I imagined the phone's mouthpiece rested against her cleavage. "You there?" she finally asked me.

"I'm here. What happened?" I took a mouth-scouring swallow of warm Coke I found at the end of the table. The drink reactivated the acid bath in my gut.

"Total set-up. The cops came right to Grady's door. Fancy mansion in Nob Hill. They got me."

"What about Grady?"

Jossie snorted. "What Grady was doing isn't illegal, baby. Except maybe back where your people are, some of them Southern states. Even if it was illegal, he owns everything in town. He's running for mayor, you know, and his future police force won't mess with him, and those newspapers he owns won't be writing this up either." Jossie's voice dropped an octave. "You can just wait your turn, I get five minutes, dig?" A background baritone responded, rumbling like a low-rider's engine. To me she continued, "Nothing's going to happen to Grady. Meanwhile I don't see him in here trying to bail me out. And I didn't dress for a jail cell. You should see what I'm wearing in here. But baby, it's better than the neon scrub-suit I've got coming."

"No, things won't get that far. I'm coming to bail you out."

We never talked about her extracurricular activities but the nature of Jossie's dates was not a secret to me. I'd known that her cabs-and-condo lifestyle wasn't maintained by the odd ten dollars she garnered from hustling drinks.

"Bail's not set. I'm still in the holding tank. You can worry about that in the morning. Right now I've got another job for you, baby.

Listen, I know who did this to me."

"Did what?"

"Set me up. Cops don't just come up to Whitmore Grady's door and knock his brass knocker looking for transvestite prostitutes, dig? I've been doing this for years. Someone knew where I would be and what I would be doing. Remember what I said about Peaches?"

—"No. You didn't say anything. You didn't seem to think me a worthy audience for your conspiracy theory."

When Jossie spoke again it was in a coarse stage whisper. "The woman is Vice."

"Vice?" I'd been keeping my voice below the television volume until then. Hugh turned to look at me, strung with nerves. Geoffrey, in contrast, turned and smiled in his sleep, relaxed as a baby. Both attitudes were typical of my male roommates. "As in sex and drug police? What makes you think that?"

"You know I've got radar. I've had my eye on her the last couple weeks. That one watches us when we're not looking. Checks out what's going on. Seems unobtrusive, right? Never says much, but she's there listening, in the dressing room, on the floor. She even hovers around the bouncers and Mose Junior. Not talking to them, but sitting where she can hear their conversations."

"So do you. Even if she were Vice, why would she be scoping Naughtyland? Lapdancing is legal."

"Stop being snide and catch up to me. Lots of girls are making dates in there. Meeting customers after hours for you know what. You may not be, but that's going on. Prostitution's still not legal, baby. Not even in San Francisco. As I am living proof of right this minute."

"You're saying some of the other dancers are really prostitutes?"

"Have I shocked Miss Cynical? I'm saying a couple of them might be making dates regularly, and some more might now and again if they need to make a slow night profitable. Dig? Don't tell me you never get asked out by customers."

"Every night. Every hour. But it never occurred to me to take them up on it."

"Well to some people with better business sense than you it does. But it doesn't matter if you're making dates in Naughtyland or not when the cops come around. They're not interested in details like that. They'll arrest everyone they find working there and book them for being present in a house of ill repute."

—"How quaint."

"Believe me, it ain't quaint in here. You sound like you don't believe me, but I'm telling the truth. If Naughtyland gets a rep as a front for prostitution, we're all going down. We're whores and the Moses are pimps."

"But Peaches, a Vice officer? She gives lapdances. Do cops have huge dragon tattoos on their rear ends?"

"Listen, take me seriously. You're the only one I trust to help me. I know something's up with Peaches." Jossie's tone was momentarily earnest and desperate, the opposite of her usual attitude-problem style. She reverted to that mode to growl at a phone aspirant, then continued. "It's my living and if we're all busted, that's your ass too. Naughtyland is going down, dig? Unless we prove Peaches is Vice. If she's a cop, Mose Junior will fire her in an instant."

"He won't fire her on your suspicion?"

"Of course not. When he could be sued for wrongful termination? Remember Lucresha, big girl who got fired after she got too fat? She sued for wrongful termination and won a hundred and fifty thou. Bought herself a house in Oakland. Use your head."

"She was smart. But how do you plan on proving that Peaches is Vice?"

"That's where you come in. We need her real name. Then we can find out if she's on the squad."

"I can't help you. I don't know her real name." For security reasons in these days of stalkers, all of us dancers knew each other only by our stage names, often even after we became good friends. I knew one hundred or so strippers, but I knew the real name of only one of them.

"I know you don't, baby. Not yet."

"Mose Junior would have her name." Or some version of it, anyway, to complete her bogus paycheck.

"Of course I tried that, sugar. He told me Peaches is fine, I shouldn't worry. If she turns out to be a cop she's fired. He won't go against club policy and give out personal information. You know he doesn't want us dancers hanging together. We might be telling each other how much we make and such. That's not good for his business."

"Why don't you just ask her if she's Vice? Don't they have to answer truthfully? Or look around for a badge. Wouldn't she have to have a badge or something?"

"I did ask her."

"Really?" I was impressed.

"She denied it, of course. But I know a way we can find out for sure.

You with me baby?"

"What's your plan?"

"Get her personnel file from Mose Junior's office. Then you got her name."

"How are you going to get her file?"

"I'm not baby, I'm in jail."

"How convenient."

"You're going to get that file. If that woman is Vice, it's your job too, remember. Maybe your ass in jail right here beside mine."

"You make it sound so cute."

Hugh was wide-awake beside me by this time, humming with tension and pretending to watch the television. I was mentally picturing Momma telling her girlfriends at the beauty shop that her only child was in jail on prostitution charges. I winced. Then I pictured her telling Eb and that was worse. Momma's third husband already thought I was a lost cause. I'd chosen to leave Ohio for Sin City. I'd traded my sturdy polyester Shoney's uniform for a work wardrobe of underwear that shouldn't rightly be made in those colors. His kids, on the other hand, worked as a bank teller and an accountant right there close to home, where they could come to Sunday dinner and help their Pop with the tedious chores of suburbia—cycling out the storm windows, pruning the azaleas, repairing the deck.

In my opinion, his kids' lives were bleak. I thought of the latest round of step-siblings rarely, but when I did I imagined two figures pacing the shadows of Dayton's cloned gray-skinned office towers, their routine as pointless as an airplane in a holding pattern. My life might have been as pointless as the next recent college graduate's, but at least it wasn't dull. But I supposed most people would have agreed with Eb and considered my career evidence of some colossal failure of genetics or upbringing, while Eb's contented brood would be judged favorably.

"There is a way out of jail time, though," Jossie was saying. "I forgot to mention the cops' special instant plea-bargain offer. Let me tell you about it, just so you know your options. You listening, baby?"

"Yeah."

"If you suck them off in the patrol car while they're hauling you in for hooking, they'll let you go."

"You're kidding."

"No. I didn't have to end up here, you see, but I turned them down. What's a girl got but her morals? The sooner we expose Peaches the better. Who knows what she'll be up to next. Get to Naughtyland tonight. The bouncers leave around four."

"How am I supposed to—" I was cut off by fierce grumbling and a crack that could have been the receiver hitting the pay phone, or a fist hitting a head.

"I said back off! All right, I've got to go, baby. Listen," she said, finally. "Take a friend."

Twenty minutes later Hugh and I were drinking coffee at a gunky window table in the Chinese Food and Donuts on the corner of Jones and O'Farrell Streets. Across Jones and half a block south was the cheap facade of Naughtyland, the name spelled out in double-high red letters on the old movie theater's cracking marquee. Underneath were the names of the dancers, listed alphabetically through N when space ran out. Stripper names have a lot of vowels and 'a's had run out with Farrah, advertised as Farrh. Greta became Gret and so on. The Live Nude Girls promise winked below the marquee. Perched on top of it were three more neon tubes, one fashioned into a curvaceous girl, the other two into the to and fro positions of her swinging hips. The red hips flickered back and forth until precisely four a.m. when the signs sputtered out.

"Now?" asked Hugh. He'd driven me to the Tenderloin in Peter and Rainbow's Volkswagen van, which we'd parked around the corner on O'Farrell.

"In a minute. We have to wait for the bouncers to leave. They've been cleaning, supposedly."

"To get the money you've saved from your locker? Wouldn't it be prudent to go now, when someone can let you in?"

"We'll be going in the back way. I'm not actually here for any money. Jossie thinks one of our coworkers might be the cop responsible for putting her in jail tonight. She wants me to get her real name. Breaking into Mose Junior's office is the only way I can get that information. I don't want to get busted for prostitution any more than the next guy. Sorry I didn't tell you before," I said, as Hugh splashed coffee onto the table from a trembling Styrofoam cup. "I didn't want you to worry. You won't be involved in any breaking and entering. I'll go in by myself."

I watched Naughtyland's front doors, but there was no activity. After a moment, Hugh cleared his throat. "Will an actual break-in be necessary?"

"I don't think Lance would just let me waltz in there and browse through Mose Junior's files. He seems like the company-loyalty type."

I'd turned back around to watch for the bouncers before Hugh spoke again. "Well, I can't let you go alone."

"What? Oh, that's sweet. But I really don't want you to get involved. I'll be fine."

Hugh looked relieved.

A dark sports car with tinted windows stopped under Naughtyland's marquee. Mose Junior exited the club, strode toward the car, flicked the butt of his Marlboro into the gutter and folded into the passenger's side. I hadn't realized he worked so late. The money count must have taken hours. That didn't look like the car of a shy brunette bride such as the one immortalized in the photo cube on my boss's desk. The other five sides of the cube displayed their team of children. Wife and kids suffocated together under the spotty plastic. The sports car took off, concussing the pavement with a bass throb from its stereo system.

A moment later Lance emerged, followed by Kevin, the other bouncer. Together they scraped an accordion of metal mesh across Naughtyland's plate glass facade. Kevin was a Goth, made up, no matter the time or occasion, in thick white pancake and raccoon eyeliner. From our distance we could see the shiny moussed stalagmites of his dyed-black hair. Kevin affixed two large padlocks to anchor the mesh, while Lance scouted out every direction, including up and down. Kevin looked nervously around before scuttling toward Market like a house-wife caught out-of-doors in her curlers. Lance followed him more slowly, looking over his shoulder every few steps.

"We closing," said the young man who squeegeed mop water towards the soles of my boots.

The coffee rippled my gut as we rose and returned to the van.

When the mopper and the nervous female employee of Chinese Food and Donuts pulled their grate down and left thirty minutes later, I had no further excuses. I took a breath and opened the van's door. That's when Yohimbe started to bark as loudly and rhythmically as a car alarm. I shut the door and she stopped.

Borrowing their van meant borrowing Peter and Rainbow's pregnant German Shepherd as well. When Yohimbe heard the van start, she howled until admitted into the vehicle. To spare the roommates her mourning, she went along for every ride.

"I can't do this if that dog isn't quiet," I said. The block looked deserted. The Tenderloin's homeless must have found it too threatening for a peaceful sleep. The donut shop and Naughtyland kept the latest hours. After the shop closed and its fluorescence powered down, bluish light from no apparent source made Jones Street glow dimly. The city never quite gets dark.

"There don't appear to be any potential witnesses to—"

"I need her quiet! Sorry." I picked a cuticle, something I did when I was nervous.

"Maybe they have a muzzle," said Hugh. He got up to poke around in the morass behind the van's bench backseat.

"I don't think they'd muzzle their dog. They'd consider it unfree or something."

"This might work." Hugh threw me a padded leather bracelet, adorned with a buckle and a small silver ring dangling opposite.

"Wow, what are Peter and Rainbow up to with that? Hippies are getting so unpredictable." I joined him and began rummaging through the back of the van myself. I found a Peruvian-style knit cap and put it on. It was itchy, had unflattering ear flaps and was woven in a strange geometry that reminded me of runes, but it would have to do. I didn't want to leave any foot-long wavy reddish-brown hairs behind me.

Hugh fastened the cuff around Yohimbe's muzzle while she looked at him liquidly. He found some pipe cleaners in the glove compartment and wired two together, then hooked one end through the cuff's buckle, brought the length around the back of the dog's head and fastened the other end to the ring. This contraption looked like it would stay on her head for about five minutes.

"Let's go." I said.

"I thought I wasn't going to be involved!"

"I just need a boost. Then you can come right back to the van."

Reluctantly, Hugh joined me on the sidewalk. Yohimbe widened her eyes and shook her nose at us, but the improvised muzzle stayed on. The air was still and held its faint smell of rotting garbage close.

In the alley behind Naughtyland, ten feet off the ground, was the window to Mose's second-story office.

"Okay. I need a boost up to that window."

"Have you ever thought that they might have an alarm at this place?"

"There's no alarm. Our boss doesn't leave any money here. There's nothing to steal except plastic tables and non-alcoholic beer."

Mose Junior always collected our one hundred dollar stage fees in time to make a night drop at the bank. Where did all that cash go, the thousands of dollars collected from the dancers every night? Whose name was on that lucrative account? A man's, no doubt.

I snapped on a pair of latex gloves that I had grabbed from a box I'd found in the van and scrambled onto Hugh's shoulders. Hugh is tall and gangly; I'm six inches shorter and not light. I could reach the window ledge easily. I tugged on the sash, but the window didn't budge. A straighter angle would give me more power to push with. "Can you move closer to the wall?" I whispered down.

Hugh staggered forward until his face was four inches from moist bricks. I strained against the sash until Hugh's complaints became dangerously loud. Why wouldn't it slip open? Then I remembered my observation of a few hours before. The thing wasn't only locked. It was painted shut. Shit.

"I need leverage, Hugh, can you not keep your shoulders so hunched?"

"You're hurting me."

"If you help me push this will go quicker. Just relax your shoulders so I can stay on them, then tense all your muscles from the ground up. Use your leg muscles, they're strongest."

I gave Hugh a break by pulling myself up the wall with my forearms crossed on the window ledge, while he kneaded his shoulders and kicked out his long legs. My breasts were crushed and my cheek was plastered against one of the window's cold panes, which soon steamed up from my labored breathing. I held this position as long as I could.

"Hugh! Hurry up!" My upper back felt like it was being hot-combed.

Hugh unenthusiastically reached up for my feet. Then came the frantic barks. From over half a block away.

"Shit!" I said.

"Blast!" Hugh froze, caught between my crisis and Yohimbe's. He stuck his shoulders under my slipping feet and said, "Lock your joints!" I stretched my limbs. Hugh rolled up onto his toes. With my body braced between his shoulders and the windowpane, the window splintered open. I grabbed the rough bricks of the window ledge and pulled myself over it. I felt the sill scrape across my torso and down to my knees. I fell onto the gray industrial carpeting, just missing the sharp corners of Mose's chintzy desk. I was still for a moment, aware of the sound my heart and lungs. Every wool fiber of the hat seemed to be worming its way into my scalp.

After a moment I cautiously walked over to the file cabinet, a two-drawer army green job with as many dents and scratches as a tank. I found the drawer marked "Human Resources" and riffled through files labeled with the unfamiliar given names of my coworkers. The latex gloves were thin enough not to be much of a hindrance and protected me from paper cuts. Onto each file was stapled a Polaroid of the applicant posing in either a bikini or in underwear. It was obvious what the hiring criteria were. I spent a moment on my picture, taken two years before, remembering how I'd sucked in and thrust out and poofed up. My hair had been shorter then, wavier, in a shoulder-length bob. Momma had convinced me to highlight my red highlights redder and the striated effect had resembled a rag rug. I didn't take her hair care advice anymore.

In her picture Peaches wore simple white briefs and a white Playtex bra of the kind that come in a box and hold for eighteen hours, whatever that means. She was standing in the corner of what appeared to be a living room. A floor lamp had been rearranged to sidelight her hi-gloss black hair. I admired again her sunlight-through-a-daisy complexion, the inquisitive uplift of her thin black eyebrows. Her ribs showed. She looked at me, or at the camera, almost mockingly. Peaches' real name was Luna Nguyen. I had found her in about three minutes.

I tucked Luna Nguyen's file under my leather jacket and closed the metal drawer carefully. The naked women on Mose's wall watched me, mute and smiling, faking seductiveness.

The paint on the office window frame was scraped and cracking from my forced entry. I hoped Mose wouldn't notice. Just then I heard loud noises from outside, shouts and speeding cars. A pair of engines gunned down Jones Street. Probably a convoy of suburban kids on their way to one of the nearby drug corners. I couldn't blame them. Suburbanite's lives demand some kind of chemical boost. I waited until the engine noises faded before I climbed through the window, hung by my hands and dropped. There was no way to close it behind me. Mose might not notice the missing personnel file, but he probably would notice the unpleasantly fresh air. A car turned into the alley. I ducked behind a dumpster, watched headlights sweep a yellow curve on the pitted black asphalt. The car stopped.

A horn honked. The sound was more plaintive than threatening. It was the horn of a Volkswagen van. I rose and ran toward it.

Chapter Four

San Francisco's jail had recently been refurbished in an odd modern style. The building was of gray steel layered torte-like with opaque windows. Its back wall was staggered outward with each floor, the fourth a scant few inches from the city's bisecting highway overpass, separating prisoners from motorists without breaking the architect's lines with visually confusing steel bars. Travelers might pass within inches of the city's most wanted and notice only the lovely frosted glass. Inmates could look out the window but see only vague swirls of the free world. Architecture of cruelty had become architecture of cruel irony.

I had to go to the fourth floor, where the so-called Alternative Population was separately incarcerated, to see Jossie. The guards called it AP. Other visitors spoke of it as the gay jail. Jossie and I spoke in a room made of cinderblocks painted with a thick coat of gray. On her side the cinderblocks propped up a uniformed guard. Our conversation was through telephones separated by riot-proof glass. My friend's face was faded as much as everyone's fades in contrast to neon orange. I don't know when prison uniforms went from black and white stripes to day-glo, but the effect could hardly be less flattering.

"They confiscated my spike heels," Jossie was saying. "Potential weapons."

"Sorry I didn't get here sooner." After my late night, I'd slept right through the morning visiting hours and the afternoon ones hadn't begun until three. "Anyway, they haven't set bail yet. You look good."

Jossie was smoothing back her uplifted coiffure. Considering what she'd probably been through, which she wasn't talking about, she did look good. She usually wore enough make-up for the erosion of several top layers to make little difference in her appearance. "It's just like the Naughtyland dressing room in here. Everybody hanging with their own race, divided up into teams, except here instead of old girls versus new girls or Asian girls versus white girls it's gays versus transgendereds

34

versus transvestites. But still everyone's in his or her separate corners checking each other out. You're reduced to your physical proportions and all you've got's your attitude."

"Our work's like jail. Great."

"Know where Grady is today?" Jossie lacked any prop with which to make a haughty gesture, so she flicked fingers and thumb upward.

"No."

"He's in school."

"School?"

"School for johns. That's where he's going while my ass is in jail. But I bet you he doesn't even go. He's got his finger in every pie in this town. Business, real estate, development, he's got stock in all of it. He's probably got stock in this jail. He'll buy his way out of their school."

"What's the school for johns?"

"They send the week's catch to some class where they have to listen to some poor streetwalker tell her sob story. I hope the hookers have the dramatic talent to make up a good tearjerker. It's supposed to keep men from using our services."

"Through empathy? There's no danger of that putting any sex worker out of business anytime soon." Most customers demonstrated a profound lack of this quality. Many lapdance customers thought I was a stripper because I was perpetually horny, or cheerfully suggested that we trade places; I could be a software engineer/construction foreman/legal aide for a day, while they sat around diddling themselves for an admiring audience. And making oceans of money. I had it so easy. I was disgusted by this insensitivity until I realized that if customers empathized with us they wouldn't be paying us. We had to be nothing like them. We took the blame for their debauchery and that was the allure.

"Empathy, right. No, dummy baby, I'm talking about school. School's all about public humiliation. They've all got to sit in a room together. Imagine the coffee break."

"You're right." We laughed. I couldn't imagine a classroom full of customers. They ignored each other at Naughtyland. The rest of us just went along with the pretense that each man there was the only one sitting alone and watching naked girls and sipping O'Doul's.

"I know I'm right."

"They'll set bail soon. How long can you be held for something like this?"

"I don't know. It's just a misdemeanor."

"Still no help from Grady?"

"You see him around here? None of my clients will touch this one. They're all somebodies in this town. Like I said, Grady's running for mayor. No, I'm counting on you, baby. I'd do the same for you." She leaned forward until her dark eyes and her nose, slimmed with strategically-placed stripes of light base, were as close to the glass as the telephone cord would allow. The guard looked at her, then back at the person next to her whose visitor, beside me, was energetically kissing his side of the glass. Jossie whispered, "Did you get the file?"

"I got it."

"No problems?"

"No."

"Her address is in there?"

"I didn't go through it, but it should be in there somewhere."

"You've got to go and confront her. Before she can work another shift. Say we're onto her and she best butt out."

"Me?"

"I've tried, baby, and now I'm up in here for who knows how long. You've got to do it before she takes this thing further and busts the whole club."

"I guess I could talk to her."

"We got evidence now; that evidence is me sitting here in neon orange talking to you on a crusty phone. Last night was not a random event."

The guards announced that our ten minutes were over.

"You doing okay in there?" I asked, as prisoners and visitors stirred and the kisser next to me slapped himself to his side of the glass in a passionate finale to his make-out session with the windowpane.

Jossie smiled. "It's not easy being a female dick, right baby? I can take it. Go on now, I'll see you on the outside."

Back home, I jostled between roommates in our small kitchen to make myself a cup of tea. I wasn't looking forward to confronting Peaches. As the water heated and I dandled my dry bag of Earl Grey pointlessly in an empty mug, I spread the pages from the file I had borrowed from Mose's office over the other three burners of our large old stove. Three paycheck records, a W-4 form, and the Naughtyland application.

I read the application. Luna was single. She lived on 1120 Prospect

Street, Apt. Two, San Francisco. Her birthday was 10-19-72. Her bra size was 34B. That was an application question. She was five feet one and one hundred-five pounds. She'd graduated from UC Berkeley four years before. Her most recent employers in reverse order were The Femme Royale, six weeks, where she interpreted the art of striptease, and The Cher Cherie, one year seven months, where she had interpreted the art of striptease.

Would a cop make all this stuff up?

"Your water's boiling. It was already hot, you know. I just made coffee." Vivian was sitting at the table, working on her endless homework. She was a graduate student at San Francisco State. With the hand that wasn't scribbling, Vivian repetitively smoothed down her slicked back hair. The coconut oil she saturated it with made her smell like a beach.

"Oh. Thanks." I filled my mug as I leaned against the stove. I now felt obligated to acknowledge her. I wasn't up to verbal sparring, which Vivian and I got into a lot.

"No classes today?"

"They're over with." Vivian glanced at me over the schoolboy glasses she wore for reading. My hair was knotted, as it gets since I let it grow, and I'd changed back into the faded black Depeche Mode T-shirt and cutoff sweatpants that I slept in. For slippers I had on the yellow Kmart flip-flops that had come in Momma's latest care package. When I'm at home, I've got to be comfortable.

"If only your customers could see you now. What girls really look like."

"You'll be happy to know customers won't be seeing me at all for a while. I've been fired, for two weeks at least—for chasing one of them out." I added an inch of milk to the Earl Grey.

"Right, your special direct-action feminism. How's that program going? Have you pounded respect for women into any thugs lately?"

Milk splashed above the rim of the plastic jug as I set it on the table, hard. "I didn't touch the guy."

"How'd you manage to hold back? Was he just too devilishly handsome? Had a real way with the chicks? Second-husband material?" Vivian didn't think much of sex club patrons. She imagined them to be social misfits who just couldn't figure out how to talk to a live, clothed girl. Some of Naughtyland's customers were like that.

To spare her from utter cynicism, I never admitted to Vivian the diversity of the men who visited Naughtyland. They fit no stereotype. I'd lapdanced for men of all ages, social classes, religions, and ethnicities. I'd heard many accents and languages spoken around the plastic tables. I'd danced for men who refused the O'Doul's because they were Muslim and for businessmen fresh from martini lunches and for tourists more acquainted with moonshine. I'd danced for Tenderloin residents who wanted to reimburse me with crack, suburbanites who offered cocaine, and rumpled graduate students who tried to sell me pot. I'd danced for grandpas, janitors, cops, Chinese men, Afghan men, Scotsmen, Maoists and fundamentalist Christians.

I'd learned not to blame them for being there. Wouldn't I unthinkingly do the same if the female sex drive were so cherished that it merited an entire industry to service it? I spent idle hours at work trying to imagine what it would feel like to have one's genitals symbolize power rather than filth. I couldn't. If I ever felt like having an all-night argument, I'd bring up the subject with Vivian. She'd undoubtedly studied something about it in class.

Instead I answered "You're right. I have no control over these violent impulses. I have to immediately attack. My father was the same way. It must be in my genes." Any reference to genetics would likely set Vivian off in a different direction. The Earl Grey made waves in the mug as I brought it to my mouth. I was shaking, and I hadn't even had caffeine yet.

"You've got it backwards. Men claim they're violent because of their genes. Women aren't supposed to have those ones, you see. Our genes are supposed to make us crave pregnancy and give us a knack for baking. You'll have to think of another excuse."

I rubbed my forehead. "Give me a few minutes. I'm not awake until night."

"Try, multiple personalities, too many Twinkies. What was it when you avenged your friend? Your college roommate, what was her name—?"

"Mellissa. It wasn't avenging. She took me in after my divorce. She was living in an apartment the size of a bathtub in Austin with her two little kids, and her husband was beating the crap out of her. He went at her in front of the babies, and I conked him over the head with a frying pan. Tyler's my godson. I wasn't going to let him watch that."

"Her savior. She must have been so grateful."

"I did it for me, not for her."

Mellissa hadn't been grateful. She'd reported me to the cops for battery, in fact. I left Texas for San Francisco realizing that I had a lot to learn about the complexities of romance. And since her husband had gone to jail for battery, I'd become a source of financial support for her and the kids. "I chased that guy last night because he stole my money. Thanks for your support. Why don't I call my boss and tell him you support his decision to make Naughtyland a violence-free zone? He'll love it. Support from academia, the women's studies department, no less. Maybe you could send him a seal of approval to hang in Naughtyland's lobby. A fist with a line through it, or something."

"In that place, the symbolism might be misinterpreted."

After a moment, we both started to laugh.

As soon as the caffeine had ignited my brain and my faculties hummed to life, I decided to treat myself to a Mexican meal at El QuakeO, the taqueria that occupied the street level storefront underneath our shared flat. I was stalling, and wanted to be fortified for my encounter with Peaches. With Luna Nguyen. El QuakeO's smell of fried pork and earthy pinto beans was scarcely thicker, and the jukebox stocked with maudlin corridos was scarcely louder in the restaurant itself than their echoes were in our own kitchen. I ate my beans, eggs, tortillas and chorizo at the counter in the narrow restaurant's window, looking through the grease spots and backward gold lettering at the eclectic mix of humanity in the Lower Haight.

Haight-Ashbury got famous in the sixties, but its bottomland neighbor never did. The Lower Haight neighborhood joins the Mission, the Castro, the Haight, and the Fillmore. Its grim square blocks are undesirable, perhaps for the simple fact of lying in between neighborhoods where one would really want to live. The area is populated with brick housing projects and neglected Victorians, unprofitable stores and vacant lots gone to seed. In recent years the Lower Haight has struggled to become trendy, giving itself the image of a street-tough version of hipness, with cafes and clubs painted black and the opening of a few tattoo parlors. The coffee in the neighborhood's cafes got stronger and three times more expensive. Black residents had been pushed out by rising rents. Young white kids in their punk, ska, or tattoo phases, gays aspiring to move to the Castro, and relics from the Summer of Love who couldn't bear to leave but couldn't afford to live up the hill now populated the Lower Haight.

Pushing the last smears of refried beans around with the thick homemade tortilla, I skipped over my imminent unpleasant task and thought about the unstructured days ahead of me. One great thing about my job was its flexibility. I could go in any day, or call in when scheduled to say I couldn't make it. In exchange, the management could do as they pleased with us as well. I had never been suspended before, but I had known other girls to beg and cry when laid off by some whim of the Moses. They had kids to feed. They had a drug habit to support, which is probably what got them suspended in the first place. Mose Junior didn't like to deal with addicted dancers, who might be unpredictable. I had bills to pay, too. Two weeks of free time would likely drive me crazy. I had a lot of nervous energy and had to keep busy. At least I had some short term plans. I'd get the story on Luna one way or another.

I cleaned my plate with a final swipe of tortilla and left a tip for Doña Rosa, the chef. I hurried to the corner, where I waited forty minutes for the J Church streetcar.

Prospect Street was on the northwest side of Bernal Heights. I got off the streetcar at 30th Street and prepared to walk up the steep hill. Bernal Hill is a bunion of granite at the south end of the flat Mission District. Victorian houses and apartment blocks climb up its slopes as far as foundations could be sunk. I walked backwards up the incline of Virginia Street for a block. City lights winked on in the dusk. Neon striped the Mission. House lights stippled the city's hills: Twin Peaks and Diamond Heights to the west, Telegraph and Russian hills to the north. Fluorescence in the skyscrapers downtown indicated the after-hours presence of workaholics. The Bay Bridge and the Golden Gate were two chandeliers cranked open over the black Bay.

I turned left onto Prospect. I soon found 1120, an apartment cube with four mailboxes and four accompanying doorbells by the glass front door. Inside a split staircase led to two doors up, and two down. The entrance where I stood was on the east side of the building, the setting sun far behind it, and the interior was dim.

I rang the buzzer for apartment two. No one answered. Maybe Luna didn't want to be seen in her current state of disrepair. But then the bruises hadn't stopped her from going to work. She didn't seem to be vain. I rang apartment one, and an annoyed female voice answered me through the intercom.

"Who is it?"

"Is Luna Nguyen still living here? I'm a friend of hers." I realized it wasn't exactly true. I'd worked with the woman for only three weeks. I barely knew her.

"Ring number two then." Click.

I buzzed number one again.

"What?"

"She doesn't answer and she's expecting me. Can you let me in?"

No answer from Luna's helpful neighbor, so I began to press the doorbells for numbers four, three, and one at random. After a minute of this, the front door buzzed and I pushed it open. I've never had a problem getting through the front door of a secure apartment building. Driven mad by the buzzer, someone always caves.

Number two was upstairs on the left. I knocked on Luna's door and it swung inward—unlocked. That was strange. In my part of town, even second-story windows were locked. I stepped across the threshold.

"Luna?" I called. "Peaches?" The apartment was dark.

I heard nothing and tiptoed through a short hallway that smelled like pizza. On my left was a living room with a plate glass window aimed north, toward the view of downtown. It gathered enough of the sunset to burnish what I saw. The room was edged with bookshelves interrupted by a thrift store sofa. The shelves were empty. Books were scattered over the floor, some open, some half-open, paperbacks and hardcovers skittering over each other in careless piles. The sofa's cushions tumbled among them. The curved lid of an old-fashioned trunk that served as a coffee table was thrown open, and the trunk's contents, papers, file folders, compact discs, were a flurry inside and around it. Two black plates lay smashed over the white papers, their debris mixed with crescents of pizza crusts.

Either Luna wasn't the greatest housekeeper or else someone had ransacked the place. I didn't know how undercover cops lived, but probably not like this.

"Peaches?" I called again.

I turned around and found a closed door to knock on. No lights were on behind it. The door cracked open at my knock to a faint smell of odd incense. A pile of clothes acted as a doorstop. I reached around the door to clear them away.

I plowed the door open. After a moment, my eyes adjusted to the dimness of the bedroom. Gloom protected the naked figure amid tousled covers on the bed, and now the smell accosted me.

I didn't need lighting to identify the figure as dead. I didn't need to see her face to identify the body as Luna Nguyen's. Her killer had left her on her stomach, her face muffled inches deep into the softest kind of pillow. Her long, straight black hair had been flung above her head, but it wasn't the hair that gave her away. It was the tattoo. Death had whitewashed its canvas. The black ink was darker, the red flickering tongues of fire more cruel, the one yellow eye more menacing without the background of warm blood in her veins. My eyes followed the undulations of the dragon's body down Luna's backside to where the tail's tip tucked coyly around to her inner thigh. Luna's muscular legs, supple enough to do splits on stage, had been left widely splayed. The dragon's tail appeared dislocated.

Luna wore one article of clothing. Soft leather string looked like a pink necklace in the dim light from Prospect Street. A triangle of the same material fell limply toward her shoulder blade. The garment, too, was easily identifiable. My pink leather bikini always lifted my spirits on a long night shift at Naughtyland.

Someone had used the top to strangle her.

Chapter Five

I sounded panicky enough through the intercom to convince the resident of apartment one to let me use her phone. I explained to her that her neighbor was dead while I dialed 911. I wasn't being tactful. If I'd thought about it, I could have predicted that Ms. security-conscious would begin to freak out, not from sympathy for the dead, but for her own threatened safety. Someone had been murdered on the other side of her sheetrock. Her background yelps lent realism to my brief report to the police.

Apartment one was laid out in the mirror image of Luna's adjoining place. But where Luna's had the look of an aftermath, her neighbor's apartment was orderly and clean. After I made the phone call I went into the immaculate cubbyhole kitchen to see if there was camomile tea. Momma always made me take camomile when she diagnosed me as suffering from nerves. The delicate yellow flowers grew wild in her lawn. She bypassed the soothing herb for stronger relief, herself. I put on some water to boil, and joined the trembling woman on her couch. Dealing with someone else's crisis is a fine substitute for dealing with one's own.

"I'm Aubrey Lyle. I worked with Peaches. Luna. Are you okay?"

"Angie Pritchett. I need a smoke. Shit." Angie's jerky movements as she searched her beige purse made a mesmerizing kaleidoscope of her robe. She wore a kimono blobbed with peach, orange, lavender, and lemon. The orange blobs matched Angie's layered hair. Pastels normally aren't my favorites, but at that moment their optimism was a welcome change from the cold scene next door.

Angie's couch faced across to the deck, just as Luna's had, but in this apartment a lined white curtain was drawn across the sliding glass doors.

"I don't usually smoke in the house, but..." She gestured to the curtain. "We shared the deck." She stood, her thin form a mast to her robe's sail as she went to get an ashtray.

I clenched my fists between my knees, an oddly calming posture. I'd never seen anyone dead before who wasn't dandied up by the funeral home. I fought the image of the blood-drained dragon out of my mind. When it wouldn't leave, I tried to make sense of it. Naked, in her bed, no signs of struggle. Only rumpled bedclothes. Her pose had been sexual. Could she have been the victim of a sex scene gone awry?

Angie returned from the kitchen with an empty Merlot bottle to flick her ash into. She lit up, avoiding my gaze. "Secure building, my ass. I'm cashing in some stock and moving somewhere with a doorman. That could have been me dead, you know. Nowadays they're just looking for anybody to slaughter, those gangs. They're coming into this neighborhood, you know. The windshield on my Lexus got scratched with their symbol, what do you call it, a tag. I drove around until I could get it replaced, just terrified that someone would see the symbol and shoot me for being some rival or something. It's totally random. Flash your headlights at them, and you're dead. This neighborhood's going to the dogs." She looked at me. "How did you get in here, anyway?"

"I hit all the doorbells and someone buzzed the front door."

She took long drags to compensate for the skinniness of her Virginia Slim. "That's what I mean. They'll let in anyone. Now a murderer." A column of ashes fell to the white throw rug under the coffee table. Angie's hands were shaking hard.

"Who's they?"

"Two families downstairs. Immigrants, you know. No speakee English."

An image of Luna's stiff body came back to me. Her body had darkened on the underside, where gravity had pulled her blood. And the strange smell. "I think it must have happened last night," I said uneasily.

Luna had left Naughtyland early the night before, long before the shift officially ended at two a.m. How long did it take bodies to begin to smell?

Angie's cigarette butt smoldered from the bottom of the wine bottle, and she promptly lit another. "Middle of the night, you think? I sleep like a log."

"You didn't hear anything?"

She shook her head and took a contemplative puff. "Girl sure caused a ruckus late yesterday evening. Didn't even quiet down when I went out on the porch for a smoke."

"What kind of ruckus?"

"A pizza party, smelled like. She and some man were in her living room, a handsome young fellow by the way. He looked rich." She leaned to tap her cigarette into the bottle, which required a steadier hand than she could maintain. The ash slipped down the outside. Angie ran her tongue over her teeth. "If it were me I would have saved the argument until after the sex. But she was giving him a piece of her mind. It was as loud as if they were right here in my place. I told them that after I finished my cigarette I was going back to my "Dallas" rerun and they'd best shush. The guy said he was just leaving."

"Did you hear what they were arguing about?"

"Oh no, I had my TV on."

"Did you know the guy?"

"Never saw him before. I didn't ask. Didn't want to get messed up with her personal life. I regret it now." Angie's face hollowed as she sucked her cigarette. "Did you see those bruises she had on her face? That's what I mean about random violence."

"Did she tell you how she got those bruises?"

"Random violence. Not like she had a boyfriend. I kept telling her the Safeway down on Mission is the best place to meet singles. Produce department. She told me some stranger in a ski mask attacked her on the street. Isn't that just typical? Not in this neighborhood, thank goodness. Somewhere downtown. Tenderloin, I think. God knows what she was doing there. She's lucky she didn't get kidnapped into white slavery, walking those streets."

An earthquake interrupted Angie. I'd been through a few of these since moving to San Francisco, so I automatically panicked and scurried in search of the nearest door frame. Angie, suddenly the calm one, motioned for me to sit, and exhaled a slow stream of smoke. "There's your cops," she said, and nodded toward her door. "On the stairs."

Sure enough, two male voices were talking to each other in the hallway, radioing for backup and for crime scene team. Then more voices arrived, asking for tape, discussing 'the body', warning each other not to touch anything. The cops were loud. Every word was clear. The walls really were thin.

I went to turn off the tea water, which had long ago come to a boil. We were beyond camomile. I opened the door to the melee of cops in the hall, and offered Angie and myself up to the first woman cop I saw.

Officer Alma Suarez, short and bulky in her gun-laden uniform, followed me into Angie's apartment to take our statements.

"Got another room here?" asked Suarez. "I need to interview you separately."

Angie pointed a lit cigarette down the hall. I knew where the bedroom would be.

Sitting on Angie's fluffy duvet, I described my quick journey through Luna's apartment to Suarez and ended with my discovery of her body. The picture of her lying dead was already growing unclear in my mind. Suarez asked me my relationship to the victim, and I answered coworker. She asked me my place of employment, and I answered Naughtyland. She asked if that was one word or two.

"Strip club?" Suarez marked her form with a pen. She didn't look up.

"Lapdancing."

"Address?"

"Jones Street in the Tenderloin." Suarez filled in her form impassively, as though all her interviewees worked at strip clubs in the Tenderloin.

"Was Luna one of you?" I blurted.

The cop stilled her pen and looked at me over the small shields of her bifocals. "Excuse me?" she said.

"Was Luna a cop? Vice squad?"

Suarez reined in her stare and the beginning of a smile. "We'll pose as streetwalkers, but as lapdancers? Your name?"

After I gave her my name, address, and phone number, the cop gave me her card and told me to call if I thought of anything else. I pocketed the card. I'd decided to leave out one small, perhaps insignificant detail—the murder weapon had been my own bikini.

Suarez went off to interpret for the two Mexican families that lived downstairs.

Angie was squared off with a dark-haired male cop on her couch when I returned to her living room. He took notes as Angie repeated what she had told me about the downstairs neighbors letting anyone in. I'd seen the people in question gathered in the hallway: two bewildered young couples with a handful of children between them. None of the kids looked older than eight. I crossed to the sliding glass door, seeking to escape the haze of Virginia Slim smoke that had curled down from the low ceiling to lung level. I tugged the door open as Angie added a few epithets about encroaching Latino gangs. Her vehemence about protecting her turf was equal to any gang member's.

The deck was a cozy size, running the length of the building but only jutting out about eight feet. Front porch-sized. No rocking chairs here, though. The deck was bare except for a metal bucket half-filled with cigarette butts and a clay window box of herbs against the left railing. Basil, parsley, cilantro. They'd all bolted in the warm April days, stalks reaching hungrily toward the sun like the arms of front-row fans at a rock concert. Dusk had fallen. The city made an arc of diamond glitters below me, an arc as wide as flung-open arms. I loved heights and views but could afford only bottomland. Luna must have spent a good percentage of her income to live where she could look out upon distant beauty rather than down on sidewalk filth. Looking at her panoramic view with the lush back garden in the foreground, I saw her point.

The cool air was scented with the cilantro and with lemon from a mature tree that rattled against the rails of the deck on Luna's side. A few late-blooming fruits still ripened between the shiny leaves. I moved closer to the scent, wanting to cleanse my lungs. As I stood at the deck's waist-high railing I noticed the lemon tree was damaged on one side. Branches were broken or splintered from the deck down to the ground eight feet below. Lemon leaves glinted up at me from the snapped-off branches lying on the ground.

Just then Luna's sliding glass door opened. A young cop in a too-large uniform joined me on the deck. He wore no gloves, and had opened and closed the door with bare hands. Any fingerprints that may have been on the metal handle were now muddled.

"Crime scene, miss. Please leave immediately. Don't touch anything. Can't risk contamination," he said, his fingertips firm on my shoulder as he ushered me back to Angie's.

Angie put me in a cab home. She couldn't believe I took the bus around. It wasn't safe, she said. She bummed an unfiltered Camel from the driver, instructed him to watch me to my door, and gave him a twenty. Though I thought Angie excessive, I wasn't as offended by the fuss as I would normally be. I was grateful for the ride. It was nine o'clock by the time I left Angie's, and I was still in shock.

No one but Hugh was at home when I returned. He made me sit on the couch and tucked my quilt around me. He made me some tea and listened in horror to my tale of finding Luna dead. Panic replaced his horror when I told him what I hadn't told Suarez: my bikini top had been garroted around Luna's neck.

"That's bad, Aubrey, very bad."

"Well I didn't kill her. I loaned her the thing the last time I saw her—Wednesday night." I sluggishly stirred milk into the tea. I wondered idly if I'd be able to keep it down. Ingesting made me think of embalming fluid. I put the spoon down and pushed the mug away.

"Your fingerprints might be all over it. They'll call you in for questioning for sure when they find them. And you found the body, that's suspicious." Hugh had a habit of pushing his glasses up his nose when he got nervous. "You'd better prepare your alibi."

"Alibi?" I began to pick my cuticles.

"What time did she die?"

"I don't know." My gorge rose as I thought of the putrid smell I had thought was incense at first. "I think maybe last night."

"And last night you were...?"

"Home. Home, except for the hour or so I was breaking into Mose Junior's office."

"My point," said Hugh.

I was beginning to get it. My head was starting to ache from exhaustion.

"The fact that you found the body and that the murder weapon probably has your fingerprints on it will make you a suspect. But don't worry about it," he continued, "you do have an alibi, however incriminating. I can corroborate your whereabouts, if it comes to that. Who could have killed her?"

"I have no idea. I barely knew her. It looked to me as though it might have been some kind of sexual accident."

Hugh cleared his throat. After a moment he said, "Who was the last person seen with her? That's always a good place to start."

"Her neighbor told me a man had pizza with her the night before she died. But she heard him leave."

"So he wasn't the last person seen with her?"

"He could have been. But I don't think Luna killed herself."

"Was she Vice, after all?" Hugh's question reminded me of Jossie.

"I don't know," I said.

I picked at the rips in the worn leather sofa inside Got To Be Free Bail Bonds, conveniently located in a trailer right across Bryant Street from San Francisco's six-story Hall of Justice and correctional facility. The trailer's few cubic yards were infused with stale smoke.

The jail was by far the classiest building in the neighborhood. Around it were abandoned lots, parking garages, the flimsy cubicles of bail bondsmen, and warehouses. A McDonald's was being built to provide for the prisoners' visitors. I waited for Gus to make the necessary phone calls. The hand-lettered signs on the trailer's paneled walls meant to reassure. Felonies Misdemeanors 24 Hours; Any Jail Any Court; We Accept Real Estate. A beanbag ashtray in a lively tartan plaid slumped on the plastic coffee table. Its gold top brimmed with cigarette butts of several different brands marked with various lipstick shades. A glossy photograph of smiling, pimply Gus, possibly his senior yearbook picture, was framed in black plastic and hung off the wood paneling behind his desk.

"Thomas. Joseph Thomas." He was saying into the phone. Was that the name on Jossie's driver's license? Did Jossie even possess such an earthly item? I tried to picture her behind the wheel of a car, negotiating city traffic. I only made it as far as the back seat of a cab.

"Okay. Bail's set and it's three thousand." Gus had hung up and was speaking to me.

"So I pay three hundred?"

"That's ten percent. Just between you and me though, they won't hold your friend much longer. Usually that type of thing, it's just an overnighter."

"Well they haven't let her out yet. She's been in there since last night, three AM."

"Might save your money is all."

"Is there an ATM around here?"

"Got to go toward downtown for that."

"Great." Five long blocks, at least.

"But look here, you got your card, I got PayPoint. Your bank will charge you a quarter." Gus pushed a calculator-sized keyboard toward the front of his desk. A blue message flashed at me: Swipe card on left. My Granny Leann had always complained that the world was getting too complicated. She would have appreciated being able to spring folks from jail as easily as rolling a week's groceries through the checkout. She'd done both with predictable regularity.

"Shouldn't take long. You want to wait here?" Gus smiled and gestured expansively to his trailer. "Comforts of home." I couldn't tell if he was being ironic.

"No thanks." Perhaps the black-and-white television that scrolled the ten o'clock news in lazy defiance of vertical hold was meant to represent the comforts of home.

"You taking your chances out there on the street. It's a dangerous world, baby." Gus handed me his business card across the desk. "Nobody knows that better than Gus."

Thirty minutes later, Jossie swept out the door of the jail, once again laminated in the gold-colored sheath dress she'd left work in the night before. I was waiting for her on the stone steps, reminiscent of those at the Lincoln Memorial, that swept grandly up to plain glass doors girded with six-foot-tall metal detectors. No detectors for those leaving, however. Jossie and I kissed each other's cheeks.

"You got money for a cab, hon? My petty cash got taken as evidence." Jossie lived in Twin Peaks, in an outrageously expensive one-bedroom condominium with an astounding view across the bay. We could share a cab as far as Church and Market, but I was planning on seeing her home. At some point I had to break the news to her that Peaches was dead and that Jossie herself was the only person I could think of with a motive to kill her. I wasn't sure I wanted to say all that in earshot of a cab driver. "I cannot wait to take a bath," Jossie added.

We settled into the back of a cab, Jossie smoothing her backside before sitting. She was cool as ever, giving directions to the cab driver who was noticing her breasts under the Mylar material of her dress. "I'm taking you to my house, baby. While I'm in the tub, you can make me my midnight snack."

I nodded. Jossie squeezed my hand, leaned back against the seat and closed her eyes, instinctively opening them when the cab driver, after negotiating the medieval labyrinth of San Francisco's downtown, turned onto her street ten minutes later.

I stood in the chilly blast of Jossie's open refrigerator, picking through the drawer for the ends of expensive cheeses curled and dry in their cellophane. The other contents of her fridge were a half-empty bottle of champagne, five eggs, five diet sodas, three corsages in various stages of wilt inside their crushproof plastic, and a wrap of white paper that I found to contain popcorn shrimp. The freezer was full of Lean Cuisines. On the counter were three bumpy brown avocados, soft and ripe, and one black banana. "Is brunch all you stock up for?" I yelled, but she ignored me. I found a persimmon-colored Fiestaware bowl and cracked all the eggs into it. Shrimp and avocado omelets with Gorgonzola seemed the only option.

Jossie's kitchen was no more than a glorified hallway, so I took the finished omelets to the coffee table in the living room. Her apartment was furnished with chairs and tables of a dark wood that gleamed without polish, apparently wrought from the vital hearts of some endangered rainforest trees. Displayed on the walls was Art, in the Latin American style of large canvases done in chunks of bright color. None of the rooms in her small place were bound by perpendicular walls. The living room was a trapezoid. In fact, the whole apartment was slightly askew, torqued between the scrap of bedrock foundation on the steep hill and the best angle for the view. The Castro and the Mission spread over the plain below us, caught inland by Portrero Hill's cigar shape. The low skyline of Oakland, as workaday as the steel tankers that hulked near it in the Bay, filled in the background, the lights softened by distance.

"Nice view, right? Now you know how it feels to be above it all." Jossie, wrapped in a black satin robe and matching hair towel, make-up retouched, arranged herself in one of the dark chairs. "This looks great. I don't want to talk about what they feed you in prison." She began to eat. She ate daintily, despite the trauma of twenty hours without gourmet food.

"I couldn't figure out your coffee maker," I said. The huge copper machine took up most of her counter space. Those few square inches of countertop that it didn't actually sit on were overhung by the air traffic of its various appendages and nozzles.

"It's an espresso machine. It's all right, I plan to go to sleep right after this delicious meal. Thanks, baby. Do you cater?"

"Maybe when I get too saggy to strip." I sighed and leaned into the chair, the back of my neck pinched against the hard slat of wood. I watched her eat, not yet touching mine.

"So did you make it over to Peaches'? I hope you were convincing. There's no way I'm going back to that hole they call 850 Bryant. First she's hitting on my regulars, and now this. She's got to get her nose out of Naughtyland. It's her or me, and it sure ain't gonna be me." Jossie's lipstick somehow refused to be slicked away by omelet grease.

"Wait. She was hitting on your regulars?" Anyone who had worked at Naughtyland for more than ten minutes learned that another dancer's regular customers were off-limits. You couldn't talk to them. You couldn't smile at them from a distance, and you certainly couldn't ask them for a lapdance. Just another of the myriad unwritten rules that kept new dancers terrified.

Jossie mmm-hmmed. "Grady himself."

"That must have been when she was new."

"She wasn't so new a week ago."

An image came into my mind. Lance, following Jossie's fondle with his slicked head.

"Did you happen to complain about that little incident to Lance?"

"He might have seen it happen."

"God, Jossie, did it ever occur to you that he might have beaten her up in return for that? Or done something worse? He's a thug, and he dotes on you. It did occur to you! That's why you were so nice to Peaches about her bruises."

"I can't help it if Lance is protective. He's looking out for me. For all of us. Vice presence in our club doesn't do any of us any good. Which is why you and I did Peaches a big favor by giving her a friendly warning in person. Just to reinforce Lance's point."

"Well I never got a chance to clarify Lance's nonverbal communication. Sorry."

"I thought you said you made it over to Peaches' house?"

"I made it over."

"And I figured you'd chicken out."

"No." I hadn't realized that was an option. I would have taken it.

"Talk to me. What happened?"

"Peaches is dead," I managed to say at last.

Jossie stopped eating and looked at me, her mouth around an omelet bite that was still attached to her plate by a string of Gorgonzola. "What are you saying?" She put down her fork.

"Peaches is dead. I went over to talk to her and found her body."

"You're kidding. Baby, that's too much."

"No." I studied my friend's face. Jossie was a bit of an actress, but her horror seemed real.

"Don't you be accusing me! I see that look."

"You're the one who thought she was going to close the place down. You're the one who accused her of trying to ruin your career."

"Well, I happen to have been in jail for the last day. When did she die?"

"Sometime that night after she left work. You were in jail, but where was Lance? How far would he go for you?" I'd seen him leave work at four that morning from my post at the Chinese Food and Donuts, but he could have left and come back before that.

"Don't you be assuming anything, baby."

"Lance seems awfully interested in protecting the rest of us strippers from a vice cop in our midst. I don't see him as the altruistic type.

By the way, there's no evidence that Peaches was a cop."

"Lance just follows orders. And she was *something*, I'm telling you. The way her eyes were jumping around all the time. It's like she was casing the joint. Scoping all of us out."

"Well she wasn't Vice."

"Then why did I just get my career interrupted by doing time?"

"Maybe it was a coincidence."

"Right. Cops coming directly to us, to a private home, Whitmore Grady's private home, that is. He's considering running for mayor, by the way, that's who he is—cops coming to his door just minutes after he shows up with his high-class hooker."

"Maybe it was some city-wide sweep."

"There were five, ten other hookers in the holding pen, all streetwalkers. A city-wide sweep would have swept up thousands."

"Well maybe one of his neighbors turned him in. You know how they get in those ritzy neighborhoods."

Jossie put a hand to her chest and looked out her picture window for awhile. She knew. More than one of her condo-encased neighbors had brayed at the monthly building meetings about her professional activities. The problem seemed to be that these short, expensive sensual encounters were taking place just a short distance from their stock-portfolioing or laptop-using or scotch-sipping or whatever it was they did in the few hours of down time granted them by their employers. Jossie just kept right on paying her outrageous condo fees and hefty monthly mortgage and flirting with these neighbors in the elevators. No way she was going back to suburban hell, she said. Jossie had spent her unhappy childhood dodging taunts and punches in the nearby suburb of San Rafael and had escaped to San Francisco long before her majority.

I tucked Jossie under layers of satin leopard-print that dressed her canopy bed. She murmured her thanks and rolled into sleep.

I found her phone by the bathtub and called the pay phone in the dressing room at Naughtyland that we weren't supposed to know the number to. Plantagena informed me that everyone knew I'd been laid off unfairly but it was just as well I wasn't at work. I was lucky I hadn't come in because it had been a lousy night. Plantagena said she could count on one hand the number of guys out there, and they were all cheap. They weren't sitting with anyone, not even with that skinny new white girl who looked like she was still in high school. It didn't help that a bunch of cops were standing around outside and one was up there in the office with Mose Junior. The boss was all pissed off about a break-in or something. Didn't he know cops were bad for business? How was she supposed to make her stage rent with all these blue uniforms cock-blocking her?

I told her I was sorry, to be careful and thanks and hung up. I couldn't bring myself to tell her the story of Peaches over the phone. I thought the girls at work should know, though, and know the truth. Whoever had killed Peaches might possibly be out for strippers in general.

If he wasn't too busy obsessing about his missing personnel file and the mysteriously fresh air in his office, Mose Junior might make an insensitive announcement—if he knew yet—timed for a moment when few customers remained to get scared away by girlish shrieks. I decided to go down to the club myself. I'd explain what I'd seen before rumors of our co-worker's murder spread.

Jossie had an interesting alibi, I thought, as I shouldered on my leather jacket. Had she killed the suspected Vice officer to protect her livelihood? Had she then called the cops on herself to ensure an alibi so solid it was already in the police database? Jossie was rash, I thought as I let myself out of her apartment, but firmly against jail time. Besides, she'd been at work until two and in the holding tank by three thirty. And whoever had killed Luna had been looking for something.

Chapter Six

Lance was guarding the front door when I arrived at Naughtyland after midnight.

"Who is it?" he said as I closed my eyes to avoid his penlight. "Oh, it's Aisling. I didn't recognize you with clothes on. And because..." The pinpoint was replaced by a bright flash. I opened my eyes to Lance commandeering a fresh Polaroid as it ground out of the staff's camera, "...until you're back at work, you're eighty-sixed." He added my photo to a collage of bouncees pinned to the wall in the lobby. "So you'll just be leaving."

"It's been so nice not seeing you. I've got to talk to the girls." I settled myself in a lean against the lobby wall. "And I have something I have to say especially to you," I added, in an eye-batting tone.

"Move," he said. "You can't stand between me and the door. I need the door in my line of vision." I didn't move. "You're not going in if you're not scheduled. To get past me, you got to pay your fee."

A customer came in. I recognized him as one of the club's regulars. He was an elderly gent with white hair and a body mass collapsed waistward. He visited Naughtyland at least once a week. He always took a seat at the stage to see the Asian women, and retreated to a table for anyone else's show. When asked for a lapdance, he would drag the unwitting proposer into a discussion about God that would last as long as the dancer's patience or graciousness allowed. We called him The Converter. All the dancers who knew him avoided him. I smiled sweetly at The Converter in compensation since Lance was energetically frisking the old man, tossing his polyester pant legs up over his thin brown socks, snapping aside his suspenders to pat down his antique short-sleeved shirt. I was sure this harassment was a show for my benefit. After a peek under the old man's fishing cap, Lance let The Converter pass inside.

"You assaulted Peaches," I said.

To my surprise Lance didn't deny a thing. "Yep," he said.

Five or six barely-legals were coming through the front door. Lance gruffly demanded then checked their IDs. The Friday night crowd was never my favorite. Young men travelling in hunter-gatherer packs were notoriously rude. I watched them shove each other through the curtained entrance, already hooting, their postures slouching toward Neanderthal.

"Well? Why? You're supposed to be everyone's security, not just Jossie's avenger."

Lance kept his eyes on the front door, his surveillance on the street. "You're assuming I started it. Maybe she started it. Ever thought of that?"

"She started it. Right. How? By being in front of you when you started throwing punches? You're the hired thug." I'd kept my eye on Lance over the few weeks he'd been working at Naughtyland. As a bartender, he'd worked near the stage and had watched naked girls for eight hours with an intensity that had led to complaints from us dancers. Mose Junior had reassigned him to door duty for fear of sexual harassment lawsuits. I had no idea why the Moses didn't just fire Lance. They must have worried that they'd never find an equally intimidating replacement.

"Hey, look who's talking. The fired thug. Trust me, babes, I was helping you out. She's not what she seems to be."

"I've heard the cop rumors. I don't believe them."

Lance shrugged. He angled himself toward an incoming crowd. None of the small group of thirtysomethings that pushed past me failed to arrive at Lance's side without an ID already meekly offered. The bouncer ran his penlight over each of their faces and pulled the last man aside to pat down his Dockered ass. The Docker-wearer lifted his arms automatically. He looked vaguely terrified.

"Was that really necessary?" I asked, after the group had passed sheepishly through the curtain. "We don't want to scare off these guys, you know."

"Are you aware of the number of concealed weapon permits in the state of California."

"No."

"You'd be properly scared if you were. Are you finished with your interrogation?"

"God. No. Where were you last night? Did you kill this Vice infiltrator to help me out, too?"

"Where do you think I was? Some of us still have jobs."

"Did you hear me? Peaches is dead."

"You're lying." His expression didn't change, but the bouncer's stare flickered away from the street.

After a moment, I began searching my pockets for cash. "I want to get in and tell the others. Look, here's fifty bucks."

"Keep looking. You know Mose Junior wants a hundred every time he sees one of you dancer's faces." He was still gruff, but his speech had lost its crispness. His face had paled to an even greater contrast with his aviator sunglasses.

They weren't his rules. Mose Junior did want his hundred every day he saw a dancer's face. I suppose our boss feared we would sneak in, sneak a few lapdances, sneak out, cheating him of his cut.

I kept an emergency stash of twenties duct-taped inside my boot. I had to dip into it to pay him. Lance counted the bills and creased them into the pocket of his black and white camouflage combat fatigues. I took a steadying breath before I joined Naughtyland's Friday night.

Painted-on bat wings rode up Kevin's forehead when he saw me.

"Hey!" His black lipstick gave a high gloss to his smile. He was pouring an O'Doul's into a half-pint glass, the non-alcoholic beer's label turned carefully away from the crowd. You wouldn't have known cops had been there before. Naughtyland was now packed. Every seat was full. A double ring of men barnacled the stage. I couldn't see who was dancing, only the disembodied masts of two thin legs hoisting silver spike heels. The shoes were a pair of mine. Whoever was up there was flat on her back.

"Hey," I said.

"What's up? You back?"

"Another couple weeks." Kevin shook his head in sympathy. He added the full beer glass to a circle of others on a cork tray. "Listen, you were working last night. Was Lance here the whole time?"

Kevin nodded. "I heard he turned you in."

"He never left work? Not once during the shift?"

"Nope. Why?"

"I've got something unpleasant to tell you," I said.

"What's up?"

I told him about finding Peaches. He was still for a moment. Then tears made a wash of his thick black eyeliner. The kohl turned to gray runnels as it collected motes of the white pancake he used on his face. I handed the tray of non-alcoholic beers to an annoyed pair of fraternity boys who'd come ranting for their drinks. Kevin had fallen to a squat against the wall.

I went around the bar to him. "You okay?" I've never been good with crying people. I handed him a cocktail napkin.

"It's my fault," he whispered, after I bent down to hear what he was repeating. "I shouldn't have let her go with that guy."

"What guy?

"The guy who gave her a ride home."

"When?"

"Last night. She left early in some guy's car. I should have made her take a cab. And the driver, I recognized him. He's been in here a few times. A customer." He swabbed his eyes, making a marble-cake pattern of his make-up. "I knew it was bad news," he whispered.

"A customer?" That was weird. Normally, dancers fled from customers when we met up with them out of the club. I'd certainly never known a co-worker to consider riding home with one. Most of us went home in cabs. Few spouses or friends were willing to show up at two in the morning to give rides, and cabs were a safe alternative. They were numbered for identification, and Kevin, concerned for our safety, studiously wrote down the cabs' numbers and passengers before the drivers took off. If anything went wrong, cabs could be traced.

"She told me it was okay. I had a terrible feeling about it."

"What did he look like?"

"Youngish hippie type. And the car was a white Toyota Camry."

"Well that ought to help the police. You can't possibly blame yourself for this." I squeezed his thin, trembly shoulder.

Cameron came over for a Coke. I told her the news as well, and left the two of them together.

Why had I taken this on myself? I thought, as I elbowed my way to the dressing room through a rowdy crowd thick as mud. I'd wanted everyone to get accurate information, not gossip, not rumors. But for someone at a loss among the crying, it was going to be an miserable night.

A pounding on my door the next morning sat me straight up in my futon.

"Wake up darling! There's some cops at the door for you! Should I invite them in for tea?" Geoffrey, with his apoplectic laughter, smacked the door to my bedroom open and crumpled into my room. My most social roommate was still dressed in Friday night attire, cuffed dark jeans below his leather jacket and a ribbed underwear shirt. The shirt had come untucked, a high state of dishevelment for Geoffrey. Basketball shoes with double-tall soles aggravated his stumbling.

"Just getting home?" I groggily flipped through the baskets that contained my clothes to find an outfit. My bedroom, small enough to have been originally designed as a closet itself, had no closet. I'd half-expected to be woken by cops pounding on my door. I really should have laid something out before I'd gone to bed. "What is it, three?" Wasn't that the time favored by police for dragging people away?

"Oh, later, I think. Or earlier, would you say? I had the most fabulous evening. At some point, we were up in Twin Peaks just being gathered into the fog. Couldn't see a thing. Just dissolving. It was marvelous." Geoffrey held on to the door frame. He appeared to be melting down it.

"You don't have to yell, I'm right here. Did you happen to drop some acid? Along with the booze I can taste coming off of you? You don't normally enjoy nature." I pulled on a pair of black rayon bell-bottoms.

"You know I would never do drugs, unless we were completely out of chocolate."

"Right." I exchanged my grubby Depeche Mode T-shirt for something more form fitting and bright. "Does this look okay for an interrogation?"

"Stop! Stop changing! Go just as you were! That rumpled look is fabulous!" My roommate had by this time sunk all the way to the floor. He crawled across it to my futon. He hoisted himself onto the mattress, dragged my quilt over his legs, and began to rock himself to sleep.

I decided the rumpled look would do for my hair. I checked the time as I passed through the living room on my way to the blue uniforms, rigid as two fence posts, that waited outside the security grille at the bottom of our stairs. It was nine o'clock.

A black-and-white idled at the curb. Officer Suarez jumped behind the wheel. A male cop even burlier than she was steered me from my front door the few steps into the cruiser's backseat.

"We'd like to ask you a few questions," he said. That seemed obvious. I picked my cuticles while the male cop seated himself shotgun and Suarez pulled into the street. There was little traffic this early on a Saturday morning. Or perhaps what few cars there were pulled in panic to the side to let the cruiser through. I'd never ridden in a cop car before. Instead of being completely fenced off with steel mesh, the front seat was divided from the criminal element by sliding panes of Plexiglas behind the two officers' heads. It was like being taken away while ordering from a Tastee Freez counter.

"I'm flattered that you brought backup. Who's the sidekick?" I'd wanted to say something equivalent to 'who's the chick?' but there are no mildly disparaging slang words for "man" in English.

"My name is Officer Michaels." He had a deep voice and a thick neck, and concentrated on looking out the window. The fog hadn't burned off yet; the sky was the color of a switched-off light bulb. I hadn't dressed warmly enough.

"Where are we going?"

"Bernal Heights Station." Suarez answered.

"What's this about?"

Suarez glanced at me in the rearview mirror as she made a turn onto Valencia Street. "What do you think? The Luna Nguyen case."

"I already told you everything I know about that. I found her, remember? I gave you a statement. May I say, you were a lot friendlier then."

"Well, new evidence came up. Let's not talk about it further, no one's read you your Miranda rights yet."

"Miranda rights? You haven't arrested me. Shit, what kind of new evidence do you have?" How could they have evidence that I'd killed Luna when I hadn't?

"Detective Deegan of Homicide will tell you all about it."

"Do I need a lawyer?"

"I don't know." Suarez paused dramatically. "Do you?"

Bernal Heights Station was on Cortland Avenue, a home-towny kind of street on the other side of the hill from Prospect where Luna had lived. I looked glumly out the cruiser's window as we passed a small library, a cafe with gingham curtains, a senior citizen's center and an organic food store. The only building on the street that wasn't cute was the police station. Suarez pulled into the parking lot of what looked like a compact motel: a two-story rectangle painted in fading atomic blue, with external concrete stairs zigzagging in front of it. "Bernal Heights Police Station" was affixed in foot-high gold letters to the front. Officer Michaels curtly ushered me through the empty tiled lobby and past the reception desk staffed by one bored dispatcher into a tiny gray room furnished with a table and Detective Deegan.

"Aubrey Lyle" said Officer Michaels, and immediately took leave of us. I began to regret his relatively benign presence after a moment of silence in the company of Deegan. The detective sat on a metal folding chair facing the door, two files in front of him. He was a guy you wouldn't notice if you passed him on the street. Average height, brown hair cut long on top, late thirties. His clothes were earth tones pressed into creases. They gave the impression that he wore a belted cardboard box.

After that uncomfortable sizing-up moment, he spoke. "Detective Deegan, homicide. Please sit." He gestured toward a chair with stained upholstery and metal arm rests.

I didn't sit. "What's this about?"

"Just have a few questions about the Luna Nguyen case. Please," Deegan rose, playing the gentleman, and again waved his arm at the hard chair. "Sit."

We both sat, slowly. Deegan had spoken slowly and calmly. It seemed like he was trying to strike a soothing tone, but he overplayed it. He reminded me of a purring lion.

"You worked together at," he peered at his file, "Naughtyland?"

"Yes."

"And why would a lovely girl such as yourself be involved in that business?"

"Is this part of the interrogation? I'm not answering that. It's irrelevant."

"It's just a friendly warning. We're always finding bodies in this city, and a good percentage of them are members of your profession. We find so many dead prostitutes we got a name for them. Zeros. And they don't die without taking a few punches first, or worse."

"It's nice to know you handle the death of those citizens with sensitivity. But I'm not a prostitute, I'm a stripper."

"Same idea. Do your parents know about this little escapade of yours? Is it a rebellion thing? They must be worried about you. You're not safe out there, little girl."

"I don't fetishize safety. And I'm not good at being worried about." I recognized that Deegan was baiting me, trying to get me angry. I suppose emotional inquisitionees spill more of their guts. I didn't elaborate, and Deegan didn't say anything. The long silence that followed was another tactic, I thought, to keep me talking.

Momma did know about my job. I'd told her about it as soon as I'd started stripping, and she never brought it up again, perhaps because she was in denial or perhaps only because her pills evaporated her memory. She had protested about my safety during our one conversation about it. I'd tried to explain to her that I thought the you're-not-safe argument was just another way to keep women out of a lucrative job, and for that matter, to keep women out of the neighborhood, the

Tenderloin, that men used as a shopping mall for sex and drugs. Personally, I hadn't felt more "safe" in my jobs that had required clothing. I'd just been poorer.

"You found the body, yes?" Deegan caved.

"Yes." I pushed the image of Luna lying naked and discolored out of my mind. The body.

"How well did you know Luna?" He continued, without the polite pause that is customary after a mention of the dead. In fact, Deegan seemed to be developing a habit of beginning his next question before I had finished my answer.

"Not well at all. I met her about a month ago."

"How did you two meet?"

"She took a job at my work. Naughtyland."

"Was the night you found the body the first time you had been to her apartment?"

"Yes."

"She told you her address?"

I didn't answer right away. The new evidence Suarez had mentioned—perhaps Mose Junior had reported Luna's employment file stolen. But how could that have been traced to me? There must have been something else.

"Ms. Lyle?" I'd run out of time on Deegan's conversation clock. I'd hate to play chess with this man.

"I got her address from her file at work. Have you interviewed other people from there?"

"It's being covered in the investigation. Why did you go to Luna's house that night?"

"Just to talk to her."

"About what, if she wasn't your friend?"

"I don't see why it matters."

"And does it matter or not that you assaulted a man the night before?"

"Well, no, but I didn't assault anyone."

"You've been laid off work because you assaulted a customer."

"I followed him. He stole some money from me. He got away."

"You're saying you've never committed assault?"

"I certainly didn't assault that guy. Even though he deserved it."

"Then how do you explain this?" Deegan opened one of the files on the table and turned it around. He read the top page for me. "Booked for assault and battery, Austin, Texas, February seventeenth, nineteen ninety-five." There lay a fax of the report and a fax of my ten fingerprints. He sat back and looked at me with his detective stare.

My southern accent gets more pronounced when I'm under stress, and I had noticed its appearance in my last few responses to Deegan's rapid-fire questions. People that aren't from the South themselves often perceive me as dozens of I.Q. points below average when they hear me speak with the slightest hint of a drawl. People that are from the South often do so, too, since the Kentucky hill drawl I picked up from Momma is low-prestige on the drawl hierarchy. I feared the detective was making this dreadful mistake. I took a breath.

"Okay. I didn't just fall off the turnip truck onto the corner of Haight and Ashbury or something. The charges were dropped for that—" I pointed to his file "—it was years ago, and I don't know what it has to do with the present. Why am I here? This is ridiculous harassment."

"I'll tell you what it has to do with the present." Deegan spoke lightly and calmly. He tapped his pencil slowly on the fax of my prints. "It proves you are capable of assault and battery, for one thing."

"Assault and battery! I swung a frying pan at the guy! The only thing that got battered was his ego, and it was big enough to take a few hits. Mellissa dropped the charges the next day!" Deegan knew all this; it was all in the faxes in front of him. He couldn't be serious.

"There's more. Your prints were all over that room."

"I told you, I found her body!"

"Your prints were on the murder weapon."

Shit. Okay. "They were on the bikini because it was mine. I'd loaned it to her."

Deegan raised his eyebrows, as if incredulous. This guy should have been a lawyer. "It was yours?"

"I loaned her the bikini. But someone else used it to kill her."

"How come you didn't make that fact part of your statement to Officer Suarez?"

"Because I figured it didn't matter. I know I didn't kill her. Why would I kill her? What's my motive, Detective?"

Deegan pushed his glasses up on his nose and stared at me coldly. "Jealousy. She made more money than you did. She had a customer you wanted for yourself. You couldn't handle your girlfriend dancing for men. Money. You needed money for drugs, you knew she'd have cash. An accident. You two were into some kinky sex and things went awry." His pause after "awry" became a silence. "In that case, you could plead manslaughter. Shall I go on?"

"No, there's no need to go on." I had heard too many whispered male fantasies in the dark cubicles of Naughtyland to be completely surprised by Deegan's conclusions. They were common. Women are jealous and possessive, strippers do drugs and are into kinky sex, behaviors made likely because of abusive backgrounds. What was frightening, if unsurprising, is that he was prepared to accuse me of murder based on his own stereotypes. What else did he have to go on? He'd thought about my "motives" long and hard, maybe even fancied himself one of those brilliant detectives who works up a suspect based on their psychological problems. "Troubled relationships with women" inevitably ranks high among the criminal's neuroses. Apparently I was no exception.

"Good work. Lesbianism, drug use, kinky sex and petty jealousy. You're definitely on your way to tracking down whoever killed your zero. Let me give you a clue, detective. Women don't become sex workers because we have psychological problems. We do it because we're poor, to make money."

Pencil taps against the clipboard, which had kept tempo throughout the interview, stopped. Deegan pinched the pencil in midair. He looked at me oh-so-quizzically. "I'm not an old-fashioned thinker. Isn't it true, Ms. Lyle, that you and Luna Nguyen were close friends? You seem to be quite interested in her, for someone who hardly knew her. You went to her home. She was bruised a couple days before her death, and you are capable of assault and battery, as we have seen. Your fingerprints are all over her bedroom and on the underwear that was tied around her neck. How am I expected to view this evidence?"

"I don't know. As a visual aid when you're jacking off?"

Deegan pursed his lips. His straight hair hadn't moved throughout the interview. It must have been sprayed. "Let's move on then, Ms. Lyle. Where were you the night of the twenty-sixth? That would have been last Thursday. Between midnight and one a.m."

We were all off the hook, I thought. Jossie and Lance and I had all been at work.

"At Naughtyland."

"Who can verify that?"

"Any of my co-workers or my customers. Hundreds of people saw me there."

"Saw quite a bit of you." Deegan made a few notes on his clipboard. He squeezed the clip open to even up the edges of his papers. "I'm sure I'll be seeing you again," he looked at me dismissively.

I got up and walked out.

Chapter Seven

It was time for brunch when I got out of the police station. The fog had retreated but I still shivered at the unsheltered bus stop a block west of the station. A few patrons sat in the gingham-curtained windows of Cortland Street's cafe, eating steamy oozy egg casseroles and drinking lattes. They looked warm. They looked like the citizens the police protected and served, not those they interrogated. The twenty-two bus hadn't come after ten minutes, so I decided to walk. It was a mile or more home.

That joker Deegan was never going to figure out who had killed Luna. He'd certainly enjoy interrogating hundreds of strippers, though. I got the sense that the murder cases involving zeros were never seriously pursued. The public had never gotten over the idea that sex workers deserved whatever we got. The papers regularly ran tall headlines about prostitutes' bodies being found. It seemed to be a monthly occurrence. If the cases were ever solved, that didn't make the news.

I passed a newspaper kiosk and decided to confirm my cynicism. *The Chronicle* mentioned Luna's death on page one of the Metro section, below the fold. At least I suppose it was Luna they were talking about, as her name was not mentioned pending notification of relatives. "Suspected Prostitute Strangled," read the headline. After what Deegan had told me, I wasn't surprised. "Definite Stripper Strangled" just didn't catch the eye of today's reader. "Woman Killed in her Bernal Heights Home." Times and dates and noncommittal quotes from police soon gave way to juicy details. "The young woman's unclothed body was found in her bed. She apparently died of asphyxiation after a ligature was tied around her neck. Time of death has yet to be determined. San Francisco police declined to say if any suspects have been identified. Sources indicate that police have not ruled out autoerotic asphyxiation as a possible factor in the death."

I wadded the paper between my hands. I don't know where it landed. I sucked in a breath and resumed walking, no longer feeling the cold.

Walking failed to give a steady rhythm to my thoughts. Why mention that Luna had been naked? Whoever wrote the unsigned article must have been dying to let his dirt-craving audience know that the "ligature" in question had been a bra, but was stopped from revealing this juicy bit of evidence. And "autoerotic asphyxiation"? Please! Of course the police hadn't ruled it out, because if they'd had any sense they wouldn't have considered it in the first place. Boys in their teens might get off on choking themselves, but I've yet to hear of a woman trying it. Even as corpses, women are just more fodder for John Q. Public's erotic imagination.

It had looked like a sex killing, though. But maybe that was just what the killer, whoever it was, had wanted it to look like. Another dead prostitute was just that.

I was making some unconscious decision during my walk, because at the end of it, I found myself standing outside 1120 Prospect. I stopped and spent a moment looking at the scene of the crime. I had two weeks on my hands. I'd make sure Luna's case got solved. I began by ringing number one's bell.

Angie answered my buzz with typical exasperation, but she did invite me in. "What are you doing here? Come up in here out of the cold." She buzzed me through the outer door and was waiting for me at the top of the stairs, dressed once again in her pastel kimono. A Virginia Slim dangled from her right hand. Her fingernails had been subjected to a manicure, professional length, lollipop pink. She hadn't thought about how that color would look against her candied yam hair dye. "Aubrey, did you say? With all the chaos before, I never got your name. Forgive the mess, hon, I'm moving out." Angie waved me into the apartment.

Stacks of boxes leaned against the living room wall where the entertainment center had been, and a pile of clothes drifted several feet up the wall in the corner next to the couch. Angie had apparently lifted her ban on smoking inside permanently. Smoke hung around the track lights. Angie gestured to the couch. "Have a seat. Cigarette?"

"I don't smoke, thanks."

"Don't start. Well, as you can see, I'm getting out." She waved her hand expansively, gesturing to the boxes. Smoke trailed in the air behind the path carved by her long nails.

"Where to?"

"Noe Valley. Now there's an up-and-coming spot. My new place has hardwood floors, bay windows and it's a secure building. Really secure. And I'm on the top floor. No deck though, but I'm getting used to life without it."

The deck was curtained off or we would have been able to see Noe Valley, a gentrified neighborhood a few blocks to the north and west. I thought of Victorian hardwood floors ruined by hairy white rugs. I hadn't absorbed the details of Angie's decor before. Her living room could have had a theme: contemporary igloo. White curtains drifted into white shag wall-to-wall carpeting which was layered over with hairy white throw rugs. The coffee table was a glass kidney shape with clear spear-like legs stabbing the shag. Other furniture was either glass or white upholstery so puffy it looked to be holding its breath.

"Still not going out there?" I asked, indicating the concealed deck.

"Can't. It's all taped off. A genuine crime scene. Of course I haven't told my mother. She's always telling me to come back to Illinois. As if! When I left Plainfield, I left Plainfield forever." Angie plopped her cigarette butt into the Merlot bottle, now almost half full of the slender lipstick-marked stubs. "She'd flip if she knew there's police tape right outside my window. Tea or coffee?" Angie stood up.

"Tea would be great. Thanks."

My hostess went into the hall-like offshoot from the living room that served as a kitchen. As though her kitchen were actually another room, she talked louder as she put the kettle on. "Yeah, whoever got to Luna apparently made their getaway over the deck. He had a long drop, or she did. I guess it could have been a woman who killed her. Those gangbanger girls will do anything for their boyfriends. Well they're getting this white girl out of their neighborhood." She opened the carton of milk she'd extracted from her refrigerator and sniffed its contents.

"I came here to talk to you about that. Luna left work that day with a man driving a white Camry. Do you know who it could have been?"

"White Camry. No." Angie showed me a basket full of tea bags to choose from. Since she had little yellow envelopes of Earl Grey, I chose that. Her words and her kimono drifted after her as she returned to the kitchen. "Whoever got her would have to have been someone lightweight or sneaky, since I didn't hear anything. Maybe they used a ladder. Do you think a ladder could reach up to third floors? My new place is on the third floor. Here you are." Angie handed me a steaming ceramic mug the color of butter. The tea bag surfaced in the water, hemorrhaging a brown stain. "Milk?"

I nodded. Angie returned with the open carton and set it on her coffee table. She didn't seem to be joining me for tea. She tapped a Virginia Slim out of the pack and looked me up and down as she took her first drag. "You want to look through that pile? There's some clothes I'm giving away. Can't move everything, you know."

I looked politely toward the tangle of clothing against the wall. No one else had quite my style. I rarely wanted any castoffs that were offered to me. I only pretended to participate in the female ritual of swapping clothes. Angie was obviously a yuppie type who probably went to work in pastel dress-for-success suits and white running shoes. Since I had only seen Angie in her Monet kimono, however, I couldn't be sure. The pile confirmed my suspicions. Heaped into the corner was a jumble of mix-and-match outfits in sea foam, eggplant, dusty rose and beige. The only bright spot in the sea of washout was a spot of peppermint-pink leather peeking out from the bottom. I leaned over the couch's armrest, my eye caught.

"What's this?" I pulled at the scrap of pink. Out came the bottom of my leather bikini.

I set my tea and the bikini bottoms carefully onto the glass coffee table, sat back and steadied my hands. How weird.

"Oh those. Aren't they hideous? I found them drying on the deck. I told her if she kept putting her underwear out there, I was going to start confiscating it. Imagine, crazy-looking panties flapping in the breeze for all the neighbors to see! And every time I went out for a smoke I had to think about her crotch."

"That pair is mine, actually. I loaned them to Luna."

"Take them, then. You've saved them from some trash-picker. You can't throw anything away anymore, have you noticed? Anything valuable on the street, and the whole area's crawling with people looking for gold in your garbage. I'm waiting until the day I leave to put out my trash, and the neighbors can deal with the aftermath. Oh, you want something else of hers?" Angie padded toward her bedroom, trailing smoke.

She returned, flicking through a pile of glossy junk mail—coupon pages with rectangles cut out and flyers advertising whimsically patterned personal checks. "I put it here somewhere. Where I wouldn't lose it, hah! Right. I almost threw away this whole pile, course you can't throw anything away anymore with the new recycling campaign. More containers on the sidewalk to tempt the unwashed. Here you go." Angie handed me a cassette tape without a case. Its label curled off the black plastic cassette. "'80s music' was printed on it in purple felt tip.

"This was Luna's?"

"Yes. She insisted I borrow it, she thought I would love it. I didn't have the heart to tell her that unless it was country music I wasn't interested. Well I did tell her, but she made me take it anyway. Practically forced it on me. I never did get around to listening to it. Well," she stubbed out her cigarette and took her air neat for a moment. "Good luck to you. I'm off, got a meeting with some movers about my poundage. Hoping to fudge it a little. You've no idea what it costs these days to move."

I took a quick swallow of scalding tea and wished Angie luck in her new place. She once again called me a cab and gave me a twenty to pay for it, writing her new address on the bill. She tucked me into the cab with a warning never to come into the neighborhood again. Between the smoke cloud around her face and her powder-puff slippers, Angie resembled a tall Q-Tip waving good-bye.

I decided that I liked Angie Pritchett. She reminded me of the good souls who got their hair fixed in my mother's beauty shop back home.

I smoothed the label on the tape while the cab driver whisked down Bernal Hill then chuted the roller coaster hills of Guerrero Street through the Mission.

I asked the driver for the favor. He obligingly ejected the Indian movie soundtrack from the car's tape deck and inserted Luna's tape.

"Boy George, whatever happened to him?" he asked me. "All these great singers that you never hear from now."

"I think he kicked heroin and then made some kind of comeback," I said.

The driver hummed "Do You Really Want To Hurt Me" along with the tape until we reached my apartment on Church Street, where he ejected it and, reluctantly, handed it back.

Inside, I collapsed onto the green couch. After a few moments I stuck my hair up in a topknot and went to the kitchen to look for a can of Coke. Our refrigerator was crammed with half full bottles of wine, crusted condiments, and bowls of leftovers with crumples of aluminum foil inserted as covers. In the back, stuck on their sides to the bottom shelf, were two cheery aluminum cans. I took them both out and chaindrank them. Afterwards I was queasy.

I realized the apartment was relaxing and quiet. Alarmed, I went to check on my roommates and see if any of them had a cassette player. Maybe there was some clue in the mix with Culture Club. Only Geoffrey was home, sleeping quietly on my futon, bedding tangled around his platform basketball shoes. He smiled softly in his sleep. Drunken revelry never made him vomit and he never had a hangover, moral or physical, the next day.

Zan had a CD boombox on the nightstand on her side of their futon. Its cassette drawer was open, with a tape still inside. As I pulled Zan's tape out, the thin brown ribbon spooled out behind, stuck in the machinery. Hope she wasn't too attached to that Natalie Merchant album, I thought guiltily, as I slotted the eviscerated cassette back into its plastic drawer. I'd have to listen to it in Peter and Rainbow's van. I couldn't risk ruining Luna's tape in Zan's machine.

A scrawled note was attached to my bedroom door with a chewed wad of gum. The handwriting was Vivian's. *Check your messages*, it said. *Some hysterical person keeps calling for you. Hope your visit with the police was free of fisticuffs.*

Where was the sisterly concern, I wondered as I punched in the voicemail number. I made a mental list of my hysterical acquaintances, wondering which might have called.

It had been Jossie. I called her at home.

"Oh, there you are. At last."

"What's the matter?"

"I called Mose Junior to get off the schedule for next week. I'm gone from Naughtyland until I can get myself a lawyer."

"A lawyer? Why?"

"Don't get smart with me. You know what I've been up to and we know the place was under surveillance."

"It wasn't under surveillance, not from the cops anyway. Peaches wasn't Vice."

"I still know she was up to something." Jossie paused. "Well it doesn't matter anyway. That place is crawling with cops now, of the uniformed kind. Half the force is hanging around inside Naughtyland, this time officially."

"Right, the big investigation. Did they question you?"

"I'm not dealing with any more cops, baby."

"Smart thinking." I couldn't picture Jossie getting wrangled into a cop car just for questioning. She didn't do too much against her will. "Listen. Kevin says Peaches left that night with a customer who drives a Toyota Camry. He says the guy looked like a hippie. Know who that could be?"

"One of her regulars. He comes in to see her all the time. Drops at least sixty on her. That's per visit I'm talking. Why, is he a suspect?"

"Don't you think he should be?"

"Not if he's her Vice contact."

"What does he look like?"

"White. Looks poor, but he's not."

"Can you give me anything else?"

"He needs a haircut—a dog groomer wouldn't notice the difference."

"Is his hair brown? Black?"

"Just frizz, far as I can tell."

"You're not being very helpful."

"Look, baby, we're just tense. There's been a murder, right? Actually, I've been calling to tell you about Luna's memorial. I hope you don't have plans for later. I saw the announcement in the paper, which made a point of asking friends and co-workers to attend. It's today at three. Here's the address. You should check it out."

The memorial service was at Luna's father's home in Berkeley.

"See. That doesn't sound Vice, asking us to come to the memorial," I said, and promised to go.

"Well, we'll see, baby, you never know. I've got to go now. A girl's beauty regimen takes time, but it's always so well spent."

We hung up.

When Hugh found me in the kitchen a few minutes later, I was using tongs to put the bottom half of my pink leather bikini into a turkey-sized ZipLoc freezer bag. I explained that I'd come across the bottom half of the murder weapon and wanted to deliver it to Suarez as evidence.

"You realize you're now tampering with evidence. You can't turn that in. Haven't you ever heard of the evidence chain?" Hugh's glasses slid down his nose when he got excited.

"No." By the time I removed the kitchen tongs, the panties were smashed into the corner of the bag.

"If where evidence has been, who collected it and by what methods, where it was stored, etcetera, is not documented, it can't be admitted. You should have left that where you found it and called the police."

"Well, I didn't know. I've never heard of any evidence chain. This isn't exactly evidence. It was laundry, brought in by the neighbor. I thought it might have useful fingerprints on it. Anyway, it's mine."

Hugh regarded the underwear as if it were a grenade. Since it was of the thong variety, there was hardly enough square yardage to contain an entire fingerprint. "Well, it won't help Luna's case now," he said.

Chapter Eight

The address Jossie had given me for the memorial service wasn't anywhere near public transportation, so Hugh and I took a taxi from the Ashby BART station. Hugh had agreed to be my escort. All of my roommates were also my friends, but Hugh was the friend whom I counted on to accompany me to potential ordeals. He'd go anywhere with me, no matter how uncomfortable it was sure to make him. Geoffrey balked at anything that wasn't obviously fun. And unlike Geoffrey, Hugh was always demure and remembered his manners, even if he didn't dress nearly as well. Vivian would have had an analytical field day at a stripper's memorial service. Zan would have tried to take care of my feelings to the point of annoyance. I wasn't good at being mothered.

I wore a demure black dress, ankle-length, with darts at the waist and short sleeves. Hugh wore a black nineteen-fifties style suit that didn't look too bad, except, like all of his clothes, it was too big. Hugh was so slender and tall that he could never find anything that fit right at the thrift store. But the employee discount deal was too good to pass up.

The homes in the Berkeley hills all seemed to be either adobe-style Spanish revival or boxy, brown-shingled Craftsmans, gardened with pine trees, neon flowers, and groping cacti. The landscape which only eked out threads of green, seemed barren, the homes' material foreign. When I had first moved to California, I'd walked around with a jarring feeling that I was living on a movie set, or maybe in Spain. Red clay roof tiles, perpetual sun, blondes, surfboards and skinny-legged palm trees—familiar, yet unreal. It turns out I knew California intimately before I ever lived there. I knew it well as backdrop to countless television shows and movie scenes and it seemed fit only for memorized lines and bit parts—not for life. Its soil could barely support a deciduous tree. Since then I'd learned to appreciate a lifestyle free of winter, humidity and bugs.

The cab driver dropped us off at a small stucco home. The house was low to the ground. Rectangular pots of bonsai trees surrounded ceramic Buddha figures on the front lawn. The front door was open.

The huge room the foyer opened onto was crowded, but the noise level was at a low murmur. Two distinct groups of mourners had formed in front of the picture window. Middle-aged folks dressed in earth tones stood in a circle in front of the view of the Golden Gate bridge and green hills to its north. A few of my co-workers, looking great in clingy black outfits and styled hair, huddled opposite the older people. I went over to them and exchanged murmured greetings, hand-squeezings, and some air kisses.

We silently admired the view. I didn't often get over to Berkeley and certainly never to the toney Berkeley hills, and I was unprepared for how beautiful my adopted city looked from there. The San Francisco Bay and the mountainous headlands tethered to the peninsula by the Golden Gate Bridge were empty, vast shapes; the water was silver and the mountain a silhouette in the afternoon sun. The city itself huddled tight on its peninsula, as though that small landmass had been a magnet collecting filaments of steel that would soon overburden it with skyscrapers. The skyscrapers, at that hour and season, wore a shawl of fog, and the skyline blurred like a developing photograph.

But I'd lost Hugh. I found him near the door to the foyer, alone and shifting nervously from foot to foot. A bearded white man with receding hair and his hands in the pockets of his perma-press trousers walked towards us. He wore brown workboots, freshly polished, and a brown-and-white striped oxford shirt with a square-cut matching sportcoat. The clothes were stiff. Only the boots were broken in.

"Thank you for coming." He spoke quietly. "There's no need to introduce yourselves. You're in a safe house here. I'm Murray Lebowski, Luna's father."

We shook hands with Murray. Hugh and I politely didn't introduce ourselves.

Why didn't we need to introduce ourselves? It was kind of a relief. I never know how to act at normal mourning rituals. And I had the feeling that the Lebowski household was rather non-traditional.

"Refreshments are in the dining room, and a memorial to Luna is in the backyard—please visit it. I believe in simplicity, so no service or anything will be held." Murray's eyes were blue and sad. He gestured toward the buffet table and rejoined the circle in front of the view of the bridge.

Hugh seemed reluctant to join the cluster of strippers whose high heels, densely packed as a bed of nails, threatened the Lebowski hardwood floor. I suggested that we visit the dining room.

In the dining room a rustic oak table was arranged with a platter of white and yellow cheeses, several blue and white teapots with small matching cups, and a pile of unwaxed fruit, held in place with a vine of purple grapes. The food and tea were displayed with balanced precision, like a still life. Perhaps that explained why no one had disturbed either food or tea. I certainly wasn't going to be the first. Even Hugh, who was usually hungry, didn't disturb the sculpture.

"Hugh, what did he mean by 'this is a safe house'?"

"Look at this." Hugh nudged me. He pointed to a portrait, done on a grand cult-of-personality scale. A man's head was in black silhouette against red. The piece took up half of the wall opposite the buffet table. Whoever had allowed that example of poor taste to flap against their wall could not have been the same person who had so artfully arranged the simple food in front of us. "Che Guevara."

"The biggest Che I've ever seen!"

"The national hero of Cuba. A revolutionary. An asthmatic doctor from Argentina who joined Castro to overthrow the repressive Batista regime of Cuba in the nineteen-fifties—"

"I know, Hugh. History major, remember? Why is there a ten-foot-tall Che silhouette in Murray's dining room?"

"He's a hero to many. An icon of revolution, and considered a martyr of it."

"I know that, too, but that thing's the size of a sheet! Who's in the picture next to him? Is he an icon too? Doesn't Murray have any family portraits to put on his walls?" Did Luna grow up eating her mac and cheese under the inspection of Che?

We approached the five-by-seven-inch framed portrait that made a relatively small dot in the middle of the white space on the other half of the wall.

"Ho Chi Minh," we whispered together. I knew his face well. The Vietnam war had been a subject I had taken several college classes on. My father, Early Lyle, had been there, but never talked about it, and when I was younger I was curious to know what exactly had gone on over there, and if it might account for why he was such a shit. I'd concluded that it might.

Murray came to usher several people from the dining room outside. It was time for us to visit Luna's memorial.

The memorial was made of redwood planks. It was the size and shape of a telephone booth. It had only three walls. A plank on bare ground inside it served as a bench. A bouquet of incense sticks smoldered in front of it. That was all I could see from the end of the silent line, which began a respectful distance from the booth's opening and wound across the manicured yard. Murray's outdoor plants all seemed to be in miniature, bonsais and small round cacti, except for the rough brown column of a colossal redwood tree. I stared up at the redwood which filtered the strong sunlight, as Hugh and I waited for our turns to sit inside.

Murray was the first to go into the memorial booth, and then went back into the house alone. The next few people in line spent several minutes each inside the booth. Then they sat on the ground or walked around the small garden. No one was talking. It would be at least an hour before my turn came. I decided to go in and see Murray. Hugh looked to be daydreaming, possibly solving some differential equation in his head. Or perhaps he was entranced by Moana's black miniskirt. She stood in front of us. I decided not to disturb him. I found Murray in the living room. He was alone. I offered my condolences.

"Thank you." Murray stood propped against the window. He asked me to have a seat and offered me tea, which I accepted.

I sat and he left the room. Now that competing cologne and essential oils had gone outside with the crowd, the house smelled of wood smoke. All the seats in the large open living room faced the picture window. They'd been moved from a conversation pit configuration to accommodate the mourners. I picked one end of a plaid sofa, and when Murray returned he took the overstuffed chair next to it.

"I put some water on," he said. For a moment, we both admired the view.

When the pause felt too long, I introduced myself and said, "I worked with Luna."

"I build geodesic domes," said Murray. "Run a little company. Dharma Geodesic Domes."

"Nice name. No dome for you?"

"That's more of a country house. But no, I've never been interested in owning one myself. They leak. Let me check on that water."

He left again. I looked over the photographs that stood in frames on the end table. One was of Murray alone standing in a redwood grove. He looked a few years younger. The other was a casual shot. Luna and a friend had their heads bumped together, both looking over the frames of their sunglasses and smiling goofily. Behind them, a football game was in progress. Next to her friend's head I recognized the plastic shimmies of a cheerleader's pom-pom. They were red and white. Luna looked softer, her face a bit chubbier than the woman I'd known. Her friend was stunning in the way you don't want your best friend in high school to be. Magazine-cover beautiful. Her sunglasses were the black wraparounds made popular by various mid-eighties icons. Looking over them, her eyes were cobalt with black lashes. Her blond hair was thick, frizzled by a permanent into an approximation of the pompom held next to it. She had cheekbones. Her lipstick was too dark for a teenager, especially one with her pale complexion.

Murray returned with a cast iron teapot and two palm sized porcelain cups on a wooden tray. "Green tea. I hope you don't mind?"

"That's great." I'd never had it, but I liked any tea. I'd picked up my tea habit from Conor, my first husband, who'd had his Ma send care packages of his favorite from Ireland. His favorite was the cheapest pence could buy, packaged in a box decorated with an Indian woman stooping over a tea plant. He called it "the tea of the vanquished colonial." "Irish Breakfast," he'd scoff at the emerald green Twinings package, "what shite."

"Taste okay?" Murray was looking out the window.

"Yes, thanks. I was just noticing your pictures. Who's the girl with Luna?"

"Carina Smyth. Her best friend for years. All throughout high school and before that, I think. They were inseparable. They went on to Cal together. But I think they had a falling out in recent years. I haven't seen her in a year or so."

"She's not here today?"

"No, I invited her through her parents. I'm not sure she ever got the message. Lydia and John didn't seem to pay much attention to her, growing up. She used to come over here for dinner a lot. She said she liked my cooking, but that couldn't have been it." Murray smiled gently. "I'm a woeful cook. By the time they were in high school, they were cooking for me. Carina always came up with some crazy concoction like pasta shells stuffed with peanut butter or tofu bread. Luna just followed along. She always looked up to her."

"I'm sorry for your loss."

We admired the view some more. Massive container ships moved in slow formation around the bay by the port of Oakland.

Before I could ask Murray his opinion about who had killed his daughter, he started talking. "It's my fault. Maybe I was living vicariously through her."

"Your fault?"

"I adopted her, you know," he said. "She never knew her real name. I brought her back from Nam in seventy-four. She'd been orphaned. Her mother got killed. She took Nguyen as her last name as a teenager."

"You're a vet?" I couldn't imagine Murray, builder of geodesic domes and bonsai gardens, slogging through jungle swamps with intent to kill. "My father was, too," I added. Early Lyle had been a plumber's apprentice and eighteen in 1967. Draft bait.

"Was he drafted?"

"Yes."

"I volunteered. Marines. My parents came from Poland, you see, and I grew up hearing how terrible Communism was. How the Russians had ruined their lives. I couldn't wait to get to Nam and fight it hand-to-hand. Revenge. I was a political innocent. That changed soon enough." He took a sip of his tea. A few clear drops of it remained in his mustache. "I came back in sixty-nine, got active in war resistance. Vets against the war. But Berkeley radicals didn't want people like me in their movement. They didn't want to know what had really gone on over there. They called me a baby killer. Told me I should have gone to Canada or something. Anything to avoid the draft. They didn't understand the idealism that I had that made me want to go. They only validated their own particular brand of idealism. I quit the movement and started to build geodesic domes for the war protesters to live out their utopian fantasies in. Business was great. After a couple years I had more orders than I could handle. I could afford a child, and god knows, I'd done my share of fooling around over there. I went back to adopt. When Luna became political I certainly didn't discourage her. It was something we could share, and I thought maybe she'd have more acceptance and success than I'd had."

Murray's tears had started halfway through this confession. He wiped one from his beard with the back of his hand. I went over to him, trying to think of some "There there" gesture appropriate to losing one's only daughter. I couldn't think of one, and when a stout woman in a fancy moss-colored blouse approached us and captured Murray in a hug, I left them, relieved, to visit Luna's memorial.

Dear Dad, I love you, how are you, I am fine, The End was penciled in painstaking block letters on the cheap gray newsprint of grade school. Loopy purple letters on a page ripped from a college-ruled spiral notebook told 'Robbie' of her dreams to visit Vietnam. An unfolded note, still creased in the complicated pattern that proved it had been wadded up to escape a teacher's eye, invited Carina to Iceland Skating Rink for a thirteenth birthday party. An acceptance letter from UC Berkeley invited Luna Nguyen to attend in Fall 1991. Inside Luna's redwood memorial, pages of writing made a geometric wallpaper on the planks.

Thumbtacked photographs covered an adjoining wall. A faded square picture showed a toddler Luna running away from Murray's outstretched hand, dressed in small green overalls, smiling toward the camera. In another small square she playfully covered her father's eyes with her hands, while both of them laughed. Glossies taken from a more modern camera showed Luna in poses in front of Iceland, skates slung over a shoulder, grin showing off her braces, one arm hugging a huddle of friends. In another photo, a grown-up Luna smoked a cigarette at a table in front of a cafe, dressed entirely in black. Next to her was Carina Smyth, recognizable from her blue eyes, looking defiantly at the photographer and leaning jauntily back in her chair, her hair dyed a fabulously artificial cherry red.

A conical straw hat hung on the third wall. Early Lyle had had one too. It was the Vietnamese farmer's hat that he had called a 'non la'.

The breeze changed direction, and smoke from the incense threaded into the memorial booth. The scent was familiar—from Luna's bedroom, the thick perfume that had blended with the stench of her decaying body. They say smell is the most primitive of the five senses, wired directly to some residual reptilian part of the brain. I ran from the beautiful memorial and retched into Murray's delicate, dwarf garden.

I hugged myself for steadiness against the bumps and jostles of the subway ride home. Hugh attributed my complexion to nausea, but it wasn't only that. Luna's memorial service depressed me. It reminded me of another funeral—my Granny Leann's. That one had been horrible. Momma's doctor had upped her dose to help her cope with the tragedy, and my Kentucky cousins, assured of a higher profit margin from her prescriptions than from their rusty marijuana crop, had stolen her pills. She'd been cold turkey during the service. I had to rush to town during the subsequent reception to get her a refill, town being an hour away on winding coal-camp roads and the pharmacist reluctant to dispense stimulants to a hysterical girl at that habit-forming age. By the time I coaxed the pills out of him and got back to the gathering, Momma was clammy and shivering on Granny's couch, the uncles that booze hadn't yet killed were whirligiggly drunk, and the younger generation had disappeared. They'd gone over to the wet county in Cousin Larry's hatchback to secure more beer.

Then there was my father, dead somewhere too, who knew where or how. If there'd been a funeral for Early Lyle, Momma and I hadn't been informed.

Hugh wasn't much cheerier, and we rode the subway home in silence. Back at the apartment I found Peter and Rainbow trading bong hits in the bathtub. I asked to borrow their van. It had been years since I'd driven a car so I just sat in it, draining the battery by listening to Luna's tape and staring at the Polaroid that had been attached to her Naughtyland application. A stitch of rust just over her hair marked where the staple had clipped it to the questionnaire. I could show the photograph to her former co-workers at the other strip clubs she'd put on her resume. Maybe someone would remember her and have a clue to her killer.

The tape was nothing more than eighties hits in succession: Duran Duran after ABC after the Thompson Twins. I clicked it off after eighty-seven minutes. I just couldn't suffer through an entire four minutes of Milli Vanilli. I yanked the tape out of the deck in frustration. It had to mean something. Had she given it to her neighbor to keep it safe? If this was why her apartment was ransacked and she was killed, I sure couldn't see the point.

Jossie's talk of a lawyer got me thinking that perhaps, for the first time since my divorce, I might be in need of one myself. Plenty of circumstantial evidence implicated me in Luna's murder. If charges came up against me, it would be best to be prepared. While Jossie would insist on counsel as expensive and proven-effective as one of her boutique lingerie sets, I'd be taking my chances with a cotton-briefs type. A non-profit existed that was supposed to help San Francisco's sex workers. I'd seen PROTECT's Tenderloin office on my way to work. Their mission was to give sex workers skills so that we could get badly paying but morally reasonable secretarial jobs. Perhaps they had legal referrals. When I woke up the next morning, I dressed to visit them as well as Luna's two former workplaces.

PROTECT's office was on Turk Street, near where Leavenworth crosses it. They'd taken over a small storefront that looked like it had once been a convenience store. Posters slathered on with wheat paste covered the front windows. The posters promised help in getting out of The Life—counseling, job interview clothes, childcare, detox. One poster included a grainy black and white head shot of a man, his mouth open and eyes a-flutter and a finger on the way to wiping his nose. A candid, apparently. WATCH OUT FOR THIS MAN read the caption. HE'S A 'FREAK.' The door was unlocked.

Inside, two facing desks heavy with computer monitors and stacks of cardboard boxes crowded the long, narrow space. Cables and wiring made a booby-trap of the floor. No one seemed to be in.

Whoever had left the door unlocked and no one home was taking a big risk in this neighborhood. It wouldn't be long before someone showed up. Meanwhile, I could take a closer look around and try to figure out what PROTECT was all about. I circled one of the desks and looked into an open box on top of a stack. It was full of packets containing condoms, bleach, and small tubes of lubricant, the kit made ubiquitous in San Francisco by the AIDS epidemic. Other boxes contained disposable cameras. They take surprisingly good pictures, but I'd always thought them wasteful. Why not just buy a real camera? I asked this very question to the young blonde woman who emerged from a door in the back of the room.

"Um, hello? I'm sorry....have we met?" she answered.

"Sorry. My name's Aubrey Lyle." I tiptoed through the wiring to shake her hand. "I'm a stripper at Naughtyland, not a prostitute, but I was wondering if you could help me."

"Oh, hi, I'm Sandy Larson. I'm just a volunteer?" Every statement a question, Sandy looked about twenty-one and wore unripped jeans, spotless white aerobics shoes, and a sweatshirt with a perky logo: Walk-a-Thon for Youth '95. Her blue eyes were big. In my black flared pants, dark lipstick and tight shirt, I must have looked somewhat qualified for PROTECT's services. Sandy looked at me, chewing her unglossed lip. "Are you here to volunteer?"

"I'm here to enquire about a lawyer and to report the death of a sex worker. She was a stripper at Naughtyland."

"I'm sorry, we don't have legal advice. Was the sex worker the one we read about? Yesterday' s paper?"

"That was her."

"You know, my boss already called the police. We offered to help them track down some johns. We have a database. I don't think they've gotten back to us."

"A database of johns?"

Sandy gestured to the tower of boxes of disposable cameras. "That's what those cameras are for. We give them to street prostitutes to take pictures of johns. It's a safety issue. Then we scan in the pictures. Would you like to take a camera?"

"No I wouldn't. They take pictures of all their customers? Doesn't that scare away business? And isn't it a violation of rights, or something?" I was all for prostitutes sharing information about dangerous patrons, but with PROTECT's penchant for wheatpasting, I wouldn't trust the organization with a catalogue of portraits. Relatively innocent johns could someday find themselves outed, their mimeographed faces hanging crookedly in storefronts all over town. "I depend on porn addicts for my living. I don't want to be snapping their pictures for possible public humiliation," I said.

Sandy's expression reminded me of a popped balloon.

"Look, I don't think your photos would help in this case anyway." I felt like patting Sandy's hand. She was obviously from a well-scrubbed background, trying to do her part to help the down-and-outs, probably against her mother's better judgement. "My friend was a stripper, not a streetwalker. The paper may have said she was a suspected prostitute, but I don't know who suspected her of that. I don't know if you do any work with strippers, but the cops don't seem to be too serious about solving this case. I thought maybe you all could put pressure on them or something."

Sandy tugged on a string of blond hair that had escaped her ponytail. "We work mostly with prostitutes. Our mission is to reeducate street prostitutes to give them different opportunities. We want to give them choices. Choice is a privilege." Sandy rattled off the memorized mission statement. She was right, though. I'd decided to work as a stripper, but I'd had other choices—however limited those opportunities were for computer-illiterate history majors. Luna had presumably had choices too. But she had still been murdered.

"Are you saying you can't advocate for a stripper, then? We're talking about a murder here! The murder of a sex worker!"

"I'm sorry. Would you like to be on our mailing list?" Sandy blushed.

I was just scaring her further with my escalation technique. I took the clipboard she handed me and began to fill in the blanks: street name, phone number, name to ask for over the phone, address, name known by at that address, street/house/massage parlor, circle all that apply. Sandy gave me a business card with PROTECT's logo and number on it. While I was scribbling in my names, I asked if perhaps they had a white Toyota Camry in the database. Sandy, insensitive to my dripping sarcasm, was earnestly punching the computer keyboard before I'd finished the question.

One minute later, she handed over a dot matrix composition of a Camry, a street corner, a hairy left arm hanging out of the car's window, and a clearly uninterested working girl leaning against a row of Victorians. Street light seared the car's windshield. The driver's face was invisible behind the glare. If that photo was representative of the contents of PROTECT's database of johns, no privacy rights were in danger of violation.

"Good luck."

We shook hands. With an audible sigh of relief, Sandy opened the front door for me.

I stepped out into sunshine. By mid-April, San Francisco's weather had finally come around to what I liked to dress for. My black rayon shirt was enough to keep me warm. I turned up Turk, waded through fast food litter and sun-baked pebbles of chewing gum, toward the guy who lived by the newspaper kiosks at the corner of Leavenworth. If odors were light rays, he would have been ground zero of a nuclear glow. He lived on a milk crate, and his occupation was growling at himself.

I wasn't sure exactly where to find Luna's old clubs, but had a vague idea that The Femme Royale was the one with the tall neon can-can leg for a sign, located a couple of blocks to the north. I walked there slowly, musing about work. It had been three days since I'd been suspended. The Femme Royale would probably be happy to hire me for ten days. Maybe I'd borrow a costume and audition. But I wasn't sure if they were a 'suck and fuck' club, or just lapdancing. At some of San Francisco's adult theaters, the fee that dancers paid to work each shift was extortionate. The only way for the women to pay both the boss and their bills was to give customers those illegal extras that the men incessantly proposed. Tricks were turned right there in the cubicles, rather acrobatically, I supposed, since the square yard of floor space was furnished only with a spindly chair. Going above and beyond the call of duty in that way was discouraged on the premises of Naughtyland, if for no other reason than the Moses' paranoia about legal issues.

If I did accept a job at another club, though, the Moses would never hire me back. Once your stripper name was misspelled across Naughtyland's marquee, you were their superstar and no one else's.

Working elsewhere was forbidden. I knew that the Moses would find out immediately if I started to dance somewhere else. Some kind of invisible network linked San Francisco's sex clubs together. Hirings and firings were common knowledge. Perhaps it was just gossip that spread the word, but if you became known as a troublemaker or drug user at one club, you wouldn't get hired anywhere.

I'd stayed at Naughtyland so long because it was the busiest lap-dancing venue in town. Money would be less anywhere else. That was a problem with Momma wanting that new car and with Mellissa and her kids depending on me. She and her brood had moved back in with her parents in Austin, and I sent her a few hundred dollars a month with a note saying spend most of this on yourself. I needed a Naughtyland income. Besides, if I quit Naughtyland I might be black-listed throughout the city, and no club would hire me.

From the looks of the Tenderloin's buildings, the decaying district had once been fashionable. On every block, beautiful turn-of-the-century facades rose above street-level's convenience stores, Vietnamese restaurants, and adult theaters. These buildings dated from the days when urban architecture aimed to dazzle pedestrians rather than those driving by on the freeway. They had details like notched cornices framing their roofs, gargoyles or stone ivy carved out of their corners. But few passers-by looked up to see the old splendor. A crowd of Vietnamese schoolchildren, each small torso doubled in size with a backpack, was hustled past me by two anxious women, who herded them into a tiny park already filled with loiterers and portable home-steads. The park's latrine perfumed the block.

The Femme Royale looked dead when I arrived. Strip clubs often have a drab feel about them during daylight hours. The neon signs hang limp against the sunlight. And like speakeasies or gay bars, some sex clubs sport a nondescript facade to foil cops and protect all those furtive customers. So, although there wasn't much activity around The Femme Royale, in fact its windows were blacked in and a heavy-gauge chain sagged through the handles of its adjoining doors, it wasn't immediately obvious to me that the place was closed. And not just for church, but apparently for good.

A young Asian man carrying a paper grocery bag was walking quickly towards me.

"Excuse me," I said and he stopped politely. "Do you know how long this place has been closed down?" I indicated the building painted black, its thousand-watt cursive logo and jaunty can-can leg forever winked out.

"Let me try to remember. Two or three months, I guess." He deliberately kept his gaze above my chest level, and slightly to the left of eye contact.

"Do you know why it closed?" I moved my head to try to meet his eyes.

"Nope. It was there one day, gone the next. Not like I go there." He shrugged.

"No community petition, anything like that?"

San Francisco was a boomtown again, thanks to the computer industry, and even the Tenderloin was filling up with middle-class evictees as rents in the clean neighborhoods doubled. Sometimes the new residents got feisty about the concentration of liquor stores and sex parlors in the cheaper part of town.

He laughed and looked straight at me. "No. I don't think so." He switched the bag to his other arm.

"Thanks. Sorry to keep you."

"No problem."

"Wait!" I called, and ran to catch up to him. "Do you know where the Cher Cherie is?"

He thought for a moment. "Try up Taylor...wait, is that the one with the union? Yeah, that's on Taylor."

"Thanks again." Not that he ever went there. I turned around and walked west to the intersection with Taylor Street.

Chapter Nine

Outside the Cher Cherie's double door a barker chanted "San Francisco's only twenty-four hour live nude show!" with an exuberance unusual for the service sector. Wearing a wide-lapelled blue suit and a color-contrasting bow tie, he gestured with skinny arms toward the club's flyspecked doors. His brown hair was as shiny as his patent leather Doc Marten boots. "No admission fee. Twenty-four hours of peeping pleasure. Guys and girls welcome too." He bowed at me. I pushed past him into the red-carpeted lobby. I didn't need a reception. Was this a strip club or a hot dog stand at the carnival?

It took me a minute to sort out the lobby, a mirrored triangle with its apex opposite the front door, curtained off in red velveteen. An appropriately unbubbly bouncer stood next to the curtain. His thin black-clad body was reflected several times in the angles of the mirrors, giving the impression that a small army of similarly stern young men was ready to dampen your libido for you at the slightest provocation. Pasted to the mirror on the lobby's left were at least fifty Polaroids of the club's dancers, all in bikinis and posed in whatever extreme posture they felt accentuated cleavage. The dancers had each scrawled a message in a shade of dark lipstick beside their photo: "Cum see me! Love, Creemie." "I'm Delicious! Bubb'licious." "Put me back in your life! I'm Spice." "On your knees, naughty boy! Lick my boots. Love, Portia."

"You going in to see the show, or what?" interrupted the gatekeeper. "You can't loiter out here." He pointed to another sign, on the mirror opposite the collage of desperate bosoms. No Loitering.

I collected myself and produced the photograph of Luna that had been part of her personnel file at Naughtyland. I felt a little guilty about showing my only picture of her around, since in it she was wearing nothing but frumpy undergarments. But if this guy knew her he'd seen her in less.

"I'm sorry, I didn't mean to loiter. Can you tell me if you know this woman?" The mirrors made my walk over to him resemble an infantry charge. I put Luna's picture into his outstretched hand.

He glanced at it and shrugged. "I just started working here. Don't know her. Sorry. You going in, or what?"

"I don't know. What's the deal with this place?"

He slouched against the mirrored wall, the slump of his spine pile-driving his fists into his black Ben Davis pants pockets, and spoke his well-rehearsed spiel in a monotone. "Cher Cherie is a fantasy island of sorts. Several of our lovely young ladies are within today just waiting to fulfill your every fantasy. Private booths are provided for your viewing pleasure. Just step within and choose your personal fantasy playmate."

"Wow. Is Bubb'licious in today?"

He showed no reaction. "Due to security concerns I am not allowed to reveal the work schedules of our lovely young ladies. Just step within to choose your personal fantasy playmate."

He made it seem easy. I pushed my way through the red curtain.

Inside was a humid, gloomy terrarium the size of a parlor. Weak ruby light shone from one bulb. The floor's worn carpet was black, and so were the low ceiling and the exposed bits of the walls. The gamey smell of sperm clogged the condensed air.

The terrarium was in the center of a ring of tiny booths. Eight windows and corresponding narrow doors opened onto it. Some of the windows were curtained shut with thick jungle-green drapes. The others framed lingerie-clad women of various sizes and expertise, all lit in diffuse red—like fast food left under a heat lamp. The women were confined among tapestries and throw pillows in miniature, red-upholstered rooms. If one of them were to stretch out her arms, her fingertips would touch either side of her tank.

Cher Cherie's architecture made it plain that its customers were to pick out a woman like a woman might pick out an ice cream flavor. Two customers were with me in the terrarium, surreptitiously checking out the six or seven fantasy possibilities while ignoring each other and me. We placed ourselves apart in the sex-scented airlock like fellow travelers in an elevator. My companions were casually dressed older gentlemen. One was Asian, the other white. I studied them before I studied the women. The two men were expressionless.

I looked at the strippers. A variety was on offer: a white woman wearing white lace, a black woman wearing black leather, a petite Asian woman in red high heels. All looked out at us with expressions of hope and horniness, only one of the emotions genuine.

One of the men tried the door next to an anorexic, incongruously busty blonde. The other seemed interested in a frail Asian woman whose nameplate read Lotus. Lotus was sucking her finger like a lollipop as they gazed at each other through the pane of glass.

A woman with roughed-up black hair and glossy red lips raised her thick eyebrows at me and waved from behind the nearest window. According to the hand-lettered nameplate affixed underneath the pane of glass, as if to describe the strange habits of some exotic reptile in a city zoo, her name was Mamacita. Mamacita indicated with happy gestures that I should open her corresponding door. I did.

Inside the armoire-sized cubicle I entered, the floor appeared clean of suspicious puddles. Fresh disinfectant prickled my sinuses. I faced a curtained-off window identical in size to the ones that advertised the girls to the lobby. Its lower edge was at crotch level. A plexiglas box with a slot cut out of it and a padlock hanging from its hinged lid was on the window's right, next to the back wall. I sat on the built-in wooden bench next to a family-sized box of Kleenex.

Nothing happened.

Money, I thought. "I need the money first" is the mantra of this industry. I poked a ten-dollar bill through the slot in the plexiglas box.

The curtain parted and the brunette smiled at me with such enthusiasm that the gloss on her lips spun light like a disco ball.

"We never get girls in here! It's so good to see you!" she said. The words came out fuzzily and after a slight time delay through some kind of intercom. "I'm Mamacita. You want to see a pussy show? Twenty dollars, but I'll give you a girl discount." Mamacita flounced the hem of her white lace garment, flashing me.

"Oh, no, that's okay, I wouldn't want to work you too hard. I'm actually looking for someone who used to be a performer here. I have a picture." I held the Polaroid of Luna up for the stripper to see. Mamacita's slack expression of disappointment clashed with her optimistic make-up. She scanned the photograph, absently rubbing lipstick off a tooth.

"Don't know her. I just started, though. I was working at the Femme Royale until they closed it down. The money was better there, lapdancing."

"She worked there, too. Sure you don't recognize her?"

Mamacita shook her head. "Sorry. You should ask one of the girls who's been here longer. Lotus, or Azote. They're on shift. I bet they know your friend. They've been here forever."

"Thanks." I smiled at her and stood to leave.

"But you don't want a show from them. Between you and me, they're old enough to be coming in here with walkers. I'm nineteen. For real. I do dildo for thirty."

I once again declined. Mamacita waved goodbye and plunked herself down on a plush throw pillow that was imprisoned with her. She sat like a little girl, knees pressed together, fishnetted calves angled outward, toes turned inward to made a wedge of her glitter platform shoes. She pulled a sandwich out of a paper bag and was taking a bite as I closed her door behind me. Ham and cheese, it looked like.

Lotus was now unoccupied. I stepped into her cubicle, identical to the one I'd just left. Her inner curtain was already open, and she gestured a small hand to her plexiglas box. This visit could get expensive, I thought, as I put a ten through the slot.

"My shows start at twenty," fuzzed the intercom. Lotus's voice was forceful. She hadn't bothered to stand up, but reclined over an arrangement of pillows, legs crossed and kicking one red-high-heeled foot. "Forty for dildo. Sixty for dirty talk. Domination extra. Anything else we can negotiate."

"I'm not here for a show," I was suddenly nervous. "I'm wondering if you knew someone who worked here." I stuck the photo to the glass between us, then noticed that the window was splattered with filth and peeled Luna's picture off of it.

"My shows start at twenty," Lotus repeated. Another of my ten-dollar bills found its way into her box.

"I know her. That's Peaches. Better talk to Azote about her." A bell made a soft mechanical ding-dong.

"What was that?"

"Time's up," Lotus mouthed. I could no longer hear her. The intercom appeared to have been timed out of commission. Lotus closed the curtain.

"Shit."

A leather briefcase was nosing the cubicle's door open. Its owner, a tall white businessman in a suit, propped the door open with it until I stepped out. Didn't want to touch the doorknob with his hands, perhaps. Surprising, considering what those uncalloused hands would clutch next. I hoped Lotus would give him the expensive punishment he deserved.

I took shallow breaths while I waited for the curtain over the nameplate "Azote" to open. Even half-lungfuls of air brought me too closely in touch with the viewing area's ripe smell. I was on the brink of hyperventilation when a blue-jeaned man with curly blond hair slunk out of Azote's booth and flitted out the door. A moment later, her curtain opened to the lobby.

Azote kept her back to the lobby instead of her breasts; she displayed her shrink-wrapped hamstrings and calves. Burnished black hair hung straight down to the waistband of the black vinyl thong that outlined the anvil cheeks of her ass. Her back muscles bunched as she rhythmically whipped the mirror on the booth's back wall, making her own full-length reflection tremble with each sting. She looked straight into her own dark eyes, dragging the limp leather across the floor, cocking her right elbow and cracking the whip forward while her reflection shimmered from the whip's contact. Her movements were as rhythmic and incessant as a metronome. She was completely absorbed in her activity.

I entered her cubicle, inserted a twenty, and pushed aside the giant box of Kleenex to sit.

The curtain was brusquely swept aside. Azote looked down at me. Holding with both hands onto a bar anchored to the ceiling, she was flexing her deltoids. Shiny pink toenails contrasted with her glittery silver high heels. Her whip curled up on an upholstered pillow behind her. From my position on the bench, I was eye level with her muscle-ringed kneecaps.

"You here for an interview? You can schedule with my secretary. The guy at the front desk will give you the number. I'm only doing paid ones now. Otherwise, masturbation shows ten, dildo shows twenty. For two minutes. Domination extra." I pondered my choices, then remembered why I was there.

"Sorry. I heard you used to work with this woman." I fumbled around my various pockets for the picture of Luna. Where had I put it after wiping Lotus's window scum off of it? My two minutes were ticking away. Sometimes I thought I should start carrying a purse. But then I'd have yet another place to paw through for lost items.

I found the Polaroid in my breast pocket. I stood up to plaster it against the glass at a height that Azote wouldn't have to stoop to see, and found myself facing the striations of her inner thighs.

The woman seemed to still herself for an instant, an accomplishment in stilettos. Perhaps competing muscle groups had found a momentary equilibrium.

"Did she send you to me? You know we can't talk here."

I cleared my throat. "I knew her from Naughtyland, we worked together. I know she used to work here. Four, maybe five months ago?" The timer's bell interrupted me.

Azote coolly pointed to the plexiglas box. That couldn't have been two minutes. I stuck in another ten. I couldn't afford to talk to this woman much longer. Maybe she would agree to meet in less expensive circumstances.

"Do you know she's dead?" At five dollars a minute, I wasn't going to hem and haw.

"I heard." Azote's expression didn't change. "Did she tell you about me? We'll have to meet on the outside."

"That would be great."

"I'll let you know where and when. Leave me your name and number." Azote looked at the blank wall behind me for a moment. I wondered how well she could see me. Lighting was dim, stronger on her side. She was probably seeing her own reflection.

The electronic bell rang again. It was obviously calibrated with less concern for the actual count of seconds passing than for maximizing profit. Azote closed her curtain.

As soon as I exited her booth, a businessman in the lobby tucked his head and launched himself into it. He shut the door behind him with a shaky slam.

Azote hadn't described how I was supposed to leave her my name and number. Fortunately, writing in reverse is one of my talents, practiced during long winter hours on the school bus back in Ohio when the heat of my fingertip traced obscenities backward onto its frosty windows. I took out my lipstick, the shade, Firefight, a dark ruby-brown, and scrawled in reverse across her window. Call Aisling. I wrote my phone number underneath it. I'd wanted to add something more, but I couldn't think of what and I was afraid the bell would ring and the computer guy would lurch out the door. Besides, my brief message had smashed the Firefight down to a useless nub. Hip lipstick brands just weren't constructed for writing love notes on glass.

I pushed the sweat around on my forehead with my non-absorbent sleeve. My walk home corresponded with the fifteen minutes of uncomfortable heat delivered by a spring day in San Francisco. At least this particular walk was from one bottomland neighborhood to another, and I could avoid strenuous hills.

As soon as I got home, I made the mistake of answering the phone.

90

"I thought you'd forgotten your old momma. You're talking to a size eight! These pills just take away my appetite. Betty brought me some homemade stewed tomatoes the other day over to the beauty shop and they were the best I've tasted in years, but I just couldn't eat more than two bites. My old size tens are hanging off of me. It's been so hot here it gives me the chafes. And Eb out there in his garden all day. I told him he better hop to if he wants pumpkins this year. Hot there?"

Momma's latest drug combination gave her a lot of energy.

"Oh, let's see. Yep, sunny, yep, in the seventies. Like every other day." San Franciscans are deprived of complaints about the weather, which can make small talk a challenge. Fortunately we have the cost of housing to gripe about.

"Aren't you lucky? Who'd 've thought I'd have a daughter living in California. My daddy went out there once on his motorcycle, looking for work. Back during the Depression. I don't think he found any, though, at any rate he turned tail and came home before long. He never did trust a bank. Then when he died, a few years later Momma was writing a letter on his old secretary and bumped a secret drawer with her elbow, and out came a packet all wrapped up in tinfoil. Momma got so scared she about jumped out of her skin. She was afraid it was drugs, you know. She got Rudy to unwrap it for her, poor Rudy, and out fell almost fifteen hundred dollars. No one ever did figure out how he saved that much, but it put Rudy through college until he dropped out. Daryl Junior too until he dropped out. What do you think about that?"

"I've heard the story before, Momma."

"Of course you have. How else are you going to remember it for future generations? When are you going to get yourself a man, Aubrey? That Conor was so sweet, you know how I liked him. Didn't you want to have his little babies? He was Catholic, though, wasn't he? I warned you about them. They may believe in birth control before marriage, but once that knot is tied, they want more troops for the Pope."

"Did you visit Dayton Airport one too many times in the fifties, Momma? They were doing experiments in subliminal brainwashing over the PA. Maybe you're the one who should have married him."

"He got an older brother? No, Eb and I are doing well. He's taking a catnap. He goes to bed around ten o'clock, before that we have a little sherry. No harm in that now, miss teetotaler? You should see the darling little glasses I found at the thrift shop to drink it in—"

The beep of call waiting interrupted her. Normally I ignored it when on long distance, but I told Momma I should take the other call. I clicked over.

A husky voice said, "Aisling. Azote."

Since I couldn't believe she had called me back so quickly, it was a moment before I could collect myself to say let me get off the other line.

"Momma?"

"What took you so long? Don't you want to talk to your old momma? I was just watching here on the TV, the latest thing in Japan is jellyfish. They're a favorite pet there. Very relaxing to watch, but so squirmy!"

"Momma, I've got to go."

"Oh, well, if that other call is that important, don't let your old momma keep you."

"I'll call you next weekend, okay?"

"That's good. Do you have MCI? Because they're only five cents a minute on Sundays. My calls to you are only a couple of dollars—"

"I've got to go, Momma!" She hadn't been this way before Doctor Hillman had put her on anti-depressants. Still, I preferred this momma, who never listened and never shut up to the one of my childhood, who had spent the days drooling onto her pillow, rising only to paste together peanut butter sandwiches for my dinner. I remembered her slouch in her chenille housecoat, her feet pale and skinny in her fuzzy slippers. She'd rarely actually dressed. That had been Early's wife.

"Hello? Azote? Sorry about that."

"I can't talk long. I'm on my ten minute break at work."

"Should I meet you there?" I wasn't thrilled about returning to the mirrored land of wind-up girls in music boxes, but wherever Azote was, I would go.

"Why don't you come to this address later? I'll be home around eight. 2444 Jackson."

I repeated the address. "Thank you so much for calling me back."

"See you then." She hung up.

Number 2444 Jackson was in Pacific Heights, a posh neighborhood near the tip of the peninsula that San Francisco is built on. The steepest streets in town lifted the citizens who could afford those addresses far above the view of the Golden Gate bridge, the green hills of Marin county, Angel Island and Alcatraz. Angel Island was a green

cone of wilderness that matched the mainland hills to its west. Its landmass was unjustly deprived of the modern distinctions of county, city
and town by the tectonic whim of a fault line. Immigrants had been
processed and quarantined there, as they were at Ellis Island on the
other coast. The newcomers must have looked as longingly toward the
fledgling San Francisco as earlier San Franciscans looked toward the
unspoiled mountain plopped in the middle of their Bay. Alcatraz is a
boulder in comparison to Angel Island; a bare chunk of granite with the
abandoned prison clinging to it, both rock and building the color of a
seagull. I got off the twenty-two bus at Fillmore and Jackson.

Jackson Street was residential, though several signs on doorways
advertised psychologists' and doctors' offices. Azote's was a two-story
Queen Anne Victorian, restored and beautifully painted, but even so,
not the most beautiful Queen Anne on the block. I stepped between
the two pillars that framed the door like magnolia trees by the planta-
tion porch and rang the bell. A security light scrubbed me clean and
whitewashed an arc into the gray and violet color scheme of the
facade.

After a moment, a slight blond man in a tight black maid's dress and
flounced white housekeeping apron answered my knock. He turned
away without greeting me. His dress was backless, held together by a
crisscross of laces down to the waist. Below that, it was not held together at all. The white ribbons of the apron's tie fell graciously in such a
way as to cover the crack of his ass, but this effect was certainly no
more than an accident of gravity. The man started down the dark hall
to a wooden doorway of dim, warm lighting on the right, and I supposed I was to follow. I did, staring up at the polished banister of dark
wood that ascended on my left into second-story darkness. My boot
clattered against tin as I stumbled over the hallway's sole furnishing and
spilled a small collection of riding crops and stiff canes from an umbrel-
la stand. My guide doubled back and silently tidied everything up.

Azote lay on a divan that was centered in a wood-floored parlor.
The windowless room's only lighting came from the flames of two can-
delabras. A metal cage crouched against the floor in the corner. The
cage was empty.

"Hello," said Azote, perhaps to the housekeeper. She tossed aside
May's *Cosmopolitan* and removed a pair of rhinestoned spectacles.
Her long dark hair was coiled onto the top of her head and skewered
in place with a sharp chopstick. The man in the maid costume knelt on
the hardwood floor in front of her bare feet. He picked the right one

up off the cushion and began to rub it.

"Come on in," she continued. "Make yourself at home, there's some cushions there. Billy Boy!" I avoided looking at his bare backside as he left her foot. Another man, who wore nothing but a pair of white cotton hiphuggers that were decorated prissily with tiny yellow flowers, took Billy Boy's place at Azote's instep. I hadn't seen underwear like that since I was six years old and had gotten them in three packs from Penney's.

Billy Boy crossed the spacious room to get me a throw pillow from a stack of them in the corner. He plumped it up beneath me and took my hand to help me lower myself to a sitting position. He executed all of these maneuvers while crawling on his knees.

"Thanks."

"Just pretend they're not here, if you want. It's their trip, know what I mean? Are you hungry? Let me offer you something."

It was well past my dinnertime, but I certainly didn't want to offend. "Okay."

With a push from Azote, the flowered underwear man left the room through an archway that must have led to the kitchen. He returned in an instant, followed by a hirsute white man in a diaper. The diapered man entered the room with a tray, which he squatted to place on the floor between Azote and her attendants and myself. His abundant black chest hair was a startling contrast both to his skin, which hadn't seen the sun, and his garment, still apparently unsoiled. The wooden tray held a languid orchid reclined on a single leaf and an artfully arranged variety of sushi. Thick translucent slices of pink and gray flesh curled over wads of rice. Two rows of these morsels intersected each other on the tray like a geometry problem. A pile of peach colored strips and a green blob accented the angles.

The chef backed away silently.

"Another terrible meal. Try again at breakfast." The chef bowed to the sushi and retreated. "Did Luna tell you about me?"

"Not exactly." I didn't want to discourage Azote from revealing information by telling her the truth. Luna had certainly never mentioned a dominatrix friend she was dying for me to meet.

"Have some, it's delicious." Azote leaned over from the couch and poured soy sauce from a bottle into two small bowls, all of which the chef had thoughtfully included on the tray. "He's a great cook. Don't know when he found the time to learn, though. High-powered job. He's the CEO of a venture capitalist firm downtown." Azote rolled a shrimp-topped rice ball in the soy sauce with a pair of wooden chop-sticks, without losing a single grain of rice, and poked it whole into her mouth. "Some people are just ambitious, I guess. Go ahead, try it."

"Nice place." The ceilings were high and would allow for a lot of light had natural light been allowed. Two paintings on cloth in an Asian brush style hung lightly from bamboo dowels against the walls. Simple yet elegant, and these days, not inexpensive.

"Thank you."

"Do you have roommates?"

"No. I live alone."

"Great." I didn't mention that she couldn't very well have room-mates with all this carrying on. "Great neighborhood." I fumbled with a piece of the raw fish. By the time I plucked it out of the dish of soy sauce it was dark brown and too salty. At Azote's urging, I followed the morsel with a peach strip. It tasted sour, like the red pickled eggs sold from flyspecked jars on the counters of every convenience store in Kentucky. I set my chopsticks back down on the tray. "So I'm kind of looking into Luna's—"

"She went by Peaches when I knew her. So, what did she tell you about me? Billy Boy, get her some tea, don't be rude."

"No, I'm okay." Billy Boy was already padding from the room, dou-ble time.

"Sorry. Got to teach little boys manners, you know." Azote winked at me and ate another morsel of sushi.

"About you? Nothing."

"She told you about her organization, didn't she?"

"What organization?"

"She must have told you about the union. What did Luna tell you about the union?"

"The union?"

"Yes, the union. That's why you came to me, isn't it?"

"No. What's the union?"

Azote stared at me as Billy Boy squatted beside us. He set a teapot and two cups on the floor and poured. I couldn't help but wonder if when he was done, Azote would rip the steaming teapot from his hands and douse him in the boiling liquid for his own pleasure, but that didn't happen. My imagination was getting carried away. The man set the teapot on the floor after pouring, and quietly returned to kneeling by the couch.

The tea was jasmine. "Do you have any idea who I am?" Azote was asking me.

"Besides a well-to-do dominatrix?" I took a sip of tea for effect but it was too soon and I burned my tongue. Azote showed no reaction.

"You ever hear about the strippers unionizing? It was all over the news a year, year and a half ago. The first sex workers to have representation by a trade union were at the Cher Cherie. It was international news. I was quoted in the *New York Times.*"

"You were quoted?"

"My picture was in there, too. I was one of the organizers. I got interviewed a lot back then. My name was all over the place." Azote took a last bite and stretched out her arms above her head so I could see her biceps, trapezius and deltoids, attentive under her skin like the quivery legs of racehorses. "I always knew I'd be famous one day. Business has really taken off since then." Azote gestured at her ceiling, which was one of those plaster affairs that look like they were molded over a plumped-up cushion, and then to her gleaming hardwood floor, to indicate that her fabulously expensive home had resulted from that increased business. "You never heard of me?"

"No." When I thought of union organizers, I thought of Mother Jones. My Grandpa Daryl had had a photograph of her on his living room wall, next to a yellowing newspaper halftone of Eleanor Roosevelt. Mother Jones had come to organize the coal miners when Grandpa'd been a teenaged miner. Back then mines caved in routinely and killed miners, or if they lived the work gave them black lung. Miners were paid not in money but in coal company scrip. In Grandpa's photograph, Mother Jones sat astride a mule, staring staunchly at the camera through steely eyes and little granny glasses. She wore brogans and long skirts. Her boys got themselves shot up by sheriffs all over Appalachia, according to Grandpa, who threatened me with the same fate whenever I disturbed him at his crossword puzzle. Back then the law mistook union organizers for Communists, but didn't give a darn whether you were one or the other or both when they were taking aim. Stripping was a mixed career bag, but compared to all that it was roses.

What would Mother Jones think of Azote, a union organizer with her own band of slaves? I doubted Azote would be able to identify either a brogan, a Communist, or a mule. Perhaps I wasn't giving her enough credit.

"So you're a bit like Mother Jones?"

"Who's she? I'm not a mother. Luna and I organized workers at

Cher Cherie into the National Brotherhood of Service Workers International, Local Sixteen."

"Brotherhood? That hardly seems appropriate."

"We gave them national attention. But you never heard of us?"

I shook my head.

"No one was talking to you girls at Naughtyland about joining a union?" She pinned me with a stare.

"No. Why would we want to join a union?"

"Why wouldn't you?"

"We make a lot of money there. Nobody's complaining. In fact, outside interference is the last thing a lot of those girls want."

"Maybe some girls don't make as much as you. Nobody's complaining? None of Luna's friends, people she hung out with there?"

"She didn't really have any friends there. She'd just started. And anyone who doesn't make money just quits. Goes back to waitressing. We don't get any wage to increase. It's understood we just work for tips. What good would a union do us?"

Azote sipped her tea in silence for a while, staring into the candelabra behind me. I sipped my tea back. The notion of unionizing Naughtyland seemed absurd. What would the National Brotherhood of whatever negotiate for us? That johns give us bigger tips? Besides, the dancers would never go for it. The club's workforce came and went unpredictably. It was more like a drop-in center where a quick buck could be made than a voting bloc or a 'shop.' And the whole idea of a union would seem too working-class to the girls. It was just the kind of thing most of us were trying to escape.

"Do the girls there like your management?" Flowered-underwear man whisked her empty teacup from her fist and refilled it.

"Well enough."

"Listen." Azote tweezed a clump of rice that looked like it was sprouting green hair. She pointed it at me as she talked. "Some of the union rhetoric might have sounded good to the girls. No more arbitrary lay-offs. No more favoritism of the busty girls and the blondes. No more fucking the boss to get a reduced stage fee. No more sexual harassment from the male employees. Talk like that hasn't been going around your place?"

"No. Without those perks, what would be left? That's the way the whole industry works."

"Exactly." Azote fed herself the ball of hairy rice. "The seediness is half the allure. Know of anyone that kind of talk would appeal to?"

"Most of the women I work with think of themselves as hot-shit dancers, not Brotherhood members."

"It's just as well. You can't unionize strip clubs anymore in this town. Ever hear of the Femme Royale?"

"Yes, as a matter of fact—"

"Shut down the instant the owner found out someone was trying to organize it."

"You're kidding."

"No. All those girls without a job at all. The owners would rather have no club than have unionized workers. If anyone finds out someone's been talking union at a club, that dancer has had it. Blacklisted. She won't work anywhere in this town again. And word has it the union isn't interested in taking on any more sex workers. Got it?"

"Yes," I said slowly, not getting it.

"Billy Boy, don't just cower there, show her out."

But I didn't quite get it. Was Azote warning me? Why did I get more of the feeling that she was sizing me up?

Chapter Ten

Hugh drove slowly down Church Street in the van we had again borrowed from Rainbow and Peter. They'd been asleep in it, since it was midnight by the time we found their parking place on Fillmore, but were unperturbed when we woke them and I offered them my futon. Good sports, they had obligingly shuffled toward the apartment clothed in nothing more than a wrap of their respective batik tapestries. The van still smelled like smoke from its owners' nightcap.

After I'd returned from my strange encounter with Azote, I'd recruited Hugh for another chore: to help me find the location of Luna's last customer's white Camry.

After going over the PROTECT printout with a magnifying glass, I'd identified the street that the Camry was on as Treat, in the nearby Mission District. My plan was to find the cross street then ask any prostitutes that might be working that corner if they knew the driver of the Camry. If johns had the regular habits of lapdancees, everyone who worked the corner should know the guy, perhaps by name.

There wasn't much automobile traffic. On the east side of Mission Street the neighborhood was quiet. Few businesses enlivened the blocks. That part of town had yet to be gentrified with the créperies, espresso bars, and retroware shops that made the other side of Mission Street the latest hip spot for adventuresome white folks to resettle. The east side still had a reputation as Latino gang territory. An occasional low-slung vehicle pulsed by. Tired old Victorians shouldered down the blocks like a chorus line of grandmothers. Their windows were all dark.

Hugh stopped at the corner of Twenty-first Street. Across from us was the scene recreated by the computer printer, complete with cast of characters. A Buick sputtered at the intersection and a curvy figure hung into its window, her miniskirt reflected our headlights. Our view was soon blocked by oncoming traffic. The driver of a red Mustang, eager to avoid a head-on collision and to get out of the neighborhood quickly, honked vehemently at us.

"Let me out before you take off," I opened my door.

"What about me? You're not going alone."

"Yes I am. We can't approach a hooker together, a man and a woman. She'd think we were looking for some annoying I-want-to-see-my-wife-do-a-girl deal. I have to go alone. Just us girls. Besides, you have to keep Yohimbe company. She'll wake the whole neighborhood."

"Okay, but I'll come back around for you." Hugh looked relieved.

"Take your time."

Hugh drove away under fire from the Mustang's horn. I stepped onto the sidewalk just in time to avoid being hit by the honking driver, and to see Shiny Miniskirt settle into the passenger seat of the poorly-maintained Buick and be whisked away.

Alone, I waited on the corner for what felt like half an hour. Hugh certainly was taking his time. For company I had a carousel of cars. The same drivers kept creeping past the corner, hunched into their steering wheels, furtively cruising. I must not have looked enticing. Not one of them pulled over.

Other than engine noise from the johns who circled the block like sharks around chum, the neighborhood was quiet and dim. Not many streetlights were provided and half of them were burnt out. Down the block, a rhombus of blue television light flickered through a window onto the sidewalk. An occasional rumble indicated a truck crossing the highway overpass a block to the north. The air was cold enough to raise goosebumps under my scoopnecked stretch pullover and leather jacket. I walked in a small circle to keep warm.

After another few minutes the television light went out. Then three women joined me at the corner. I'd watched the first make slow high-heeled progress from a block down Twenty-first Street. A yellow cab had delivered the second. Both were looking me over when the Buick returned, coughed, and disgorged Shiny Miniskirt.

"Hi everybody," I said.

"You working?" the cab's passenger asked. She was tall, with a brown pageboy haircut. Her eyes ran up my body while I looked at hers. I saw a thin white woman jacked up on high heels, mid-thirties probably, wearing a pastel miniskirt and white hose, torso cupped with open layers. The shirt closest to her skin was of sheer white material that showed off her navel. She saw a white brunette who wasn't much of a threat to her income—not enough make-up to hide the eyebags, unflattered by her black ensemble, too covered up even though her stretch pants didn't begin to meet the hem of her shirt. But younger and a newcomer, both appealing to johns. Fresh-face here would have to be finding herself another corner. At least her expression suggested that's what she saw. I think I shook my head.

Shiny Skirt laughed, white teeth flashing below her curly hairdo. She was shorter and plumper than her colleagues. Her flesh mounded like a baking biscuit between the hems of her halter-top and waistband. "She looks like she's from PROTECT, but they're not out this time of night," she said, threading her arms through a down jacket.

"Um, no, I'm not from any group. My name is Aubrey Lyle. I'm a stripper at Naughtyland and I'm looking for a certain man who comes around here. Would you mind helping me out?"

"A stripper, you're kidding," said the tall brunette. "You sure you're not Vice?"

"Yeah, one of those cute little cop-hookers who traps johns?" The third woman was younger than the other two, with a girl's reedy shape and bottle-blonde hair. Her feet must have been killing her from the long walk in spike-heeled patent leather thigh-highs. "You sure dress like one."

"Look, I'm not a cop."

"Tuesdays and Thursdays are Vice ops," said Shiny Skirt.

"Looks like they got a new day," said PageBoy.

"Okay, I don't really see why you would help me, but here's the story. I have a photograph here, well it's just a computer printout really, of a guy who was the last person seen with a woman I worked with. Her name was Luna Nguyen. She was murdered. He comes to this corner."

I showed the paper around. The three women glanced disinterestedly from the image to the empty street. No business was driving by. What had happened to the circling sharks?

"I'm sorry for taking up your time, but if he's a killer he could be dangerous to you, too. Do you recognize him?"

Silence. All three of them looked up the street, in the direction cars would approach from. The teenager picked at her nail polish. PageBoy lit another cigarette.

"You buy me a cup of coffee, I'll tell you what I know." The blonde teenager, having no things to gather, was already crossing Treat at her stumpy pace. I followed obediently.

The fluorescent lights of the Binkee Brrgrr were the lone spot of brightness on the flat mile-long stretch of Mission Street. Not that they were warm and comforting—somehow the opposite. My teenaged companion and I settled into two bright orange plastic molded chairs at the sea foam green counter and I ordered a coffee for her. Lemon-scented cleaner, its kick as strong as smelling salts, abraded my sinuses. The several other Binkee Brrgrr customers were asleep.

The place was eerily quiet. The only sounds were the song of fluorescent lights and the footfalls of the middle-aged Asian proprietor, off to fill our order. I asked my companion her name. She just shrugged. No conversation was forthcoming before coffee, I gathered. Her hair glowed greenly under the artificial lighting. She played with the zipper of her thigh-highs. Its small metal teeth flaked her nail polish into a drizzle of red dandruff.

The coffee came in a styrofoam cup. She added two packets of sugar and inches of cream. She stirred, sipped. "So, this guy. I've seen him lots of times, he comes around that corner a lot, cruises Mission too. He always asks us where can he find Sugar. That's the girl, the one in your print-out."

"You recognize the car?"

"Sure."

"What's he look like?"

"The guy? I don't know, balding, old. Maybe forties. He don't want me. I never look at him. Can I have a donut?"

I sighed. "Sure." I felt in my jacket pocket for another crumpled dollar bill.

I watched her stick a tongue into the fat donut's middle and lick out the yellow custard. Powdered sugar dotted her faded purple lipstick. She looked at me when she was finished. I bought her another.

"Do you know his name?"

"Nope."

"He's not a cop?"

She blew out a breath. "He don't act like one."

"Does Sugar go with him?"

"I don't keep track of her dates."

"Would Sugar know his name?"

My companion shrugged. "She might. They don't always tell us their real names, you know."

I knew. "How can I get in touch with her?"

My informant pushed the last shiny arc of a honey glazed between her speckled lips. Her expression became serious as she slowly chewed. She cleared her palate with a swallow of coffee. "Sugar won't talk to you. She's gotten hauled in by the cops so many times, she's real suspicious."

"I'm not a cop. I'm a stripper. Watch, here I am not showing you a badge."

My companion shrugged again. "When she gets beat up, she always says its you guys that do it."

"Us guys? You mean the cops?"

"Sure. You don't treat us with kid gloves, you know."

My face must have registered my surprise. My companion turned away, unimpressed with my innocence.

"That's all I can really tell you. Sorry." She spoke to her styrofoam cup.

"It's okay." I was suddenly aware of the listening pose of the proprietor. I grabbed a napkin out of a holder. "If you see Sugar, could you tell her I'm looking for her? Here's my name and address." I wrote them on the napkin along with the words not a cop underlined for emphasis, and stuffed the message into her hand. The girl nodded as I rose from the hard cup of the garish plastic chair.

I left my informant in the chilly light, sipping her cooling coffee amid the dozing patrons. She didn't look at me again.

Her avoidance of eye contact with me became more awkward for her after fifteen minutes or so. I was still outside the restaurant, an animated presence on the other side of the plate glass, jumping to keep warm and flailing my arms at the one cab that passed. It was already occupied. Perhaps she felt she couldn't leave until after I did. Unhappily for both of us, no other cabs apparently wandered the heart of the Mission at two a.m. I leaned on a mailbox, hunkered into my leather jacket.

Hugh would be around eventually. He got hungry with alarming frequency and Binkee Brrgrr was the only place around still open. He wouldn't have just abandoned me, but was just a bit absentminded. He was probably parked under a streetlight reading one of the paperback mystery novels he always carried in his pocket. Maybe he was taking Yohimbe on a tour of nearby attractions—San Francisco's original Mission Church, the horsy statue up near Market, palm-lined Dolores, the Street of Sorrows. But still, it had been almost two hours since he'd dropped me off. I hoped he was all right.

My fears for Hugh changed to irritation when the van moseyed up to me twenty minutes later. Hugh reached over to unlock the passenger side door. I wrenched it open.

"Where the hell were you?" He'd turned down the volume on the music, which was Rod Stewart's "Do Ya Think I'm Sexy?"

"Pardon, did I leave a damsel in distress? You told me to take off. But Yohimbe and I got hungry. She's in a delicate condition, you know."

"This isn't eighties music."

Yohimbe good-naturedly refused to move her heavy frame from the front passenger seat. She slobbered onto my shoulder as I squeezed between her and the dashboard, then between Hugh and the two-and-a-half-foot-long gearshift lever to get to the tapestried bench seat. Hugh opened his door and climbed out. "I know. It's the radio. Your tape ended. It broke, I'm afraid."

"What?" I pulled it out of the tape deck. An end of raw tape fluttered out of the cassette. It was tipped with about a foot of clear leader.

"That's one endorsement for CD technology. I'll be right back," said Hugh. "The old girl here really loves a cheeseburger. I think Peter and Rainbow have her on some sort of vegetarian diet. Not good for a pregnant pup. Did you notice the customers in this place? Down-and-outs, and a lady of the night."

I chucked Luna's tape into the glove compartment as Hugh looked over the down-and-outs and the lady of the night. I suspected he was getting his vocabulary from the Brother Cadfael mysteries he so loved. The sleeping piles of rags that used the Binkee Brrgrr as a motel may have smelled medieval, but there was nothing romantic about them. And my informant was no lady, but a teenager. That coffee I'd bought her would stunt her growth.

"The so-called lady of the night in there was talking to me about the guy in the Camry. She was telling me just how little she knew about him."

"What did she say?"

"She doesn't know his name. He does come around to pester them a lot. He apparently does business with a prostitute named Sugar, who is black and blue sometimes but blames her injuries on the cops. Sugar can't be reached for comment. My informant says the guy's not a cop."

"Was that in question?"

"Not really. Jossie's still convinced that Peaches was Vice, and therefore any regular of hers must have been a Vice contact."

"Interesting."

"Those women think I'm a cop posing as a hooker to catch johns. No one is going to talk to me."

"Is being a john illegal?"

"I don't think so."

"But in order for them to talk to you, you've got to blend in without seeming like you're trying to blend in."

"Right."

"Well I'm off." Hugh gathered his courage and entered the Binkee Brrgrr. I watched with amusement as he tried to avoid my informant who was now breaking up her styrofoam cup in a slow spiral. Hugh stood as far from her as possible to place his order.

Whatever Hugh ordered was taking a long time to cook. Perhaps the grill had to be fired up. I closed my eyes, but sleep was impossible against the low back of the bench seat. It was as cold as outside in the van. I straightened up. When I checked on Hugh's progress, he was wrestling change out of his pocket and avoiding not one but two streetwalkers.

"I didn't tell her nothing," my informant was saying, as I pushed back into the restaurant.

"It's okay, Charlene," said her companion. "You did the right thing, getting her name." The woman sitting next to Charlene had luxuriant brown hair pinched into ponytails that began high on her head and fanned halfway down her back. I was happy to see that she wore a coat, a long black cashmere with darts so that it skimmed her waist, then flared in an echo of the shape of her long hair. Capri pants poked below the coat's hem. She'd hooked the chunky heels of her strappy open-toed shoes over the bottom rung of her molded chair. Her toe-nails were painted green, in a medium bright shade I recognized as "Pomelo." She crossed her feet as she listened to the teenager I'd been talking to, who now had a name, Charlene.

"She said she wasn't a cop. I didn't tell her nothing."

"Hi, Sugar," I said. The ponytails swept the air as she turned around. "I'm the one who's not a—"

"Cop. Glad to hear it," Sugar said.

As soon as I saw her face I recognized her. Though the photographs of her had placed her in a more wholesome context, there was no mistaking those wide cobalt eyes. I was face to face with Luna's childhood friend.

"You're Cari—"

"Sugar," she interrupted, her voice a notch louder than mine and

firm. I flushed at the faux pas I'd almost made. "The girls told me someone was asking about Luna. Have a seat." Shiny buttons down her
black bodice imitated the brilliance of her eyes.

I sat. Charlene got up and scrambled out the door.

"I didn't mean to scare her. She really didn't tell me anything. She
was extremely unhelpful."

"Good," Sugar smiled. Her features were burdened by the fluorescent lighting, so I couldn't tell at first how stunningly beautiful she was.
The photographs at Murray's house had hinted at it. Her face had bone
structure and her skin was unusually smooth. Her blue eyes looked
from under slender eyebrows of the same autumn color as her hair. Her
dress and coat fit her carelessly, yet fell in the right ways across her
angled shoulders, her parted legs, and her cleavage, their long-lined
drapes echoing the slender lengths of her limbs. Even if I hadn't seen
pictures of her as a confident teenager, I would have guessed that Sugar
had never experienced an awkward phase.

Beauty certainly wasn't a job requirement of sex work, any more
than youth was. But occasionally I'd meet someone in my profession
who could have been making a fortune as a model, with no more
demanded of them than to make love to the camera with their perfect
pouts and to pose their perfect bodies over piles of Parisian leaves.
Sugar fell into that category.

"We have the same color hair," she was saying.

"That's true," I said. It seemed odd small talk. But I've never been
fluent in it.

"Mine's Miss Clairol Moonlit Brown with Flame highlights. Yours?"
She wrapped a swatch of mine around a finger.

"Growing out from a perm and a lightening in Autumn Mist."

"You knew Luna?" She held onto my hair.

"I found her body."

Sugar grabbed my arm. "Tell me about it."

I described the scene as gently to Luna's friend as I could. Sugar did-
n't help me make it easy on her. She kept asking for more details,
including the position of the body, the condition of the rooms, had they
been ransacked, was anything missing, did it seem like whoever murdered her had been looking for something.

I told her the place looked like everything in it had been gone
through twice.

"Then they didn't find it." She untangled her shoe heels from the
chair.

"Find what?" Sugar was already standing. She tucked her ponytails under her coat.

"I've got to get out of here, sorry. Look, I'll be in touch, okay?"

She whirled and left. I wasn't even sure she had my name.

After I regained my wits I slid out of the molded seat and followed her out. She was trotting south on Mission Street, toward the wedge of pinpoint lights that scaled Bernal Hill.

"Wait," I called after her. "I wanted to ask you about this guy." I held up my creased printout. I felt ridiculous, since the identity of the man in the Camry seemed the least profound of my questions at that point. But Sugar turned.

"Whatever you do, stay away from him," she yelled back. "I'm sure he has something to do with Luna's death." Then she turned the corner at Twenty-first and was gone.

I woke up early the next afternoon, feeling sorry for myself. Monday morning blues affect even late sleepers and the unemployed. My inconclusive meetings with the people I'd found to have connections with Luna proved that I had little talent for investigating her death. I felt the doldrums of empty days stretching ahead of me, bereft of meaning or what passed for it, routine. I would have sunk into my futon if it had had any give. Peter or Rainbow's back wasn't very forgiving either. I couldn't tell exactly which one of them was pressed next to me, and which one had gotten stuck next to the wall. The two of them were a tangle of dreadlocks and hemp-scented tapestries.

I comforted myself under the circles of purple and brown cotton that interlocked into the wedding ring quilt my Granny Leann had made. The quilt's pieces were cut from tough old cloth. Granny never threw a scrap away. Her quilts paired textured polyester doubleknit from her daughters' grade school dresses with denim from her youngest boy's bellbottoms and flowered feedsack from the clothes her own mother had left behind when she'd died. Granny had stitched together these fragments of her loved ones obsessively, and made sure every family member had several of her handmade quilts.

She always gave a double wedding ring as a wedding present. Diabetes had killed my maternal grandmother two months before that blessed event had happened to me. Granny Leann had spent her last days piecing my wedding ring quilt, spending precious motes of energy on the task. My mother often suggested that this effort had killed her.

I forced myself to get up and fight back guilt with my standard remedy of Earl Grey. Mondays were normally good days for me at Naughtyland, and I worried about how much money I wasn't going to make. I decided to treat myself by going out for my customary cuppa. That way I could pay several dollars for it while risking a Gen-Xer bartender's morning mood and a bouffant made of milk.

By the time I got home it was late afternoon. Geoffrey was sitting on the couch with an empty highball glass in his hand. He was pale and still.

"I thought I had problems. You look like you've seen a ghost."

"That dog is giving birth under our kitchen table. It's the most disgusting thing I've ever seen. Aren't they supposed to do that in a barn or something?"

"God. Where are Peter and Rainbow?"

"Oh, they're in there. Take a peek. But may I suggest you don't go all the way in."

I cracked open the swinging door that separated the kitchen from the living room. A cloud of smoke hovered above the kitchen table. Yohimbe was on her side on a piece of cardboard under the table, as Geoffrey had said. The dog looked at me wide-eyed and silent. Three log-shaped puppies, two brindled and one black, wiggled by her belly. Peter and Rainbow were leaning against the stove, keeping their multiplying dogs company and trading hits off of a three-foot-tall green plastic bong.

"Check it out!" Peter gestured to Yohimbe and the puppies. He spoke without exhaling, to preserve the smoke.

"Great. Congratulations. Three times." It looked like the kitchen would be off limits for making dinner. The floor was clean enough, but the smoke would be giving second-hand highs for hours to come.

"Oh, German Shepherds typically have ten or more puppies," said Rainbow. "You'll owe her many more congratulations before she's through."

"The smoke helps her birthing pains," added Peter.

"Great. Well, keep it up then." I shut the door. "We are soon to have eleven dogs as houseguests," I said to Geoffrey.

"I know. What's that old saying? How do you know your houseguests are hippies?—they're still there. We could add a new caveat. Their one dog becomes eleven." He reached for a half-full bottle of Stolichnaya that was wedged between the cushions on the couch. "Why did I ever invite them to stay?" He swallowed straight from the bottle.

"They're your houseguests?"

"Oh, yes," he packed drama into the following sigh. "Peter's one of my oldest friends. We grew up together in Pacific Palisades. He was my dealer in high school. Do you know where Pacific Palisades is?" He hoisted the Stoli bottle once again, aimed its mouth toward me.

I shook my head.

"Cheers." Geoffrey usually only drank wine, and that with meals. He did other drugs, but feared that alcohol would make him fat.

"She was eating the—" he gagged.

"Geoffrey. Why don't we just get out of here for a while? I'll take you out for dinner. Spaghetti?"

"Don't tease. I've been through a horror. Take me to Giorno's."

Geoffrey and I avoided anything red at Giorno's, a small Italian restaurant that remained unpretentious even though it was located in the Castro. Geoffrey recovered enough after the walk to the restaurant in the fresh evening air to regain his appetite. By the time we walked home, the night was just beginning to chill.

"Can I complain? It's never warm here," Geoffrey whined. Neither one of us had worn jackets. I tucked my arm into Geoffrey's and pulled us together for warmth. "Stop! People will think I'm straight!" he teased.

"You can't complain. Ever been to Texas?"

"No."

"So hot in the summer that you can't walk two blocks without a gallon jug of water to replace lost sweat. You go down to the swimming hole, and it's tepid as spit. Unrefreshing as a room temperature Coke. You're doomed to stickiness from March to October. In midsummer it feels like your body is merging with the air, it's so humid. The kids spend the summers attached by a straw to Big Gulps the size of their heads."

"Well. When were you in Texas? Don't apply for a job with their promotional bureau."

"I was down there a few years ago. My college roommate Mellissa is from there. She's got a couple of kids now."

"Heterosexual hell. I'm sorry to hear it."

"I'm godmother to her oldest, Tyler. A boy. She's doing a great job with them."

"Don't tell me you believe in motherhood!"

"Like I need kids. I've got Momma."

"Right. Anyway, there's a certain event that has to happen before a Blessed Event. I'm not sure you've heard about it. Sex?"

"Very funny. With you for a roommate, I've not only heard plenty about it, I've heard the live version."

"Well it's a good thing you have me to tell you the truth about your life. Nobody else will confront you, even loverboy Hugh. How long has it been? Who or what are you holding out for, Miss Celibacy?"

"Hugh's not my loverboy."

"Oh, honey, you need me worse than I thought. Well that's a fight for another day. Right now I'm talking about you not getting laid."

"Well, for one thing, no one wants to date a stripper."

"Don't play victim with me. Everyone wants to date a stripper."

"That's another point. Anyone who wants to date a stripper, I don't want to date. Most people don't want to have a partner who's getting naked for money. There's no illusion that I'm exclusively 'theirs.' I've never met anyone who didn't have a hard time with that. Remember Herr Doktor?"

"Och, oy. That was ages ago. I warned you about dating Eurotrash."

"Some people can just admit they don't want to share their girl-friend, right? He was the opposite. He loved bragging to his cowork-ers that he was dating a stripper. They were all grad students who never left their labs. It made him seem daring or something. Then one of them slunk away from his beakers and saw me at the club. Herr Doktor got grumpy at me about it. At me! He didn't go so far as to call me a whore, but I could tell he really wanted to say it. So I went ahead and reminded him that's basically what I am. You should have seen the look on his face."

We laughed.

"Bastard," said Geoffrey. "I never knew it ended like that. I was right to take him to the Ladies Room at that bar. He was scared of all the drag queens. I made him use it, too. And he was the type who couldn't pee in front of people."

"That's basically the way it went with the other little flings I've had since I started stripping. While everyone here tries to be progressive and free love, they can't handle my job any better than the corn-fed Ohio boys back home. And in Ohio, they'd just tell you straight out. Here I'm supposed to congratulate people for being tolerant enough to date me. I'm supposed to help them with their 'issues' around it. Fuck that. I'm the one with a tough job. I don't go whining to them about 'issues.' Until I find someone who can support me about my job, dating's not worth it."

"Well," he said as we turned onto Church Street. The odor of pinto beans, marinated in lard, cooking in El QuakeO downstairs welcomed us home. "I think you're meeting the wrong kind of people. How can we get some of those corn-fed Ohio boys out here?" Geoffrey squeezed my arm. "Seriously. You're right. Maybe being a stripper is like being a fag. You out yourself to someone, and they immediately configure you into some outlandish sexual position in their mind, and there you stay in their mind's eye, naked among satin sheets or spread-eagled in some seedy bar, doing things that are still illegal in their home state. It's alluring, or revolting, but in either case they can't get it out of their head and it becomes hard for them to see you as a whole person."

"Maybe so." I squeezed him back.

Chapter Eleven

Geoffrey headed straight past the kitchen door and down the corridor to the room he shared with Hugh, putting an open hand against his temple to block peripheral vision of the kitchen, stopping only to extract his Stolichnaya bottle from the couch. I heard Zan's cooing and poked my head into the birthing room to say hello. Zan was holding one of the puppies close to Yohimbe's head. Yohimbe rolled her eyes to meet Zan's, but didn't lift her head off of the floor. Seven other puppies now wriggled by Yohimbe's belly.

"Look out," said Vivian who was behind me with towels and a cardboard box.

"Wouldn't it be interfering with nature if she gave birth in a box?"

"It's okay. I cleared it with Peter and Rainbow." Vivian pushed past me. Zan placed the towels, then the puppies into the box among folds of towel, then had to take them all out again so Viv could cram Yohimbe in first. "Nothing bigger in the alley," she grumbled. "Damn Safeway's started locking their dumpsters." Yohimbe fit in if her spine curved like a strung bow. Repositioned, her head fell wearily against the ground as her eight offspring were reintroduced to nursing. Peter and Rainbow could manage only silent half smiles as Viv and Zan assured the comfort of their new grandchildren, and Zan dragged the box back under the kitchen table.

"Are you two the midwives?"

"Right. Just by default. Between Geoffrey's retching and Hugh's fainting the boys have made themselves pretty useless."

"Hugh fainted?"

"You know he can't stand the sight of blood," said Zan.

"Right, I forgot." Hugh had sliced his finger once instead of the carrot and fainted immediately onto the kitchen floor. "Is she done yet?" I asked, indicating the largest dog.

"I guess the placenta would be the last thing out, and there's been no sign of that yet," Zan answered.

"We should save it and bury it beside a tree," said Peter.

"Yeah," agreed Rainbow.

What tree? I thought. A few diseased palms divided traffic in Market Street a block away, but their roots were entombed in concrete.

"She'll eat it," said Zan. "We used to raise puppies when I was a kid."

With that I let the kitchen door close and went off to look for my own little bit of nature, Hodge, who refused to take one step out of doors, either to sniff the breeze or to shit into soil. He chemically sprayed and soon killed any plants that were introduced into the apartment by those who thought urban decay and root rot could mix. Hodge had denounced his origins and embraced the modern urban lifestyle as firmly as the rest of us San Franciscans. I found him sleeping on my down pillow.

Once it was sufficiently dark to appear in eveningwear, I took the Twenty-two bus the short distance to Sixteenth and Mission. This is where the Mission district begins. Panhandlers congregate, the BART stops and bus routes intersect a hammock of electric wires above the intersection. Low-riders prowl, prostitutes beckon. Latino drag queens head to Esta Noche, Gen-X slackers to Muddy Waters, gangbangers to McDonalds and the newest wave of immigrants to the neighborhood, young computer professionals, to We Be Sushi.

Despite Sugar's enigmatic warning, I was once again in search of the Camry driver. Whoever he was, he was my only lead to Luna's killer. Or else he was Luna's killer. I hiked up my thigh-high black fishnets. In any position other than legs-in-the-air, thigh-high stockings inevitably sagged. I was attracting plenty of attention. For once I couldn't blame bystanders for staring. I wore a shiny red cropped leather jacket, Geoffrey's dancing gear. The jacket's narrow cut didn't begin to meet over deep cleavage created by a frilly black Wonderbra. My fishnets ended before my black miniskirt began. I felt far more lewd than I ever had naked and spread-eagled at Naughtyland. I had considered dressing in the off-duty pom-pom-girl style of PROTECT's Sandy Larson, but I didn't own a sweatshirt. I ended up dressing in a way that I hoped would inspire confidence that I was no cop.

I walked quickly the several blocks to Twenty-first and Treat. The evening air was in motion, about to thicken with the fog that was pumping over Twin Peaks. The moist chill penetrated clothing. What a night to be outside in pink hotpants, I thought, as I recognized my young informant who stood alone on her habitual corner. Her brown roots weren't as obvious outdoors. Charlene stared at me sullenly as I approached. I waved hello.

"Hello, how've you been?" I said, with Midwestern cheerfulness. Maybe she was a runaway and would respond to the friendly cadences of home.

She shrugged. High heels clattered around the corner, and we were joined by PageBoy. Neither of the women's outfits was adequate for the chilly evening. Neither was mine. My hands were stiff from the cold.

"Hello," I greeted the newcomer.

"It's the Vice girl. Back again, eh? You're fighting a losing battle, chicky." The brunette hugged herself, lit a cigarette, and looked down the one-way street in the direction from which cars would approach.

Several losing battles, it seemed. "Anyone seen Sugar lately?"

The brunette answered me. "You tell us how she's doing, Miss Vice. At least she's keeping warm in jail."

"Jail?"

Charlene's damaged hair didn't move much with her nod of agreement. "Yeah, you got her where you want her. If you want to talk to her so bad why don't you just visit her cell? Stop playing games with us. I never should have talked to you."

I was starting to feel guilty, like I actually was a cop. "Sugar's in jail?"

Nobody bothered to answer. Both my companions were busy with the surveillance of passing traffic. PageBoy tossed her cigarette into the path of an oncoming sedan and smoothed her hair. She stepped into the street to negotiate. As she was getting into her newfound customer's car, a pick-up truck, bulbous as overstuffed furniture, squealed to a stop behind it. Neither the teenager nor myself made a move. On my part, this was from nervousness.

"Hey, someone working here, or what? I pay fifty," said the truck's driver. He was a youngish white man in a baseball hat. "Come on, hurry. You, blondie, you coming or what?" My remaining companion pushed out of her slouch against a parked car and trudged to the truck's passenger side.

I was alone. Business was good. I hunched over to try to get the cloth of my shirt to meet the miniskirt's waistband. This exposed my back to a slash of cold. No sign of the white Camry. I began to consider the gawking driver of the red sports car that circled by every three minutes as company.

My grandmother's fake-gold Timex read nine-thirty when a car once again pulled up. The driver ignored me. Shiny Miniskirt emerged. The car sped off, leaving her to totter to the sidewalk in four-inch red heels. Her choppy movement made her various strata bounce: soft curly hair, rayon-swaddled breasts, stretch-knit-seized hips. I was ambivalent about the company. I didn't remember her as the friendly type.

"You again? Give it up, sister."

"Nice to see you, too."

"What are you doing here dressed like that? Look, I don't know if you're from PROTECT or if you're Vice, but you're scaring away business! Trying to catch johns! Personally, I can take care of myself. Sugar feels the same way. She don't like newcomers, not new cops or new whores or new do-gooders. I don't care if she did used to tell us to work with PROTECT. She won't be too happy about this." The woman planted her hands on her hips, inch-long purple nails curling against the clingy red rayon.

"Sugar told you you should work with PROTECT?" I'd gotten the impression she was rather independent.

"Until she figured out they were scaring away customers for good. She's just trying to get us to look out for each other. She got us to form little groups, now we bail each other out of jail. She thinks us girls should stick together because this is a hard life. You Vice don't make it any better."

"I'm not Vice. Look, have you seen Sugar? I need to talk to her."

"Not since I saw her in that picture you were showing us. They say she's in jail."

"For what?"

She just rolled her eyes at me.

"If she's in jail, why don't you bail her out?"

"She told us not to this time. It's a protest or something. Sometimes I don't understand that girl." A shake of her curls emphasized the point. "Who'd want to do extra time?"

"Have you seen the Camry lately? That was in the picture too."

"What is this, some cop inquisition mind-fuck? I know what was in the picture. All this talking is bad for business." She glared at me as a Lexus passed by, its driver presumably put off by the sight of two whores carrying on a conversation.

115

"But you don't know anything about the man who drives it? He was the last person seen with my murdered friend."

"Sugar, she don't gossip about her customers." My companion was looking intently at an approaching brown station wagon. As the vehicle slowed, she moved at a fast hobble to intercept it. She consulted with the driver for a moment, gripping the station wagon's windowsill to maintain balance and at the same time dangle cleavage. I used the same posture to scare up lapdances. Nods were exchanged and she was in the passenger seat, then whisked away.

In the next half, hour Charlene and PageBoy rejoined me. Both made a point of standing as far away from me as they could and remain on the same corner. My sports-car-driving friend seemed to have called it quits for the night without getting lucky. Neither woman spoke to me. The blonde smoothed her pink hot pants over her thighs and paced the curb, coltish in spike heels. The brunette jostled past her to lean into car windows. After a convoy of no-takers, she launched into conversation with a youngish white man who perspired behind the wheel of a white sedan. On closer inspection, the sedan proved to be a Toyota Camry.

Impulsively, I ran to join the brunette outside the Camry's window.

"Take me, take me," was all I could think of to say. PageBoy shook her head at me in disgust. The driver was asking her the whereabouts of Sugar. She shrugged indifferently.

"Sugar's not working tonight," I offered, cringing with self-loathing. My tattle had violated several articles in the stripper code of ethics. Never reveal the work schedule of a co-worker. Never hit on someone else's regular. But here he was, Peaches' final customer. Probably. His forearm crawled with sand-colored hair, but how different are hairy forearms from one another? He could have been anybody. At that moment, he was chewing his lip and looking away from us. A circle of heat flared near my ear and I imagined it to be a physical beam from PageBoy's glare. But it was only the tip of her cigarette.

He motioned me into his car.

I clutched Geoffrey's slippery red leather jacket around my torso as I scurried around the front of the Camry and got in the passenger side. I had a vague awareness that I wasn't giving myself time to think. The brunette retreated. They'd really hate me now. Whether I was Vice or whether I was just new competition, they had reason to resent me. Sugar could promote solidarity all she wanted, but the reality was that streetwalkers, like lapdancers, compete with each other for customers and for money. Sisterhood is not powerful among sex workers. We can't afford it.

Only Charlene voiced a protest, though. As the Camry turned the corner, I could hear her faint warning, "Dude, she's Vice!"

The car thrummed over the Bay Bridge and up the four-lane highway to the Caldecott Tunnel. What had I gotten myself into now, I thought, nervously biting my lip. I flipped down the sunguard and rubbed at my dark lipstick as I looked into the small vanity mirror. It was a bit late to be concerned about the whore veneer. I certainly wasn't going to fuck this guy. I hoped he didn't have that in mind. I stared at myself in the mirror. Of course he had that in mind. He thought I was a prostitute! He was taking me to some no-tell motel out in the middle of nowhere this very instant. I didn't even know how much I was supposed to be charging. There had to be some way to take control of the situation, and I would think of it momentarily. Meanwhile the man nosed the car into the narrow Caldecott and cleared his throat.

"You can call me Bob."

"I'm, uh, Cindy."

That was that. We were headed into the depths of the suburbs at a relentless seventy miles an hour.

Bob pulled off the highway about twenty minutes later. We had failed to find a topic of conversation. He exited onto a wide suburban street. A couple of closed steakhouses were tucked in beside the highway. Beyond them, dark low-storied office buildings looked out over bland acreage of asphalt and young landscaping. Streetlights of stadium intensity illuminated the sterile scene.

We passed under concrete supports for the BART tracks and to the left I saw a sign reading Walnut Creek Station. No creek or walnuts were evident. In the tradition of manufactured suburbs, the name seemed to represent whatever natural phenomena progress had replaced.

I picked my cuticles as Bob nosed the Camry into the parking lot of a hotel half a mile or so down the street. The hotel apparently shared the same inspired architecture as the office blocks. Several low units with concrete balconies clustered around a drive-up office. The complex was unified with islands of grass and saplings. Streetlights crowded around it like eager butlers. Bob drove up to one of the cubes of rooms and swung into a parking space. After the rip of the emergency brake, there was silence.

I looked toward the street. Deserted. If I leapt out of the Camry, there'd be no one to flag down. Nowhere to hide, either. The network of streetlights could have been specially designed to discourage fugitives.

"Want some herb?" Bob's voice was slow, and so were the movements of his hand as he unbuckled, reached to turn on the interior light and popped open the car's ashtray. Several flattened inch-long roaches wilted therein.

"No thanks, you go ahead though." I looked over my john for the first time. Jossie had been right about his hair. It was frizzy to the point of being almost colorless, like the carbonated head of a fountain Coke. He wore it long to compensate for the receding hairline. His face, thin, pale, and freckled, was at that moment unflattered by the sodium lighting. His eyes matched his face, a bleached-out color, pupils passing for two more freckles. He was thin, dressed in a T-shirt and used overalls and the type of sandals that Velcro around the feet. The Velcro threatened long brown hairs that grew from his toes.

The overalls made me think of Momma. She was appalled that they had become an urban fashion statement. "Down in the hills," she'd say, referring to her native Kentucky, "we were always trying to get something to wear besides them coverall things."

Bob held an unsteady match an inch from his lips to light the pitiful remains of a doobie. It would make things easier if Bob smoked enough so that he couldn't get it up.

I turned away and took a deep breath. Despite Sugar's warning, he didn't seem like a sex killer. I could handle this guy. I tried to ignore the one fact I knew about him: the last woman known to have gotten into a car with him was now dead.

The match flame almost went out several times before he could keep his hand still enough to light the joint. Perhaps he was as nervous as I was. He offered me the soggy, smoldering butt, then deposited it into the ashtray when I declined.

"Your first time out?" His voice was neutral, maybe even nice.

How could he tell it was my "first time out"? I'd have to start acting more confident. But it probably wasn't me. With the regularity that Bob cruised Treat Street, he would know every hooker that came and went.

"Not exactly," I said.

"Nothing to be nervous about," he said, though he didn't seem convinced of this himself. "It's room 117." Bob still hadn't looked my body over too closely. I'd expected to be examined like a slaughterhouse-bound cow at some point; after all, he was paying a lot of money to rent my various parts. At least I assumed it would be a lot of money. I got out of the car and followed him across the parking lot to the first floor hotel room.

The key was one of the credit card type and Bob stuck it into its slot, withdrew it and pushed the door open. Inside, he headed for the bed and began to smooth out the gold polyester bedspread. I shut the door, noting that it opened easily from the inside without deadbolts to flip. If I had a hankering to make a run for the parking lot, that shouldn't be any problem. The problem would be where to go once I got out there. Fellow humans didn't seem to be part of the local landscape.

I found the remote control to the 1970's television and tuned in a porno channel. That seemed like something a genuine prostitute might do. On the small screen, a curly-headed eighteen year old with arcs of blue eyeshadow was sucking on a huge purple erection, heroically maintaining a lusty expression as her head and her loose blonde curls were tossed hither and yon from careless thrusts. I punched the volume louder.

"Come here, baby," said the television man.

"Ooh yeah," said blue eyeshadow, mouthing the words around the cock.

"I've got a confession to make," said Bob. His soft voice barely carried over the wordless moans from the television.

Experience suggested this would be a graphic, sexual kind of confession. I spoke quickly to cut him off. "And I've got a confession I want."

I approached Bob quickly, which perhaps accounted for his confused, then panicked expression. I decided I had better gain the upper hand considering the situation I was in, which was in a lonesome motel room with a potential slayer, so as I ran toward him I shucked off Geoffrey's red jacket, then my midriff-baring shirt. By the time I reached Bob I was whipping off my bra. I used it to garrote his neck.

My stranglehold was coincident with the porno movie's cum shots. I yanked the bra tight during the male's elongated grunt. I pulled Bob backward until he was down on the bed during her dubbed-in screams. The man narrated the actress's climax, "Yeah, that's right. Let me drink all your squirt, baby."

"What do you know about Luna's death?" My left knee was on top of Bob's crotch. I gave that part just enough pressure so that he knew I could fine-tune it up or down to encourage his cooperation.

Bob clutched the bra, a genuine Wonderbra, rather expensive, and looked up at me in googly-eyed panic. "Luna?" His voice came out high-pitched as he struggled to swallow and breathe.

"Don't play dumb with me. I'm talking about Peaches, Naughtyland, your favorite stripper. You gave her a ride and no one saw her alive again. Where did you take her? What did you do with her?"

"How do you know Peaches?"

"I'm a fellow stripper. I worked with her, until she died. Someone choked her just like this." I tightened the improvised ligature, pulling its ends. Its two u-shaped underwires pronged my captive's skin and stretched around to almost meet behind Bob's thin neck. I watched his face go through the warm color palette. Then I eased up.

Bob spent a few seconds sucking air. The dialogue had started on the next porno movie, or maybe it was the same couple, more articulate when their mouths weren't full. From the television set behind us came salutatory pleasantries, then a man's flat middle-American accent in an amateurish monotone. "I've wanted to do this to you ever since I saw you on the beach."

"You're getting this all wrong." Bob rubbed his neck and stared at me like a spooked colt. He jerked his eyes away from my bare chest.

"Correct me, then."

"All I did was give her a ride home. I read in the paper that she died from a sex killing. That's all I know."

"And you're saying you're not a sex killer."

"No!"

"Most of us don't accept rides from customers. Why would she go with you?"

"We were working together. That's what I was trying to tell you."

"You were working together? I didn't notice you stripping on the stage at Naughtyland. Somehow I think your performance would have stood out."

"Not at that. Thing is I'm not really a customer. A john." His throat needed clearing, but he didn't.

"What are you talking about? You picked me up on Treat Street, brought me to a hotel room in the middle of nowhere, watched a porno movie with me, and you're not a john?"

"I'm a union recruiter. I was working with Luna on the feasibility of getting Naughtyland affiliated with Local 16 of the NBSWI." His face had recovered its pale coloring. "Can you get your knee out of my crotch now?"

"Are you trying to say you brought me out here to try to get me to join a union?" I slowly got off Bob, knee last. He nodded. I was momentarily speechless. Bob glumly watched the movie. A mustachioed blond in a Stetson hat was silently fucking a flexible cowgirl clad only in tooled-leather boots. "I figured you picked me up to fuck me."

"Just to talk about unionizing." He brushed at his overalls as if they had chaff on them.

"Why bring me all the way out here and rent a hotel to talk about a union?" I kept my bra between my fists, on stand-by.

"New philosophy of the movement. Meet the workers on their own territory. Then they'll be more receptive to your ideas."

"This is a new strategy? Sounds like a manual for horse breeding."

"New as it gets in Big Labor. That's one of the reasons I was excited to take on this assignment. I'd like to see more women involved in the labor movement. It sure could use fresh rhetoric. And women workers have even more to gain than men from unions. Sex workers are notoriously exploited, you women who work on the street worst of all. We've already had some success, with the Cher Cherie. Look, I know this is not what you expected out of your evening, but I'm not going to hurt you. Uh, want to put on your shirt?"

"Okay." I put it on, crammed the bra into Geoffrey's jacket's pocket.

"So can I talk to you about joining?"

"No thanks. And by the way, I'm not really a hooker."

I decided Bob might as well drive me home. On the way back to the city, he talked about Luna. They met when the Cher Cherie organized, about eight months before. Luna and another woman came looking for representation, and the only union who would even consider taking on sex workers was the National Brotherhood of Service Workers International, Local Sixteen. Cher Cherie became a union shop a few months later. The novelty of it, of strippers being unionized, garnered the club and the local a lot of publicity.

"I must have missed it," I said. I had only a vague memory of some mocking editorial I'd read about the subject in the back of the *Chronicle*.

"It was all over the papers for about a day. I can see how you could've missed it. Called a 'media window', it slams on your fingers after about twelve hours of spotlight. I can tell you who's managed to milk it, though, that's Azote."

"We've met. She told me she helped Luna."

"Oh yeah? Well, they were the driving force, but Luna kept a low profile. Not Azote though." Bob shook his head. "She was interviewed all over the place. It was her look, the fact that she's obviously a dom-inatrix, the titillation factor. She said the same things every time, but managed to keep the issue in the media until fairly recently. I guess that's good. But now I think the interviewers are making fun of her, in a way. All this idealism from the mouth of a perverted whore."

"She doesn't see through it?"

"If she does, she doesn't seem to care. Bit of a media hound. Maybe it's bringing her business. If so, more power to her."

"You don't see her anymore?"

"Only at our bi-monthly retreats. I'm a recruiter, so I go where the workers aren't yet unionized."

"I never heard anything about a union at Naughtyland."

Bob sighed and ran a hand through his hair. The smoothing did nothing to tame the fuzz. "Right."

"So, what, Peaches changed her mind?"

"Well, she moved onto the Femme Royale pretty fast and then it shut down. So when she moved to Naughtyland, she stalled the cam-paign. She kept saying we had to wait. She was acting all weird about it. She wouldn't visit the office, wouldn't talk to me on the phone. Finally I had to seek her out. The only place I could find her was at her work. We could talk in those little cubicles. Normally I'd never go into a place like that. She couldn't hide from me there."

That was true. Unsettling as the thought was, anyone who knew where we worked had access to us strippers during those hours we were on shift. We couldn't hide out in the dressing room when Mose Junior was demanding a nightly sum of money.

"What did she tell you in those little cubicles?"

"She said she had to wait and feel the club out."

"Why?"

"Something wasn't right, she said. I tried to make her feel more secure about it. It's normal to feel threatened in this line of work. No boss or manager wants a union. The thing to do is work as quickly as you can to garner support and get the union cards signed, that means three-quarters of the workers sign their intent to support a union. Then you're protected from getting fired. Luna kept saying she needed more time. She wouldn't tell me why. I pestered her but she wouldn't budge."

Bob drove on in silence. We were approaching the bay. Sky that had been tepid and clear became shot through with cold haze where the Pacific fog trailed its blanket inland.

We sped into the gullet of the Caldecott Tunnel and I reflexively hunched into the Camry's bucket seat. The tunnel had been excavated with quaint handtools and designed for the horseless carriages of its day, too low, dark, and narrow for its current task—funneling legions of commuters accelerating at Mach Two toward their second cup of coffee in San Francisco. The tunnel cut through the Oakland hills, a tawny ridge of dried grass and close-packed mansions that ignited each other regularly in the dry season.

"Why do you think Luna was killed?"

"It had to be work-related. Sex workers get killed all the time in this city." We drove out of the tunnel, and the city in question was the focal point of the stunning view. The black freeway curved toward it. Oakland's lights rumpled like a rug at its feet. Light globes beaded the curves of the Bay Bridge like dew on a spiderweb, tethering continent to peninsula with a frail chain. San Francisco glowed like fission on the other side of the black bay. The edges of its skyline were feathered, like a distant galaxy's, by fog. "She made a date and it went wrong. Prostitution's dangerous."

"What makes you think she was a prostitute?"

"I guess she did it on the side. That's what the paper said." Bob shifted around nervously in his seat.

"You don't think trying to unionize the club had anything to do with her death?"

"How could it? What could that have to do with it?" Bob's grip tightened on the steering wheel, his arms locked straight. "I'm an organizer, and I've never been threatened. It's illegal under federal law to fire a worker for trying to organize."

"Really."

"Yes. Since the Warner Act."

"The Warner Act."

"Part of the New Deal. A bill of rights for labor. Guaranteed the right to collective bargaining."

"That's great. But we're talking about a murder here, so it seems someone hasn't concerned himself much with the law."

Bob chewed his lip and looked worried.

"If Luna was an organizer, who would have hated her the most?"

"Who has the most at stake? Middle management at the workplace is typically the most vocally anti-union. Foremen, crew leaders, whoever works with you but just above you. They tend to feel like unionizing is a reflection on them, that they're doing a bad job. They're insulted. They feel betrayed. But owners hate the union even worse. To them it means losing control, which means losing money. They can't afford to be seen as not caring about their workers, though, and so they try to seem benevolent about the whole issue and almost always they let their managers and lawyers fight unionization for them. They stay out of it."

The Moses would hate the idea of their girls being unionized, but considering their phobias about the American legal system, I doubted either of them would risk their lifestyles to kill.

It was time to find out who the owner of Naughtyland was. Hadn't Azote told me that the owners of the Femme Royale had shut it down rather than allow it to be unionized? How far were these people willing to go to protect their million-dollar businesses?

Chapter Twelve

Bob drove me to my apartment, politely offering to drop me at the corner so he wouldn't know exactly where I lived. Another pointer from a sensitivity-training workshop, perhaps. I just asked him to take me to my door.

Geoffrey stood in front of the iron grate that the landlord had installed at our entrance as a first line of defense against the neighborhood. He was dazzling under the dim streetlight. He wore a sparkly blue jacket with a vinyl glow, a perfect match for his eyes. Buckles glinted from his belt and from his pointy-toed boots. His hair was glazed with gel.

"Sympathy fuck?" he asked me, taking my hand like a battlefield nurse dispensing mercy. "Congratulations, anyway. You're finally going braless! No wonder you got lucky. Well at least you're taking care of your needs. You're so practical when it comes to love."

He was right about the practical part. I just wasn't a romantic. My first marriage had been for the purpose of facilitating paperwork.

Before I could deny having sex with Bob, Geoffrey pirouetted and continued, "It's Eighties Night at The Stud. Is this so New Ro or what? There's my ride," he said, and waved to a beeping convertible that pulled up to the curb, pulsing a dance mix of 'It's Raining Men.' "Look at that eyeliner. Even straight boys wore it then. What a decade." He kissed my cheek and dashed for the car.

Upstairs, Hugh sat alone in one of the four permanent indents in our couch. He looked at me over his worn paperback. "Where have you been?"

"Turning tricks. What about you?"

He held up his book so I could read the title. *Life in a Medieval Castle*. "Reading, finally. Geoffrey wouldn't leave me alone."

"Was he bugging you?"

"He wanted fashion advice. I think he must have been joking."

My male roommates had a funny relationship. They were opposite in personality, Hugh shy and serious, Geoffrey flamboyant and irreverent. Yet they were fond of each other, in their own ways. Geoffrey complained that Hugh and he didn't get to spend enough time together, since Hugh was such a homebody, and threatened to start a knitting circle as an activity they could both participate in. Geoffrey teased Hugh without troubling him with the combative "honest feedback" that he enjoyed giving me. And though Hugh rarely went out with him he would wait up for him, much as he did for me, even though waiting up for Geoffrey could stretch on for days.

"How did they shit in a medieval castle?" I sat down between him and the endtable with the phone.

"That's actually very interesting. Latrines were constructed right into the stone walls..."

I listened as I found the business card in my leather jacket's inner pocket that Gus had pressed into my hand as I left his office, offering to be of service to me anytime day or night, twenty-four seven. I dialed Got To Be Free Bail Bonds. If Sugar was in jail, the public had access to her, much the same way they did to us dancers. Public property. If I could find her we could continue our conversation from the night before. I was curious to know why she had suggested that the non-threatening Bob was involved in Luna's murder.

"...into the moat, or dug out by the so-called 'gong farmer,'" Hugh was saying as I dialed.

"Got to be free Gus."

"Hi Gus. I was in there the other day for a Joseph Thomas, you gave me your card—"

Hugh stopped his informative talk.

"The brunette with the gorgeous green eyes?"

"No. Her eyes are brown."

"I'm talking about yours, sweetheart! You decide you're ready to be spoiled? I knew you'd be calling on Gus."

"It's not exactly that. Can you run a check for me? To see if someone's in jail?" I picked Hugh's book off the floor and handed it back to him. It seemed to have jumped from his hands.

"My job. Name?"

"Carina Smyth, Smyth with a 'y'."

"Jail?"

"Bryant Street I guess. What other jails are there?"

"I'll start with Bryant. I got to call over there, call you back. What's your number?"

"I'll call you. In about five minutes?" No way was I giving Gus my home phone number. Hugh was staring at me.

"Spell that first name?" I spelled Carina for him and hung up.

"Who's that? What's going on?" asked Hugh.

"That was Gus."

"You know what I mean. Who is Carina Smyth?"

"A friend of Luna's. A streetwalker."

Hugh went back to his book. He was too shy to be a very good snoop.

Five minutes later I dialed Gus again.

"That you? Okay, no Carina Smyth at Bryant. Want me to try around?"

"That'd be great."

"For you, no problem. What else would I do till the bars close? Then do we get business. Shouldn't take long."

"I'll call you back."

"Simpler to give me your number."

"I know."

When I called him back again, Gus sounded just as chipper as if it were almost three in the afternoon rather than in the morning. He had no news for me, though. No Carina Smyth in any jail on the Peninsula. He'd even checked the East Bay and Marin County as a personal favor. Was there anything else he could do for me? I said 'no thanks' and hung up the phone. I wasn't too surprised that the jail story was just that, a cover. I was convinced that Sugar was missing because of whatever it was that 'they didn't find' in Luna's apartment.

Hugh pressed a cold can of Coke into my hand. I drank it on the way to my bedroom and changed into my Depeche Mode T-shirt for pajamas. Caffeine never had a stimulant effect on me, which I attributed to the fact that Momma had taken a mild form of speed all throughout her pregnancy, the first of many little helpers that Doctor Hillman blithely prescribed for her. I must have been born with body chemistry preadjusted to the stuff. Within five minutes I was asleep.

Yohimbe's wails woke me at seven the next morning. No wonder Peter and Rainbow always put her to bed in their van. On this day, though, I couldn't blame her for being upset. She'd probably thought the birth of thirteen offspring was just some awful nightmare, and the cold light of morning had brought her back to reality. Maybe dogs don't think that way.

I sat up painfully. I was stiff from the waist down. When I kicked off Granny Leann's quilt I rediscovered all four muscles of the quad group, differentiated around the thighbone by pain. The leg pain I had first experienced when I started dancing seemed to be getting chronic. I rubbed my thighs for a moment and wondered how long I could keep stripping. I was twenty-five. Another two years? Five? I still had a smooth face and a smooth ass without dimples of so-called cellulite. How long would that last? How long would customers believe I was a twenty-one year old coed? More to the point, how long would they want to pay me to bump crotches? What would I do after this career was over?

I had to go into the kitchen for Advil. Peter was giving the dog a bowl of water, and the puppies were still at their scrabbling. One of the black ones tumbled into the water bowl, splashing it onto the linoleum. Peter fished it out.

I took the pill without water.

Just then Geoffrey ventured into the kitchen. "I'm desperate," he said. "I haven't had coffee…gad." He gestured to the puppies. "Now I remember why I wasn't going to come in here."

Peter was at the sink filling his bong. I was leaning on the table. Neither of us answered Geoffrey. I stumbled off to get dressed.

Geoffrey yelled after me, "Don't you want some coffee?"

"No."

"Why not?"

"I've got a lead."

I figured whoever owned a strip club would have to pay taxes on it. I looked up the city Tax Assessor's office in the white pages. I would finally be reading the name of the man that myself and a hundred other strippers were enriching, I thought, as I dressed for my trip to City Hall in a square-necked white cotton T-shirt over brown stretch flares, tight in the thigh.

City Hall was on Van Ness Street, not too far of a walk from my apartment. I did it briskly, to counteract my grogginess. The Hall is domed like the U.S. Capitol, marble head hunched over granite shoulders. Perhaps the design is meant to suggest that high-quality thinking goes on inside. The crowd around the edifice was an incongruous mixture of homeless men unratcheting from the night's cold weather and victims of morning commutes snuffling their lattes. I jiggled the heavy front door. It was seven forty-five.

As I walked around the block waiting for City Hall to open, I calculated the amount of money that the man whose name I was about to discover earned from one business day. About fifteen dancers worked the day shift. Because they theoretically earned less, the day girls paid less money in what was euphemistically known as 'stage rent.' Fifteen times eighty was twelve hundred. The night shift was the real money-maker. Night shift dancers paid one hundred dollars, and averaged thirty or so in number. Three thousand. Forty-two hundred dollars a day. That didn't even count the twenty dollars each customers paid to get in the door. Even on a slow day, fifty customers probably slunk in. One thousand more. Fifty-eight hundred in one day, plus miscellaneous profits from Cokes and O'Doul's.

Expenses? I thought of some as I took a second, swifter turn around the block. Lance and Kevin made less than ten dollars an hour. Taxes. Soda syrup. Electricity. The Moses' salaries. That was it. Maybe some maintenance costs, replacement light gels or something. It's not like the place was ever really cleaned. Low overhead and business was depression-proof. There's never a slow time for pussy.

Naughtyland's owner was making a fortune. Surely one worth more than the life of one young woman.

I was the first person in line at City Hall's reception desk at eight. They directed me to the Tax Assessor's office, in the basement at the end of a labyrinthine corridor that wound past Parking and Traffic and the dark chambers of MUNI, the city's bus system. At the Tax Assessor's, a young man stood behind a chest-high counter. His dark hair fell in chunks around his face and his clothing was equally aimless and loose. He swayed restlessly and I could tell that his off-hours were spent on a skateboard. Behind the counter industrial-strength bookshelves stretched perpendicular to it. The place had the look of an auto parts store.

"Can I help you?" asked the skateboarder.

"I need to find out the owner of a property."

"Address?"

Address. I'd never posted a letter to Naughtyland, and I had no idea of the address. It might have been printed on our paychecks, but those simply made the trip downstairs with me to Lance's till and I never examined them too closely. "I don't know. Got a Yellow Pages?"

He thumped one onto the counter. I chewed my lip for a moment. I've never been talented when it comes to figuring out what category something should fall under.

"What you looking for?"

"Naughtyland."

"You too?"

"What, it's a popular destination?"

"Only if you want to see the hottest dancers in the city. Hah. Another hot chick was in here last week looking up the same place. They holding auditions or something?"

"Ah, no."

"Too bad. I'm sure they'd take you. Try Nightclubs."

"Sorry, what did the hot chick look like?"

"Asian. Long black hair. Thin, smaller than you." The skateboarder looked at my chest. Leaving me with a paper and pen, he told me he was available for whatever else I needed and hopped off to help the person behind me. A line was forming already.

Luna. She'd been looking up Naughtyland's owner, too. I must be on the right track. The thought gave me a shudder.

I found Naughtyland's address, wrote it down and handed it to him.

"Be right back," said the clerk. He disappeared into the filing room. While he was gone I consulted the Yellow Pages again and wrote down two other addresses for him.

He returned with a slip of paper which he put on the counter, pinning it there with a thumb blackened from newsprint.

"There you go," he said. "Anything else?"

I looked down and I was flustered; the name was partially covered with his thumb. "Yes, these two, please." I handed him the paper with the addresses of Cher Cherie and the Femme Royale.

His thumb lifted to take the paper from me. The name of the owner of Naughtyland was printed neatly in pencil. The unconscious brace I had been holding myself in relaxed and I caught myself against the desk.

The name was Metzger & Associates Enterprises. It meant absolutely nothing to me. The address was on Battery Street.

Taxes on Cher Cherie were paid by John S. Bergen and Sons, Daly City, California. That sounded like a wholesome family business.

The recently shut down Femme Royale was also owned by Metzger and Associates Enterprises. That was interesting.

Two other people waited at the desk and the clerk moved off to help them. More patrons entered, until a line had formed almost to the door. I decided I had enough information. I would have to find out who the associates were behind Metzger & Associates Enterprises.

I had a vague idea that Battery Street was in the Financial District, an area by the waterfront where San Francisco's thicket of skyscrapers threatens to sink the peninsula with its collective mass. I looked in vain in the lobby of City Hall for a city map. Forced to trust my hunch, I hopped onto BART for the short ride to Embarcadero.

Battery was right where I'd thought it would be, a north-south street that ran into Market near the Ferry Building. The Ferry Building was one of those clock-tower structures, reminiscent of Big Ben but punier, that seem to crop up in places where a monument seems to be called for. It wasn't an unpleasant way to begin Market Street. The elevated freeway that had for some reason been built in front of it—replacing the view of the civic monument with one of crumbling concrete pilings—had fallen in the '89 quake and went unreplaced. Where the highway had been was now a pedestrian mall, and a few men in suits and women in hose drank lattes and computed, jacket vents flapping in the slow wind. They sat on the low brick walls of raised flowerbeds or on the chunks of granite which passed for benches tossed randomly about like dice throws.

The address I had for Metzger was on the second block off Market. I pushed through the revolving doors to inspect the building's directory. Nothing in the white moveable plastic lettering under M. There were fifty or sixty businesses listed, the majority as So & So and Associates. I started from the top and was working up a concentration headache by the time I found G.R.Metzger and Associates, Suite 3101. I smoothed my hair in the reflection from the glass case that displayed the directory and headed for the elevator.

Metzger & Associates turned out to share an office with O'Roarke Enterprises, according to the plastic plaque outside 3101. Neither concern valued the aesthetic experience of their office workers. The place looked as neglected as a middle stepchild. A carpet-tufted divider sliced the workforce into four single-occupancy cubicles under a bank of fluorescent lighting. Venetian blinds were snapped shut against what must have been a glorious view. Perhaps in an effort to cheer, a spider plant hung from the divider, dangling a single browning baby plant crookedly against the puce-colored wall carpeting. There was no receptionist. Metzger & Associates and O'Roarke Enterprises must not get many visitors.

I'd been hoping for a narcissistic display of the Board of Directors somewhere in the office, perhaps glossies in matching frames. A thin young man sat behind a computer in one of the cubicles. His glasses reflected the glow of his computer screen. He was playing a shooter video game. When he noticed me both went dark as he switched the screen off.

"Hi," I began, fluttering my eyelashes at him, "I'm a company shareholder, and I didn't get the minutes of the last Board of Directors' meeting. How's the new ad campaign going?"

He drummed the green plastic of his liter of Mountain Dew as if he were playing a flute. "Uh…that's not really my department."

The wink-out of the video game had revealed his green eyes and reddish brows which matched his almost crew-cut hair. He looked younger than he probably was. He looked like maybe a high school junior.

"So what do you do for the company?" I gave him a come-hither smile.

"Webmaster."

"Right, our web sites! Now that's very exciting. Can I take a look?"

He obligingly punched a few keys. The computer screen glowed to life with a photograph of a busty brunette lying spread-eagled on a bed, naked except for a pair of black fishnet thigh-highs. She had grabbed up her floppy right breast and was aiming her tongue at the large nipple. Every thirty seconds or so, the screen refreshed and her tongue's tip drew a tantalizing centimeter closer.

"I see," I said, my voice low and husky near his ear.

"This is cutting edge technology. It's video, live. Getting faster all the time. We brought in a million the first month."

I caught my breath. "Yes, no wonder the company is doing so well."

One million in a month! How much of that was going back to the brunette, now a mere inch from contact? "And how are our real estate concerns doing?"

"Real estate?"

"You know, the clubs."

"Oh, those. No growth there. Dying breed. The future's in digital." He nodded at the small screen as the cyber-starlet planted red lipstick marks in a wide-open O around her areola.

Watching stop-motion pornography together had broken the ice quickly between myself and Dave, and he accepted my offer for another Mountain Dew somewhere less fluorescent. We went to a Chinese restaurant a block away and I bought Dave a donut. Dave told me he was the only one in the office on Mondays, that he was free Friday and Saturday, that his salary as a Webmaster was unbelievable and that he was single. He also told me when I asked about Metzger & Associates that ironically, there were no associates. The company was the work of one man and he wasn't even named Metzger. Dave had thought it was weird when I'd asked about the Board of Directors since there wasn't any board.

I asked him if the man's name wasn't really Metzger, what was it?

Dave crammed the last of his donut into his mouth. He said a name around the wad but I couldn't make it out. He wiped the crumbs from his lips, swallowed, and repeated, "Whitmore Grady."

I made my excuses before he could work up the courage to ask me out.

Chapter Thirteen

According to the wrist watch on the commuter beside me, the time was ten-fifteen. Almost time for brunch.

Waiting for the bus on noisy Market Street, I wondered for a moment if Jossie knew that her former customer was a porn magnate. Then I realized I was being naive. Jossie knew. Jossie had known all along. Jossie had probably gotten her hostess job because she knew Grady, not the other way around. No wonder she'd been so interested in Peaches' activities. She was shacked up with the big big boss.

Jossie answered her door in matching body and hair wraps of curry-colored satin. The robe was a shimmery film across her torso, gapping only at the hollows made by her collarbones. The spice color warmed her gold-toned skin like the red highlights on an orchard peach. She must have been aware of the glamorous effect. Yawning, she invited me in.

"My savior," she draped herself over me in a floral-scented hug. I sank into the unbleached-linen-covered cushion of one of her living room chairs. "Had your coffee yet?"

The espresso machine was starting to hiss from the kitchen. I hadn't had my customary cup of Earl Grey or any breakfast in my rush to get to City Hall. I told her that coffee would be great and that I hoped she had some food. Despite my reputation for bluntness, I couldn't confront her right away. This was Jossie.

My hostess glided toward the kitchen, allowing the faded Persian rug to catch her hem into a short satin train. She seemed almost vulnerable, without a mask of make-up, pre-coffee, still in what she probably considered her pajamas and what was perhaps the most expensive bathrobe available at Neiman-Marcus. The espresso machine snorted. I studied the abstract canvas on the wall opposite me—two square yards of reds and yellows, screaming mouths and writhing calla lilies. The painting and its counterpart behind me were the most color-ful objects in the room until Jossie returned.

"You admiring my painting, baby?" She set two bone-white mugs tall as pint glasses and brimming with foamy milk on the coffee table. "A gift from one of my clients. I don't think it's by anyone famous though." She tucked herself into one of her glowing wood chairs. "But maybe it is. Aren't calla lilies always by someone famous?" Jossie con-templated her painting and sipped at the white foam. Even sunk into the ample cushion, Jossie kept up the posture of a finishing school graduate.

"Did you come to check up on me, baby? I'm doing fine, no per-manent damage. What's a girl got but her reputation, right? Thanks to Grady's connections, my name's been kept out of the papers." She smiled over the rim of her mug. "You could've just called."

I waited for Jossie to take a long sip of the milky brew and to set her mug back on the table, fortified.

"I found out your pal Grady owns Naughtyland."

Jossie's eyebrows rose. "My, my. You're taking this female dick thing seriously."

"You knew about Grady already."

"Of course I did. We do go way back. Your point?"

"Did you tell him your theory that Luna was Vice?"

"Yes." She took another sip of coffee maddeningly slowly, not look-ing at me but not avoiding my gaze either. "You're not touching your coffee. What's the matter, need more sugar?"

"You told him? You didn't think that might cost her her life?"

Jossie laughed softly and shook her head. A prominent vein on one slender bare foot throbbed with her slow pulse. "And they tell me I'm dramatic. Chill out, would you, baby? Accusing Grady of murder. You can get right out that door, you know." She gave me the look that grade-school principals save for kids who sass back. "I told him I had reason to believe that Vice had infiltrated his club. He's a good client. I didn't want him to get burned. I didn't want to get burned."

"But she wasn't Vice." I thought back to the night that Jossie had tenderly patted make-up over Peaches' bruises. No wonder she had been so nice. The bruises were Jossie's handiwork, too, if indirectly.

"Look, baby, we might never know now what she was but she was something. Grady thought so, too, but he wasn't too worried about it. He had Lance keeping an eye on her."

I was speechless for a moment. "Keeping an eye on her? That's what you call Lance beating her up?"

"It's Lance's job, right? He was looking out for all of us. Vice presence isn't good for business. It scares customers away."

"Your client was looking out for himself. If he had Lance beat her up, what makes you think your old friend and best customer didn't have Lance kill her, too?"

"Because Grady don't work like that. He's about money. Know what his motto is?" Jossie collapsed her spine into a godfather hunch, pointed a finger at me, and wheezed an impersonation. "If your money can solve your problems, then that's what your money is for." She regained her bearing and continued. "He tells me that all the time. Not that he needs to. I'm down with that. That's why I'm here being a working girl, to solve the problem of my survival. If I'd stayed in San Rafael, they would have killed me. Hear about the high school kid they found dripping down the wall in the boy's bathroom? They graffitied 'fag' all over him in his own blood. That would have been me. But how I do run on. Grady's my best-paying customer. If it weren't for him who knows where I'd be. Point is that he's loaded. He doesn't have to kill. He could have bought Peaches off. He could have bought the whole police force off."

"He would have had to try that, then. Peaches discovered that Grady owns Naughtyland."

"Maybe he did try buying her off. But he didn't kill her. He's running for mayor. The press is going to dig into his past. Why would he dirty his hands by getting involved in a stripper's murder? He's too clever for that."

"He's really running for mayor?"

"Why not? He's got the money, the influence."

"But he owns strip clubs. Most of the clubs in this city, in fact. He's a customer, for god's sake."

"So what? That's not going to scandalize San Francisco voters. It's okay to own a flourishing business. It's okay to be a patron of them too. In fact it's almost a requirement. The old boy network, dig?"

"I still think he had something to do with Luna's death."

Jossie patted her tall hairstyle. "Don't think so, baby. He was with me the night Luna was killed. You saw him yourself, there at the club. That was foreplay. I was with him until I got busted. I was arrested, remember?"

A few seconds of silence followed, which Jossie used to finish her coffee in quick delicate sips. Finally she broke the silence, speaking softly. "You haven't touched your coffee, girl. Be polite. Drink."

"You'd testify under oath that Grady—."

Jossie smiled and let it turn into a smirk. "Oh, delicious. Yes, indeed, with great pleasure."

I sighed.

Jossie curled her fingers through the narrow handle of the tall coffee cup and rose in one fluid motion. "Grady's not a killer. A pervert, sure. Cowardly, maybe. But not a killer," she said, and carried the mug to the kitchen.

I left Jossie's without ever drinking her coffee. She wasn't repentant enough for my taste.

It's difficult to make a haughty, grand exit when your mode of transportation is the bus. Jossie could have looked out her bedroom window and seen me huddled on the bench with other public transportation clientele, a species that she dismissed as too cheap to pay for cabs. My companions were two elderly men and a harried woman with a toddler scaling her ribcage and wailing directly into her ear. The rest of us waited in silence for the Thirty-three to hurtle us away. I watched the afternoon fog roil the wedge of blue sky between Twin Peaks. I didn't look over my shoulder to see if Jossie was watching me. I ruminated.

Despite Jossie's enthusiastic alibi, I was convinced that Grady was responsible for Luna's death. He had the most to lose from her activity. He'd closed The Femme Royale when rumors of a union had surfaced. It wouldn't take much detective work on his part, simply a glance at a list of his employees, to find a name that matched the old personnel files. He had a choice. Close another club, or kill the plague bacillus before she infected his other holdings. Was he that ruthless? He was undoubtedly a rich man who paid his lapdancers nothing at all, his bouncers minimum wage. At least he paid Jossie well, though he did let her languish in jail. Only a man with power in this town could suppress the irresistible headline: Porn CEO Caught With His Pants Down, Police Find Transvestite Prostitute in Nob Hill Mansion.

At home, a smiling Peter greeted me as he carried a tattered box down the stairs. Scratching noises from inside the box indicated the contents were puppies. Did they never stop wiggling? "We're taking 'em to the beach. Wanna come?"

"The beach?"

Peter pushed past me. Rainbow followed him with one of the tiny brindle log-creatures tucked into each of her armpits. The puppies still looked fetal. Their eyes weren't yet open. They pedaled chubby legs against her flannel shirtsleeves. Yohimbe yelped excitedly behind her masters, running down two steps then back up into the living room, then down the two steps again, her stomach flapping underneath her. Humans aren't the only species with post-partum flab.

"Yohimbe needs to get out of the house." said Rainbow, "Ocean Beach is deserted this time of day. Want to come?"

"It's deserted because it's forty degrees out there and under a mile of fog. You need a wetsuit to swim. And there's a killer riptide."

"It'll be rad. Just dress in layers."

"No, thanks."

"Sure? We're building a bonfire."

I once again declined.

"I'm so excited for the puppies to get out into nature." Rainbow continued down the stairs and Yohimbe happily clattered behind her. The phone rang. It was Geoffrey's mother, identifiable by her bass smoker's rasp. I got her son from his room and then waited there for him. I didn't want to overhear his conversation with his mother. These tended to escalate in volume and get intensely personal in content before too long, making eavesdropping awkward. If you endured the awkwardness, after a minute you were asked to take sides. There were no skeletons in the Overby family closet. They were trotted out and dusted off and touched up obsessively at every opportunity.

Geoffrey returned, animated. "Dramarama. Mother's convinced that my sister is going to marry this Frenchman she's been dating, my sister's been dating, not Mother, though that wouldn't be a first, and that Father won't come to Gina's wedding because he's too busy with his other illegitimate children. She never could accept that she was just another notch in dear old Dad's belt. Two notches. I told her not to fret. At least he keeps the alimony coming and he pays the therapy bills. I really have no complaints about him. Then she starts to wail about how he was never a father to us and her children have had to mourn this man. I reminded her I barely remember him, and I'm certainly not in mourning for some B movie actor who fucked her in nineteen-seventy. I told her she was projecting."

I couldn't imagine the voice of Geoffrey's mother fashioned into a wail. The closest I got was the creak of a rusty porch swing. "You're probably right. But why do you bait her so?" I asked.

Geoffrey looked at me like I was being silly. "What do you mean, bait? She started it."

With the puppies gone, it was safe to go into the kitchen. I opened the window wide to let the smell of dog escape, then visited with my long lost cat, who'd taken up residence on the warm spot on top of the refrigerator. I fried up some bacon, eggs and apples. I was hungry.

Our phone rang so often that Geoffrey had proposed hiring a high school student to answer it in the evenings. My spatula dripping bacon grease onto the couch, I ran to answer it.

"Aisling there?"

"Speaking." It was Mose Junior. I could tell by the subsequent pause in conversation for a hit off a Marlboro.

"You got your job back. Start back tonight."

"Wow. What's the occasion, short on brunettes?"

"Executive decision." He laughed.

I took that to mean that Mose Senior had heard about my suspension and there was some doubt in his mind as to whether it would hold up in court.

"That's great, really. I can't wait to get back to grinding my crotch on a succession of horny boys."

"No complaining. If not for me, you'd be back to frying chicken. Four bucks an hour." Mose Junior hung up.

I hung up too, and wondered about the real reason I'd been let back into the fold so quickly. Perhaps the Moses were missing the entrance fees and drink minimums of my small group of regulars. Five or six men of various ages and stations had chosen me as their favorite stripper. Some had been coming to see me for years. While I wouldn't call them friends, they were people whose habits I'd become familiar with and whose faces I'd become accustomed to, like a grouchy neighbor or a dutifully-visited aunt. I was somewhat fond of all of them. A friendly face at Naughtyland was always welcome. Also, like any business people, we strippers relied on our regulars for steady income. Since we worked only for tips, our earnings fluctuated. We could even end up owing more than we'd earned to Mose at the end of a shift. Regulars made a very risky business a little surer.

I had a couple hours until the night shift started. I called Momma.

"Aubrey, that you? I thought you'd forgotten your old momma. What are you doing this Saturday night? Eb and I are going to the stock car races, down in Huber Heights. It's so hot here, I can't tell you. I don't even go outdoors until the sun starts to set. He's out there making his garden. I'm going to be slaving in that August heat putting up thirty quarts of tomatoes. Just what gave your Granny her first stroke. So what are you up to? Got a hot date?"

"No, Momma. I'm going to work."

"If you got yourself a boyfriend, he wouldn't let you work that silly job."

"Are we time-travelling to the Fifties again? If that's true, that's another reason not to have a boyfriend."

"When are you going to get yourself a man? Why don't you go down to the adult children of alcoholics meeting, that's where I met up with Eb, you know."

"I thought you met him because he was your second husband's life insurance salesman."

"Well, we got to know each other in ACOA. We used to go to Shoney's after group. We had to be sneaky and leave separately because we weren't supposed to see the other adult children outside of meetings. We cheated, didn't we hon? Guess who's on the phone, it's Aubrey. Want to talk to him, hon? Just say hi, here he is."

This was my worst nightmare. I appreciated Eb for his pet-like qualities—he kept my momma company and fetched her Diet Pepsis without pummeling her—but we had little respect for each other. A stilted, boring, and mercifully short conversation followed. At least Momma had remarried people in the neighborhood of her own age. Both Hugh and Vivian had stepmothers that were in their twenties. Hugh handled this with characteristic awkwardness, but Viv enjoyed baiting her stepmother by calling her Mommy and bringing up shared memories of the Seventies. "Remember the Bicentennial? Were you in first grade then, too?"

I reminded myself to be the second wife in my next marriage. I wouldn't have to have the guy's kids or put him through graduate school and I'd get to spend his accumulated money. Eb handed the phone back to Momma.

"Isn't he sweet? He got me a little revolver for my birthday."

"What? He got you a what?"

"Just a little old thing. A Smith & Wesson Model 66 .357 Magnum. Matches his, except it's ladies size. We keep them there in our night tables, in the top drawers. There lays his on his side of the bed, and there lays mine on my side. We sleep better knowing it."

"You mean to say you two have his and hers guns?"

"You haven't come back to Dayton in a long while, honey. Things

140

have changed around here since your time. When are you coming this way to see us?"

I doubted that things had changed much around Ross City, twenty miles into the suburbs of Dayton, since my time, which had been only seven years before. Change was something Ross City folks were right suspicious of. In that place, anyone nonconformist enough to be a criminal would wither like the native plants in the genetically engineered cornfields that surrounded it.

"Eb is real good with guns," Momma was saying. "He's not the crazy type, wouldn't use it if not for a real emergency. He doesn't want me driving around town without one in my purse. He'll get you one too, Aubrey. Says right in the literature it's—are you listening?—'a fine revolver for urban defensive carry.' You're not safe in Sin City, ever think about that?"

"I can't believe Eb won't pay your phone bill or get you that Honda but he'll buy you a gun." One of my acts of defiance as a child had been to take Early Lyle's weapon collection, which consisted of a rusty twenty-two that he chased gophers with and a crossbow that he used during deer hunting season, and bury them under rotting leaves in the drainage ditch a few houses down the street. My parents assumed they'd been stolen by some of the neighborhood kids, who probably had in fact found them in the ditch and used them for infinitely more dire purposes than hunting deer and gophers. I hadn't wanted them used against Momma. To Early they weren't serious weapons, nothing like his M-16 had been—a real chum that was, a warm metal lifesaver.

"Well you think about it, would you. What are you doing with your Saturday night? Wish you were here, we'd go out to eat and then to the stock car races. When are you coming to see your old momma?"

"Can you not switch to third person?" Somehow it made me feel manipulated.

"So touchy! When I was a girl, the most important thing was to have a date for Saturday night. You'd wash your hair the night before to get ready, maybe get a new perm. Speaking of which, Doris down at the salon—"

A beep interrupted her. I let Momma drone on and took the other call.

"Aubrey Lyle please?"

"Speaking." The voice was familiar, older, male.

"Officer Michaels here. You have a minute?"

I told Momma I had an older man on the other line and she let me go eagerly. Michaels had called to tell me that the police investigation into Luna's murder had been dropped.

"Look who's back. I've been told to keep an eye on you." Lance smacked a fist into a palm, rhythmically, like a dance move. He was in his customary position, leaning against the plate glass window in Naughtyland's lobby, when I returned to work that evening.

Despite this threat, Lance kept both eyes on the street. His aviator sunglasses reflected the blue and red neon of the club's sign.

"Great. Like you did Luna? Nice to see you again, too." I hustled through the curtain to the club's interior before he could charge me for lateness, missed sets, or whatever suited his fancy. I wouldn't have been surprised if I were liable for the stage fees I'd missed while I'd been laid off.

After my second set that night I went out on the floor, hoping to catch sight of Hugh and Vivian who had agreed to come to the club that night. It was part of a plan I had. I wanted to know if Luna had actually approached any of the dancers with union rhetoric. Bob and Azote both told me she'd been an organizer, but I'd never heard about a union in Naughtyland. If another dancer had, perhaps she'd have clues to Luna's murder.

I couldn't find my roommates in the dark. So I joined a suited, bespectacled, ponytailed man who was sitting alone at one of the black plastic tables. I'd noticed him watching my stage show, bobbing his head along with the rhythm of my country music. My thighs were sore already, not halfway through the shift. Four days without the demands of dancing had softened them. I rubbed my quads under the table as I turned a toothpaste-commercial smile towards my potential customer and introduced myself. His gaze traveled from my voluminous hair to my lips, accented in a new shade of frosty brown called Crust of Snow, to my uplifted breasts. The point of beautification seems to be to create the illusion that you've spent your life upside-down.

I leaned back in my chair so he could admire the effects of my purple satin Wonderbra. I'd bought thong panties to match. Before I'd become a stripper I'd never imagined that one could spend so much money for an outfit of so little cloth. I gave the room another once over while he stared at the perky creations of the satin holster. Dumb smiles and big tits ought to quell any idea that I was intelligent. Men don't pay women that they think are smart to grind on their laps.

My eyes flickered to a table against the club's left wall, one set into the shadows between cubicles. Hugh was sitting there stiffly, rocking his chair back like your mother tells you not to do. His hands were stuffed into the pockets of his ill-fitting trousers. His head didn't bend forward from the straight stick of his spine; he appeared to be looking at the ceiling and probably was. His black-framed glasses reflected the swirling colored lights that strafed the club. The lively reflections provided the only animation to his figure.

From the cubicle beside him came raucous laughter and a fluttering of the black curtain as if it had been kicked. That was Vivian laughing. A moment later she followed Cameron out from behind the curtain, smoothing her hair and tugging the tousles out of her black knit turtleneck. She almost looked at Hugh but caught herself in time and returned, stifling giggles, to the table across the room where she had been stationed between lapdances for the last hour and a half. I'd made her promise not to get drunk beforehand but I wasn't sure she'd managed it. I just hoped she was remembering to ask the girls she sat with if they'd ever been asked about joining a union.

"What's a nice girl like you doing in a place like this?" The man was asking. Original thinking is hard for so many.

"What are you doing here, cutie?" I gave him my standard answer, then took his offered hand and smiled. He was a cheeseball, but from appearances, a rich one. Vivian was doing her part as a customer, but I had yet to see Hugh get a lapdance from any of the girls. I wanted to go speak to him, but the three of us had agreed in advance not to acknowledge each other during this little operation. In a rare moment of caution I'd decided that as a Naughtyland employee I shouldn't be associated with anyone asking union questions, and I shouldn't ask the other girls myself.

"You're too good for this place." He took my hand, and ran his thumb back and forth over my index finger.

"I'm sure you are too."

"My name's Kyle. Let's meet somewhere else. Not a date. Just dinner."

I shook my head and watched his eyes follow the wavelets the action made in my hair. "Sorry."

"I'm disappointed in you. I'd pay you five hundred dollars for a date."

"No. I just work here." I got up to leave. This whole conversation was like a broken record. I had similar ones about five times a shift. In fact, I wasted so much time trying to convince customers that I wasn't going to have sex with them, I could see why many girls just gave up and went along. More money and far less hassle. "I'm happy to offer you a lapdance, though."

"Okay." He followed me to a cubicle I'd chosen as far away from Vivian as possible. I wasn't sure what paroxysms seeing me with a customer would send her into. But Viv had disappeared, maybe to find another lapdance.

Kyle settled onto the chair and flipped his tie over a shoulder, then took off his glasses and put them into his jacket pocket. I plopped onto his lap and began gyrating, trying to find the beat of 'Emotional Rescue.' He clapped a hand onto either cheek of my ass and was good to go. Halfway through the song a conversation began in the adjoining cubicle, and though Kyle seemed oblivious, I could hear it just fine.

"That's twenty dollars."

"Sure, here you go." I recognized Vivian's voice. Great. Did she know I was right next door?

"I'm Salamé. What's your name?"

"I'm Marge." Marge? At least she wasn't using her real name. I'd forgotten to stress that point.

"Okay, Marge, nice to meet you. Here we go. How do you like them? Fast? Slow?"

"Oh, whatever you're into. Nice tattoo."

"Thank you." I could hear their chair scraping around. Kyle had his eyes closed and his nose stuck into my sternum. I had to be careful not to mush his glasses with my bouncing. It would serve him right for putting them in his jacket pocket on a collision course with my battle-stationed breasts.

"Oh Salamé, you're great." For god's sake, Marge, I thought. You don't have to shove it down her throat.

"Thank you."

"How do you like working here?"

"Oh I just love it." Now Salamé was shoving it back.

"I'm so glad. Boss treat you okay? I've heard that sometimes they're real sleazebags."

"No, he's okay."

"Glad to hear that." More creaking of the chair. What was Salamé doing to her? Or Viv to Salamé? The song droned on and my thighs began to scream in pain. I turned around to move the stress to a different muscle group.

"Lovely," said Kyle.

Viv was trying to get it out of Salamé without asking her directly, as we'd agreed. "So never any cause for complaint here?"

Salamé must have been wondering if Vivian was a health inspector or worse, a cop. But she had to be polite since the person beneath her was definitely a customer. Viv went on. "I heard one club got themselves unionized."

"Hmm. I don't know."

The song was coming to an end, but I decided that this was Kyle's lucky day. He was going to get more time than he paid for. I wanted to hear how our neighbor's conversation ended up.

"Never heard about them?"

"No. Do you want another song?"

"No thanks. So no one ever asked you if you wanted to join a union?"

"A union?" The dancer laughed. "Aren't those for factory workers?"

"Never mind. Thanks!" Viv was cheerful as Salamé opened the curtain.

Chapter Fourteen

I spent about half an hour and Kyle spent over a hundred dollars before I left the cubicle and he left the club. When I emerged out of the black drapery, Vivian was once again nowhere to be seen. Hugh was still at his shadowed table, still focusing his eyes at some undefined point in the middle distance. I decided to risk going over to him. I'd pretend he was a real customer. He seemed to need a pep talk.

Once there, I leaned down, hands on my knees and breasts dangling in his face. In this position breasts teetered dramatically against the plunge of Wonderbras, adding tension to innocuous proposals for a lapdance. Hugh seized up even further, which hadn't seemed possible. I could tell he was gritting his teeth.

"Hugh, what the fuck is up!" I whispered.

"This just isn't my kind of environment!" Hugh answered. I took a step back to give him air. He removed a hanky from the pocket of his thrift store pants and wiped sweat off his forehead. "I thought I could help you, but I've reconsidered."

I bit my lip. I was distracted by the nearby passage of Moana who waved at Hugh and gave me a get-lost look. As she moved between us and the stage, bars of red light reflected by the wall mirrors collapsed into the curves of her body. Her pink boa floated in front of her ample chest.

"That woman, for instance, has asked me if I wanted a lapdance a half dozen times!" Hugh indicated Moana without looking at her directly.

I leaned into him again. "Hugh, you have got to relax. Maybe you should just wait outside for Viv. Just give her your twenties. Seems like she'd be happy to sit with your share of the girls." There were twenty-two dancers on the shift beside myself, and Viv had probably already worked her gleeful way through her half of them. I wanted all of them questioned. Luna could have spoken to any one of them about unionizing.

Hugh nodded and patted his forehead again with the handkerchief. "Sorry I couldn't be more help."

"Oh Hugh." I felt bad for him. He looked like he was about to melt into the chair and would have been happy to do so.

Hoots arose from the ten or so customers barnacled to the stage as Alicia wrapped the pole with her naked body and spiraled slowly downward. I could hear the squeak of her skin stuttering around the metal. She landed smiling in a pool of dollar bills.

"Don't worry about it," I said to Hugh. "It was nice of you to try. None of the others would even consider doing this."

Geoffrey had guffawed and flatly refused when I'd invited him to be a strip club spy. Zan didn't think it was her thing, and Peter and Rainbow couldn't have passed as legitimate customers. Only Vivian and loyal Hugh had agreed to help me, and Viv seemed to be having the time of her life.

"Where's Viv? She's not making a fool of herself, is she?"

"Well, yes. She's off with another one of the dancers," Hugh hesitated. "A rather well-endowed woman."

"Huge breasts, you mean?"

"Yes."

Plantagena. The Moses billed her as Quadruple DDDD!, revealing their limited experience with terrestrial bra sizes. Plantagena herself had a complex relationship with her breasts, alternately nicknaming them her backbreakers and her moneymakers. She would no doubt be the highlight of Vivian's bawdy evening. I gave Hugh a kiss for his help as he passed me the small wad of twenties I had given him to spend on the girls. The bills were damp with sweat. Tonight was going to cost me over four hundred dollars. With a dazzling farewell smile to Hugh to fool onlookers into thinking I was merely taking a rejection gracefully I retreated to the back, where we dancers traditionally stood to hunt customers.

Peoria nodded to me in greeting. "That guy's a lost cause, huh. I've asked him about twenty times. He won't even watch the girls dancing." She watched Hugh impassively as he walked quickly toward the front door.

"I think he's sweet," I said. Peoria furrowed her plucked eyebrows.

I counted my earnings in the back of the cab on the ride home. Four hundred and sixty, plus a fistful of ones from stage tips. Kyle, though utterly tiresome as a human being, had really boosted my average. I'd earned back the money Vivian had spent for me. She had finally left shortly before one a.m., pinching my ass on the way out the door.

Zan and Viv were cuddling on the living room couch when I got home.

"I was just telling Zan how cute you look in butt floss," said Viv, referring to the cheek-revealing panties that were de rigueur at Naughtyland.

"You were awfully cute tonight yourself. Several of the girls complained of you groping. You're lucky you didn't get thrown out. The bouncers at work aren't known for their love of womankind. Well? Any luck?"

"None of the lovely ladies have ever heard of such a little ol' thing as a union."

"Damn."

"Don't fret. They have now. That should make your job much easier."

"What job?"

"You're the new union rep, right?"

"Yeah, right. I won't be following in Luna's footsteps, thank you very much."

"Well, now I understand why you don't date men." Vivian pressed her shoulders toward Zan who began to massage them. "That feels great. Getting sat on by dozens of women sure makes you sore."

I took a seat, cross-legged on the floor like a kindergartner. "I'm ready to listen, Ms. Vernon. Let the psychoanalysis begin."

Zan dropped her fingers from Viv's shoulders to busy them tracing the ivy tattoo that banded her girlfriend's biceps. I couldn't believe she was going to stick around for whatever was coming. Zan hated conflict.

"There's not much to say, really. It's self-evident," Vivian said.

"You don't have much to say? That's a first. Come on, I know some theory is bubbling through whatever brain cells the hair dye has left you."

"No theory. It's simple. Those men are there to treat you in a way their partners would never tolerate, at least I hope they wouldn't. Society barely tolerates that kind of behavior, which is why it only takes place in fetid little dark places. But you have to tolerate it. You're like a testosterone mop. When it has nowhere else to go, it slops over onto you and your fellow sex workers."

"A testosterone mop. God. How long did it take you to come up with that one?"

"It came to mind after I saw one of your bouncers cleaning up a certain splatter in one of those booths."

"Gross," said Zan.

"Anyway, you serve an important function in society and the people who sneer at you should be thanking you. But back to my point. With men dumping their libido over you like you're a human Kleenex, of course you don't want a relationship with one of them."

"Give me a break. I know not all men go to strip clubs." I suppressed the fact that I knew a thorough cross-section of them did.

"What is working there doing to your sexuality?"

"What does working anywhere do to a person's sexuality? It's work. It's my living. It's not sex."

Vivian shook her head. "I think you're fooling yourself. I think it's stifling you. It's not like you can't get laid. Why don't you ever take the opportunity?"

"Maybe I'm over co-dependents who play bad guitar and leave a wallow in my futon."

"You're so old-fashioned. I'm not talking about a relationship. With your taste in men, god knows you should steer clear of those. I'm talking about sex. I think that job has stunted your sex drive."

"Congratulations. You've dusted off an old stereotype all on your own. The sex worker who grows to hate sex. Do give me some credit," I said.

"So it's a stereotype. You wouldn't admit it even if it were true."

We looked at each other. Zan moved from tracing Vivian's tattoo to playing with her girlfriend's onyx ring.

"Maybe you're right," Vivian finally said. "Maybe stripping doesn't affect the sex drive. Women's sexuality is so screwed up anyway, who's to say what could make it worse. At least we have some experience dealing with repression and shame and all that. You know who I really worried about, there at your club?"

"I'm dying to know."

"The bouncers. The men who work with you all. Watching you girls dance then mopping up the results. In charge of keeping order in a roomful of frustrated, horny guys. If they have any respect for any of you dancers, they must not have any for themselves, as men. They must hate themselves."

I thought of sweet Kevin, troubled Lance. It had never occurred to me to put myself in their black boots. Rather than congratulating Vivian for her admirable empathy and lightening-quick assessment of Naughtyland's big picture, I'm afraid I was still smarting and rather rude to her. I stood up.

"Where's Hodge?" I asked.

"Conversation over, looks like," said Vivian. "Well if you ever want to talk about it—"

"You'll be the first to know."

"It wouldn't break you to discuss this stuff. Might even be interesting. You're so damn—"

"You're just quibbling now, can we end this?" Zan nodded towards the swinging door that separated the living room from the kitchen. "Hodge seems to have taken a shine to the puppies."

"You're not serious." I pushed open the kitchen door. Hodge sat on the kitchen table, looking down at the mother and pups. Hodge wasn't allowed on the table, but the kitchen was useless at this point anyway. Since the puppies had been born in there, I had been eating out. "Hodge, what are you doing?"

"He was sitting down there with them earlier. It was so cute!" Zan said.

"Was he swatting at them, or what?"

"Just hanging out."

I let the kitchen door swing closed. Traitor, I thought, and went to bed.

My stumble to the teakettle the next morning was obstructed by a slab of cardboard stamped with the international symbol for refrigerator. It was partly propped against the couch, but considerable overhang blocked the hallway.

"Careful, would you?" said Geoffrey, who caught the flimsy thing after I'd batted it away. "I've been up all night working on this and the glue's still wet."

Geoffrey's eyes were bloodshot. He had on his zipper-front, one-piece flight suit, the garment he protected himself with when his art projects involved oil-based paint or, more often, glue. Yet not a blotch of hazardous waste spoiled the olive-colored cloth. He pulled me around the refrigerator box to the middle of the living room. The other three panels of the box—splayed open like a cardboard triptych—blocked access to the couch where Hugh was asleep. The panels were affixed with a pattern of macaroni elbows.

Geoffrey bent around his artwork to kiss Hugh, then me, then he left.

"Aubrey?" Hugh touched his cheek where Geoffrey's kiss had tickled.

"Hugh! What are you doing out here?"

He was always groggy for an hour after he woke up. When one has an overabundance of brain cells, it takes longer for them all to switch on. He mumbled, "I couldn't sleep last night. Geoffrey's working on an art project that involved the overhead projector. The light was keeping me awake. Sleep is difficult under direct illumination from a concentrated light source."

"Well, he's done. Want to go get breakfast? I'll pay."

"Out?" Hugh rubbed his eyes behind his glasses, which he apparently wore even while sleeping, and combed his long blond bangs straight downward with spread fingers. His haircut was a cross between Beatle and bowl.

"Out. Dog hair omelet is not my favorite."

"I'll see if Geoffrey wants to come."

"Come where?" Geoffrey bounced into the living room, in a fresh outfit of crisp jeans and an undershirt. His shirts were the sleeveless, scoopnecked, ribbed kind. Vivian called them wife-beaters. He looked at the ceiling and dripped Visine into each eye.

"Out to breakfast," Hugh said.

"El QuakeO," I said.

"Well, since I'm a vegetarian, and watching my figure, I'm going to have to say no to El LardO. Besides, I always have to go to the gym after I finish a big piece. Work out the toxins." He blinked and lowered his head to look at us. "That's better. Besides, you two look so cute together. I'll let you make it a nice heterosexual outing. But Hugh, you have to promise me a date, too, or I'll be jealous."

Hugh blushed as Geoffrey crossed to him and gave him a wet kiss in the ear. "It's a wet willie until you promise to take me to a movie. Today." Hugh promised. He even succumbed to Geoffrey dosing his eyes with Visine, a rare victory.

"Where did you guys meet?" I asked them. They'd found the apartment we all now shared.

"Don't blink," Geoffrey ordered. "Aubrey wants to know where we met. How come you never told her where we met, Hugh? I certainly can't remember."

"Ow. That stuff burns."

"Gets the red out. Hold still. Let's see. It wouldn't have been at the gym, or anywhere in the Castro, or at a party. And I just don't go to the library. There, now blink. Did we meet through my dealer?" Geoffrey released Hugh who sat up, eyes streaming.

Hugh pressed the cuff of his flannel shirt to his face to absorb the tears. "We took a class together at City College, remember?"

"Right! Oh my god, can you believe I was in a class? I wanted to impress this geek I was after so I signed up for Computers for Liberal Arts Majors. And after the second session, Hugh and I went out and bonded about how much we hated the class and both quit."

"I only took it because of work," Hugh said, in defense, when I looked at him. He hated computers.

Ten minutes later, Hugh and I were in El QuakeO's sunny window seats, and the grease on the eggs was melting the light application of Firefight off my lips. I blotted ruby-brown kisses onto my napkin.

"Did Vivian have any success in last night's endeavor?" Hugh spoke between mouthfuls of Huevos à la Mexicana. Track-marks below his eyes marked the courses of Visine tears.

"She made some friends. But no, none of the dancers she talked to had heard of a union effort."

"Can't recruit for a union without telling anyone." Hugh pushed a bite of tortilla dripping with refried pinto beans into his mouth, innocent of the high lard content of both.

"Right. But I think Luna probably was. Or intended to."

"Why do you think so?"

"She used to work at a club that was closed because someone was organizing it. Before that she worked at the only strip club in town that is unionized. And remember all that weird business at her memorial? This is a safe house, and all that? Maybe he meant safe to talk about unionizing. She couldn't really talk about it openly; people get fired for that. Her dad seemed a lefty type with all that Che and Ho Chi Minh stuff. I can see her inheriting those kinds of politics."

"I doubt politics are genetic. Her father probably passed along his ideas."

"That's what I mean."

"If her father idolizes Communists such as Che Guevara and Ho Chi Minh, it would make sense that he would support labor unions. When union organizing was at its height, in the earlier part of this century, the organizers were often Socialists, or even members of the Communist Party of America. In the pre-McCarthy and Stalin eras, those parties had many American supporters. Then with the red scare in the fifties, unions were discredited, guilty by association. In the eighties they really became endangered. Remember Reagan's forced ending of the air traffic controllers' strike? He made union busting patriotic. Companies that felt threatened by organizing campaigns paid high-powered lawyers to counter-organize, and the unions didn't stand a chance. They suffered huge losses in membership. Some union leaders were exposed as corrupt, helping the attrition along. I think there's a slight upswing now in union membership, actually." Hugh took a long drink of creamy horchata. No matter how little sleep he was operating on, he never drank coffee or tea.

"To add to your spiel, this is the first decade to see unionization of sex workers."

"Not your traditional brothers, true. Which union is representing them?"

"Local Sixteen of, what was it, the International Brotherhood of National Service Workers, something like that."

"Why don't you visit them? Luna must have been on their payroll. They might know something."

"They pay recruiters?"

"Naturally. This is still a capitalist society. Unions are about making money as much as anything else."

Hugh had to go to God's Gym to meet Geoffrey, so he left after cleaning his plate and finishing my rice and beans. I stayed to pay the check.

"Man should pay," Doña Rosa said as I handed her a twenty. "Especially after what you did for him last night, eh?" She laughed.

"Right." ElQuakeO's proprietress had an odd conviction that Hugh and I were lovers, and I couldn't bring myself to tell her the boring truth when her fantasies gave her such pleasure. I thanked her and made my way the few feet up the sidewalk to our apartment's street door, where I waited for Pat D., one of our block's homeless people, to move his yard sale. It was mostly books that he'd salvaged from dumpsters. Pat D. hadn't thought we'd be up yet, and our doorstep was prime location. He picked up a thick stack of moldy paperbacks and shouldered against the flow of pedestrians. I was squatting to make a stack of his *Reader's Digest Condensed* hardcovers when I was pickpocketed. A wiggle to my jacket and a rustle of paper and the pickpocket was gone.

"Shit!" I stood as quickly as I could, my battered leg muscles protesting the quick rise from a crouch. No one seemed to be hurrying away in either direction. The crowd bottlenecked around bloom-filled white tubs of a flower seller and again between Pat D.'s yard sale and the curb, giving a thief plenty of opportunity to blend in. I stuck my hand into the offended pocket. The pocket had contained only a few loose one-dollar bills, the change from breakfast, and they were still there. I pulled them out. Crumpled among them was a piece of blue-lined notebook paper. On it was a note.

'Meet me in ten minutes at the Bus Stop Bar. Come alone. Table at the back'.

"You okay?" Pat D. had cleared his books away. I nodded and gave him the one-dollar bills, which he tried to trade for the condensed versions of *Omoo: A Narrative of Adventures in the South Seas* and *A Confederate Yankee in King Arthur's Court*. I refused to read condensed versions. If the author had sweated over parchment or typewriter or word processor to make the thing long, who was *Reader's Digest* to go chopping it up?

The Bus Stop Bar was a long, narrow dive, shotgun-shack style, on the corner of Church and Sixteenth. The place was scarcely wide enough for a pool table. They had one anyway, right inside the front door. Two boys who wore their baseball caps backward and had faces punched with piercings stretched over the felt table, scrutinizing angles. Chains affixed their wallets to their belt loops and dangled low enough to trip their feet.

The lighting was low. I squeezed past the pool game. Beyond it, a long wooden bar staffed with a Gen X bartender ran along the right wall, facing a line of booths along the left. The bartender appeared to have no customers. The pool players were too young or too cheap to accessorize themselves with beers. She nodded to me, then went back to draining the tap of pear cider. Russet foam snorted from the tap, scattering itself over her bare midriff and its prominent tattoo, which resembled a Celtic music stand. She mopped at the tap, then her abdomen with a rag.

As I moved toward the last scuffed table in the row I noticed the figure there. A votive candle in the center of the table flickered red highlights over her hands. They were active hands, fingers drumming against a glass' geometric torso, swirling it, making a whirlpool of the ruby drink. The hands were small, the nails bitten short. She lifted the drink as she watched me sit. When she set the glass down, I noticed its rim was stamped with pouts of lipstick.

Her hair was different, short and dyed black. She looked just as pretty with the new color, which contrasted dramatically with her cobalt eyes and pale skin.

For a minute we were silent. She slowly came into focus as my eyes adjusted to the dark.

"Hello, Sugar," I said.

Chapter Fifteen

"Carina will do," she said, with a slow smile. "Forgive my method of contacting you. I don't normally act so strangely."

"Oh, I'm getting used to such things. I was told you were in jail. You might want to get word to PROTECT that your human rights aren't being violated before they start wheatpasting your picture all over the place." I sat facing her. She sat where she could watch the door.

"I'm off the streets for a while. I took a job in a house, Missy Massage. I told the girls I was in jail because I figured some people might be looking for me. I'll tell them the truth when this is all blown over. I don't want anyone to find me."

"Anyone like who?" I said. Carina still held her head at the tilt required to keep long, loose hair out of her face, though her newly blackened blunt-cut ended at her cheekbones and didn't require such a precaution. "At the risk of starting all our conversations with hair talk, what's up with the new do? It could almost be a disguise. Who are you hiding from?"

"Whoever came after Luna. They'll be coming after me."

"Why?"

"Because they didn't find what they were looking for when they ransacked Luna's place. And they might think I have it."

"Who's they? Why would they think you have whatever they're looking for?"

"Look, I don't know who killed her. But I do know that Luna was investigating something right before she died."

"Investigating what?"

"That's what I'm not sure about. She got pretty secretive. I have my suspicions, though. And that guy whose picture you were showing around, he's got a role in my suspicions. Why are you looking for him?"

"I was looking for him because I thought he might know something

155

about Luna's death."

"I found you to warn you against looking for him. He's dangerous."

"You're too late. We already got acquainted. He's Bob, a friendly union recruiter. He seemed harmless. Why do you think he had something to do with Luna's death?"

"Because he's a professional recruiter."

"Like Luna."

"Luna wasn't getting paid to be a recruiter. She was a stripper."

"But they worked together. Why would he kill her? I don't get it."

"It's a long story."

"I've got time. Let me get you another. What are you drinking?"

"Coke." She handed me her glass. "I know, the stuff'll kill you."

When I came back with her drink, she said, "So what got you into sex work?" Her question caught me off guard. Maybe she considered it an ice breaker.

I'd always considered Carina's question a variation on the 'what's a nice girl like you' inquiry. Everyone who asked why I was a stripper seemed to be looking for a certain answer. Either I'd been sexually abused or I did drugs, or I was compelled to expose my parts like a programmed Pavlovian dog because I'm an exhibitionist/nymphomaniac. They don't believe me anyway when I tell them that I love it. I love doing sex work because I make enough money to be independent in a gorgeous, expensive, interesting city, and am not stuck in Dayton, Ohio at the mercy of someone else's paycheck.

"The money."

"Yeah. But there are lots of ways to earn money. Not everyone can be a stripper."

"It wasn't my girlhood dream, but I like it."

"It takes a macho girl to get on a stage and shake off whatever she's been taught about keeping her legs closed."

I laughed. "I know. That's my favorite irony about my job. That submissive innocence our customers are looking for will never match the qualifications for being a stripper."

"Are you saying you're not submissive and innocent?"

"Maybe. No, I can't be innocent. I feel guilty all the time." Momma had made sure of that. I'd made her fat. I'd killed her mother. I'd driven my father from the house.

In truth, I had tried my best to drive Early away. I felt my lungs seize at the memory just as they had been under pressure from his crossbow which I'd braced against my scrawny, then-flat chest. I was as bony as the rifle was, and at that moment, as mean. Black wing curves of the mechanical bow framed my memory of Early dropping my mother, whose face was already the color of a ripe avocado, onto the orange shag rug, swiping his forehead with a red bandanna, then banging out the screen door. I had aimed the bolt at the slump of his shoulders. They'd always been at a severe angle. His shirts barely hung on. His mother had always joked he was shaped like a turd.

I didn't shoot, and Early, of course, came back. Momma begged him. She had to feed me with his paycheck. Besides, she pleaded, she loved him. But six months later he did leave for good, then we got word he was dead. Momma got a job. Our lives improved.

"This is relevant, I promise," Carina was saying. She tented her fingers. "Most people do get into sex work for the money, of course. But Luna and I got into sex work because we wanted to be labor organizers."

"I don't get it."

"We wanted specifically to organize sex workers. Before we got into this, we hadn't done anything. We'd gone to Cal. We were twenty-two, very idealistic. We didn't want to go down to Watsonville to organize the strawberry workers. Everyone was doing that."

"Really?" I had no idea what she meant.

"Luna and I both came from upper-middle-class backgrounds. At Cal we read theory and learned that all work is basically prostitution anyway, renting your body or worse, your mind to some corporate bloodsucker. So we were jazzed on unionizing. But we wanted to break new ground with organizing instead of going the same old Cesar Chavez rally-the-farmworkers route."

"But why sex work?"

"We wanted to work with women who are underrepresented in trade unions. Sex workers, of course, weren't represented at all. I think another factor was that we were rebellious. We'd lived these privileged lives in the Berkeley hills."

"Couldn't you organize sex workers without actually stripping or turning tricks?" It didn't seem like they'd needed the money. I couldn't imagine another motivation for doing what I did.

"No. Our philosophy was that only people doing the work could organize the workers. That's straight from Marx. Besides, by the time we were actually doing the work, we needed the money. My so-called liberal parents basically disowned me after I told them about my postgraduate plans. Luna was fighting with her dad and would have refused any support from him, if he had offered her any. I'm sure he did, knowing Murray's guilty soul."

"They were fighting?"

"They always had a rough relationship. She was never sure if Murray pitied her or loved her, or if she was just his talisman against the guilt he felt about Vietnam. He took a trip back there to reconcile himself with the country or something and ended up adopting her. You can't blame her for considering herself just another step in his healing process."

"She was up for adoption?"

"What orphaned kid wasn't? Her mother had been a prostitute, then her mother was killed. Luna had that behind her, too, that she was a child of one of those couplings. Her biological father is some unknown soldier."

We didn't say anything for a while, just looked at our Cokes. For some reason, it hadn't occurred to me that Luna's father had been a trick. I didn't know how to feel about it.

"So we grew up and left home. Luna wrote Murray a letter trying to explain that she needed to explore her identity and this was how she was going to get started. He tried hard not to flip. He considered this step part of her rebellion against him. His attitude was patronizing and narcissistic. He interpreted everything she did as being about his life, not hers. People only have themselves to go on, and most don't have enough imagination to see other points of view."

"What did your folks think?"

"Like I said, they cut me off. I handled it like the adolescent I was. My parents had divorced and remarried a few times, so they were primed to feel guilty that they'd prioritized their poorly managed love lives over the various children these catastrophes had produced. I played on that. I got my mom and dad together in the same room for my big announcement, just us three without any current spouses. That hadn't happened in decades. They knew something was up. I told them that I couldn't handle spending Christmas morning with one and the afternoon with the other, plus Hanukkah with the family of my mother's second ex-husband, you get the idea. I was moving to the city. I wasn't asking for any support, just freedom to control my own life. It was a dramatic scene.

"They had fits and called me a bad daughter, so then I told them the truth. I was going to the city to be a sex worker. I figured they'd leave me alone after that and I was right." Carina smiled. "I'd handle it differently now, but my instinct was right. They don't support me and I'm happier. I'm better off without them. They're angry at me but now I'm just sad at them. They lost me. And for what? To cling to their middle class values."

I studied this person who was so secure in her right to simply leave her family behind her. Where did she get whatever it took? Was she being just as selfish as her parents had been, or was it really okay to trade biological connections for happiness? So many San Franciscans had done just that.

"So you came to the big city," I said. Carina seemed lost in thought.

"Right. We'd been looking at it all our lives. It was part of the view. As kids we only crossed the Bay to go to Macy's. But then we moved here. We started out dancing in a peep show. It wasn't bad. Customers were these blurry, slack-jawed faces behind glass. The glass got so dirty that half the time you couldn't even see their faces. We made a mistake by letting everyone we were working with know that we were there to promote a union. Of course we were fired shortly after management got wind of that.

"But that peep show changed us. It made our differences more important. The biggest one was that Luna was Asian. Stripping was a different experience for her, as an Asian woman, than it was for me as a white woman. She was exotic and she had to deal with a lot more bullshit. She was supposed to be this passive, child-like, horny love doll. Customers spoke to her in broken English, when she'd been an English major at Cal.

"It got to the point where she wouldn't admit she was Vietnamese. And customers always, always asked her, you know, what are you? I never got asked what I was. If she said Vietnamese, she'd get all this crap back, if the guy had been there, or if he'd been against the war, whatever. So she started lying, saying she was Chinese. She was a dumping ground, even worse than any sex worker's a dumping ground."

"Testosterone mops."

"Yeah, well, she was also a trauma mop, if you want to put it that way. It really pissed her off."

"Of course. You can't pay a person enough for that."

"She kept telling me I couldn't understand. I admitted, you're right, I can't, but that just made it worse. After we got fired from our first peep show, and were fighting anyway, we decided to work separately. We told ourselves it was tactics. Split up, we'd be more discreet and reach a larger group. We were known at some of the clubs already. They'd heard what we were up to and wouldn't hire us. Luna finally got work at Cher Cherie.

"I ended up going freelance. I couldn't get hired anywhere, and street prostitutes were actually getting abused and killed. I felt like action was most urgent there. And it worked out for a while. I do prostitutes' rights awareness. I tried to get the street hookers together, let them know they have rights and there's power in numbers, even without some outside hierarchy to represent them."

"You're not going for the union thing?"

"I'm not in favor of organizing sex workers with an established union."

"Why not?"

"Unions are notoriously corrupt. And to union men, whores are for fucking, not representing. They don't want their entertainment in their rank and file. They hate us. None of them wanted us. I don't know why Local Sixteen finally took the Cher Cherie girls, maybe to have a few pretty faces at the retreats. Or to gain notoriety, or money."

"You're not just a little cynical?"

"I call it healthy skepticism. You've got to know those health care workers and janitors and whoever else Local Sixteen represents don't feel much worker solidarity with a crop of strippers. The whole thing sounded fishy to me from the start. I warned Luna to be careful. If the union wanted to put a stop to further recruitment, I warned her, she was an easy target. But she wouldn't listen. She was always stubborn."

"So you think the union had something to do with her death?"

"I'm sure of it."

"Couldn't they just tell her to stop recruiting?"

"I assume they did. I assumed it again every time she couldn't explain away the bruises she kept attracting in the weeks before she died. She would never admit to having any problems with them, not to me, of course. She knew how I felt about unions."

"You think someone from Local Sixteen was beating her up?"

"I think your buddy Bob was. He had access to her. Of course anyone and everyone has access to us sex workers when we're on the job, it's every man's right to walk into that club. He came around looking for me, too, but once he told me who he was working for I wouldn't get near him. I could get away, but Luna was captive at Naughtyland."

"Bob wasn't assaulting her. The bouncer was because he thought she was Vice."

"Well, god knows, they've got plenty of lackeys."

"You've written off established unions altogether?"

"Yes. Unless one develops that's just for women, or just for sex workers. That's my long-term goal. Luna didn't agree with me. She'd gotten practical. She wanted immediate results. Unions are powerful. They've got lawyers and press packs. She wasn't convinced they were all corrupt. I tried to talk her out of it. She moved onto the Femme Royale and the place shut down. Weird, no? So she got a job at Naughtyland. She must have suspected, like I did, that someone knew about her activity and that Naughtyland would mysteriously close next."

"That must be why she never mentioned that she was an organizer to anyone at Naughtyland. She was waiting to see if the club would close down around her even before she opened her mouth."

"That would have proved someone was onto her."

"Grady," I said. "He's Naughtyland's owner, and the Femme Royale's. His company owns most of the clubs in town. Luna had just found out that information. She'd looked up the owner at City Hall."

"The owner. And you say his name was Grady?"

"Whitmore Grady. I figure he'd be the person most likely to want her out of the picture. He'd already had to close one club because of her."

"Yes, she could have thought so too." Carina's words came slowly. "That must explain the tape."

"The tape?"

"She wouldn't tell me what she was up to."

"What tape. Eighties music?"

"You have a tape of hers?"

"I have a tape of hers. Her neighbor gave it to me. She said Luna had given it to her. She said Luna had insisted that she take it. But there's nothing on it. Just songs."

"Do you keep it in your house? Where is it?"

"I have it somewhere. I think it's in our houseguests' car."

"Listen to me. Tell no one that you have it. Keep it out of your house. Do you have a locker at work?"

"Yes."

"Keep it there. That's what they were looking for, whoever it was that killed her. That's what they think I have. There's something on that tape."

Suddenly Carina ducked her head low across the table, reached her hand around the back of my neck and pulled my face to hers. For a startled moment I expected to feel her lips brush mine, but our cheeks grazed instead as Carina spoke into my ear.

"Officer Reilly's hanging around the door," she said lightly. "I've got to go. He knows me. He'll be antsy because I've been off the streets and he hasn't had a chance to book me lately. I'm going out the back way. We'll see each other again. Make sure you hide that tape like I said." She released her hold on me and slipped out of the booth, making her way through the shadows in the back of the bar to the Ladies' Room.

I looked over my shoulder. A pair of cops was stationed outside the Bus Stop Bar, talking to each other and surveying the scene. Occasionally the one on the left flicked a look over his shoulder towards me. The underaged boys continued their pool game, unruffled. I got up to leave. The bartender was mopping the Anchor Steam tap with her sodden rag. She wiped her forehead and took a rest. One of the pool players wiggled his baseball cap like a loose tooth while the other took aim, swinging his forearm from the fulcrum of his elbow. They both stopped when I approached, inspected me, then returned to their respective activities. As I exited the two cops took a step away from their posts, excused themselves courteously, and let me pass.

I examined the broken cassette tape by holding the cartridge up to the sunlight that filtered through the windscreen of Peter and Rainbow's van. The leader had tugged free from its reel, something I'd found to be not unusual with cassettes, especially ones old enough to have been recorded during the brief eighties retro trend. What was unusual, though, was that a coil of the black magnetic tape remained wrapped around the gear that the leader had detached from. It should have been empty.

I found a pencil in the van's glove compartment, engaged it in the plastic gear, and twirled it to spool out the short length of tape that remained. I spliced the tape to the leader—another essential skill for those who choose the cassette modality—using a shred of rolling paper I'd also found in the glove box. Moistened, the paper worked fine as an adhesive. I wound the spliced tape taut and plugged it in.

A hiss, then a baritone shivered the woofers and tweeters. I jumped involuntarily, then adjusted the volume. When the baritone focused it became clear that it wasn't singing, but talking. I tuned him in midsentence.

"...always nice to have company during these business meetings.

Makes the thing look legit."

A tenor answered. "Where did you find her? What a looker. I'm watching her ass as she goes, mind?"

"Don't blame you, son. I have my sources. You get what you pay for."

"Your motto."

"Far too crude to be my motto."

"Your order, Mr. Grady?"

"Miss, ah, do you have coffee in this fine establishment?"

"Yes Mr. Grady, of course we do." Miss Ah had a slight accent. Tinkles indicated the movement of table settings.

"Well then, I'll have a cup of your finest. If it's Italian Roast you'll-I've earned your tip. Anything more for you, Sam?"

"Another Mountain Dew." Sam was the tenor.

"Mountain Dew for Mr. Bowden, coffee for Mr. Grady, what for the lady?" Miss Ah sounded tired.

"Oh, what's she drinking? Bring her something sweet. Or what do you think, son, should I get her drunk?"

"Oh, that wouldn't be sporting," said Sam—Mr. Bowden.

"I bring Coke," said Miss Ah.

"Great! From now on, you make all the important decisions. Thank you, my dear."

"Yes."

"Now, Sam, let's get down to business before what's-her-name gets back. How are things going on your end. Any squeaky wheels?"

"Nope. I've got a very willing partner at ground level. The person who started it all. Azote herself."

"Interesting."

"She'd be a formidable opponent, but fortunately money talks to her and with her on your side, you've got nothing to worry about."

"You're saying your partner can keep elements in line."

"Easily."

"We're not in danger of being discovered?"

"Frankly, Mr. Grady, any trouble would come from a grassroots level and we feel confident we can contain that. I have control of my organizers, even the do-gooders. You should be able to run your campaign without worrying over anything, uh, uncomfortable being dug up. Plenty of the rank and file don't really want to unionize strippers and would be happy if the issue just dried up and blew away."

"Keep up the good work, then, and do whatever it takes to keep the unions out of my clubs. Here's my end of the bargain. You don't need to count it. You can trust me...Well, look who's back. Hi there, sugar, you kept that pretty face of yours away too long. All freshened up? I ordered you a—"

The tape clicked off.

I found a payphone attached to the plexiglas wall of the bus shelter nearest the van's parking place. Miraculously, the phone worked. I called Jossie.

"I'm just sitting here in the tub. You can't get too clean after experiencing even one night in jail."

"You talk on the phone in the bathtub? Isn't that dangerous?"

"Is it? I do know you're not supposed to blow dry your hair in here. And I never, ever do. But you didn't call just to check up on little old me, did you? I didn't think we left on the best of terms."

"It's true. We didn't. And now I have a question for you."

"Go ahead, baby. You're still my savior, you know."

"Would you still think there was no chance that Grady killed Luna if there was a piece of evidence out there that proved he was involved in some kind of corruption?"

"What are you talking about? You got something on Grady?"

"I've got a tape of someone talking to Grady."

"Don't get me mixed up in this vengeance of yours." Splashing followed, perhaps Jossie getting out of her bath.

"It's not vengeance, it's justice."

"There ain't no justice, baby."

"That's what I'm trying to correct. Look, Jossie, Luna had this tape and she may have been killed for it. Two men talking. Grady and a Sam Bowden."

"For the last time, Grady didn't kill anyone! He's got too much to lose. Besides, he was with me all that night, like I told you."

"If you're so sure, why won't you listen to the tape?"

"Look, baby. I'm out of Naughtyland for good. Know why? Grady felt so bad about me doing time for him that he's keeping me from now on. He's keeping me generously, dig. I'm now a happy bourgeois housewife, down to the details—the what's-it-called—ennui, and the vodka cocktails from the blender in the afternoon. I wouldn't put bribery past my sugar daddy, but he hasn't done murder."

"Jossie—"

"Don't get stubborn on me. I'm not fixing to nark out my man. I

love you, but I'm afraid you're on your own for this one, baby. Dig?"
Jossie hung up.

My second call was to Information. If Jossie wouldn't answer my questions, Azote probably wouldn't either, but I dialed Cher Cherie anyway.

A computer keyboard rattled. "Sexual Satiation Line or Front Desk?"

"Front Desk."

"Hold for the number."

I punched it in.

The voice that answered had been affected by a several-packs-a-day habit for years. It scratched out a greeting, coughed.

I said, "Hello, I'm Rosa Crucia from the *New York Times* and I'm trying to reach Azote. I'm doing a follow-up story on the brilliant work she did as a union organizer. I think she's just fabulous. Is she in?"

"Not in," rasped the voice, not unfriendly. I got the feeling it might have told me more, but beyond two words the effort was just too great.

"Could you tell me when she'll be there, or a phone number where I could reach her now? I have a deadline. I'd super-appreciate it."

There was a pause.

"Three."

"Three? Thank you so much. You've been most helpful." I hung up.

There was a security risk born every minute.

Chapter Sixteen

I occupied myself until Azote's shift started by replaying Luna's tape, more and more certain that Luna had been killed for having it. What I was hearing was incriminating evidence. There it was: Grady bribing someone named Bowden to keep his name clean and keep his clubs from unionizing. I'd have to track down Bob and see if he knew him. This Bowden paid Azote to discourage sex workers from joining the union she'd brought to them.

So Luna had found Grady out and threatened to make this tape public and he'd eliminated her when she wouldn't hand it over. One part didn't make sense, though. Why didn't he just use a gun? I remembered Grady dimly but as a heavyset man, incapable of the stealth that would have been necessary to sneak into Luna's apartment and shimmy down the lemon tree in her backyard for a getaway. Besides, according to his loyal prostitute, Grady had been with Jossie that night—until they were busted.

I entered Cher Cherie's terrarium precisely at three. On my way in I noticed a blurb in the lobby: 'Your performers are unexploited because we're unionized!' Was that a selling point? Did today's porn patrons want to feel assured that their fantasy playmates were unexploited?

Azote's curtain was closed. I was alone in the viewing area. Most of the women had their curtains open and were variously amusing themselves during the post-lunch lull. Lotus had put on a pair of glasses and was reading a hardcover book that promised to teach her C++ in one evening. Petunia did deltoid push-ups, her long red hair crumpling against the floor then extending the length of her forearms as she pushed her feet, legs and hips up the back mirror of her booth. SugarPlum wore a two-piece of yellow frills to accent the success of her tanning-bed sessions and was eating a banana, looking despondently out at the lack of customers. Lupita also read a book, *Organized Labor for Beginners*, turning the pages with an insertion of the red-slicked nail of her index finger. Mamacita jumped up and down and waved frantically at me, pointing at her door. I waved a polite hello and mouthed no thanks.

Just before I was about to leave the viewing area to get some air, the moss-colored curtain above Azote's nameplate was flung dramatically open. Azote stood behind the glass, ass facing out, spike heels planted apart in a shit-kicking Wonder Woman stance. She was wearing the same outfit as the last time I'd seen her at work, black leather stuff, and had already uncoiled her whip to begin her routine.

It wasn't until her whip's first strike sent her reflection and mine aquiver in the mirror that she noticed me.

I moved to open her cubicle's door, went in and quickly jammed a ten-dollar bill into the Plexiglas box. I couldn't see what I'd just paid for. The curtain that divided her pillowed cell from my wooden one remained closed. As soon as the money went in, however, the intercom fuzzed with Azote's furious voice.

"...in here and I want her out right away."

"Wait!" I knocked on the curtained window.

"Now!" Something slammed in the booth. "I told you, the union's not interested in more sex workers. Get out and make room for a real customer. You're wasting my time." She still hadn't opened her curtain.

"Who's paying you to say that?"

A second of silence followed. I recoiled before I heard the crack of the whip. It sliced the curtain. A hairline fracture popped into the glass.

"Shit."

"No one will ever believe you, Aisling."

I could see a sliver of Azote—muscles and fury—through the new rent in her curtain. At that moment the flimsy door to my cubicle snapped open, sucking the air out behind it. Wisps of my hair jumped from my forehead and neck in the momentary vacuum.

The black-clad bouncer reached in to grab my leather jacket collar. He smelled like cigarettes. He automatically raised a knee to threaten my crotch, then dropped it. "You're so outta here, dude."

I asked him politely to let go of me, dammit, but he declined to do so. I shrugged off his fist along with my jacket. The bouncer held the leather jacket hostage for me while the cheery barker snapped my Polaroid, showed me to the outer doors of Cher Cherie, and aimed me down the street. The two had the bouncing ritual well choreographed. I half-expected a bow at the end.

The bouncer and the barker stood outside to watch me walk to the corner. As I turned, they waved as they called out, "Have an unexploited day!"

At home I called Angie Pritchett, Luna's former neighbor. She didn't seem to have any idea what was on the tape when she gave it to me but I thought I'd ask her about it anyway. I got her machine.

"I can't take your call right now because I'm too busy getting ready for my housewarming party! That's right, it's tonight! Come one, come all! This neighborhood is very safe so don't be afraid to walk right up to the door. I can't say my address because you never know what wrong number might get hold of it, but the party starts at nine! See you then!"

It took me a while to come up with the right name but eventually I found a listing for the National Brotherhood of Service Workers International Local Sixteen in the white pages. An address on Trainor Street was given in the ambiguous neighborhood—not quite residential, not quite industrial—that had been scrambled up by the highway that divided the Mission and South of Market. Their office was close enough to walk to, and I set out into the bright blue day.

Local Sixteen was in a low building, fronted with plate glass and crumbling brick. Inside, two gray desks angled toward the front door. Both were stacked with papers and brochures. Between the desks, a door labeled 'Executive Offices' was closed. Four framed photographs were on the back wall—three of older men in suits and identical forced smiles, while the fourth man was incongruously young, perhaps in his mid-thirties, smiling as if to flaunt his tooth caps.

"Can I help you?" A college student sat behind one of the desks. He had shoulder length brown hair, worn loose, and round tortoiseshell glasses. He wore his red and black plaid flannel shirt unbuttoned.

"I hope so. I'm looking for a recruiter named Bob."

"He's in a meeting."

"I'll wait."

"They should be taking a break soon. Have a seat."

I did. We exchanged names. His was Ramsay.

He gestured to a folding chair next to the desk. "Welcome. We're a new chapter of NBSWI, growing day by day. Here, have a brochure. Where did you meet Bob? What's your line of work?" He rearranged one of the piles on his desk and found a brochure which he handed to me. On the front was a black-and-white photograph of a young man— same as the one framed on the wall.

I read the caption twice. 'Sam Bowden, president.'

Ramsay was looking at me, expecting an answer. I had one second to recover my control. "Right. Where did I meet Bob? I met Bob when he mistook me for a hooker. I'm a stripper."

"Oh yeah," Ramsay was rearranging his discomfort so I wouldn't notice. "That's cool. I didn't know we were bringing in more exotic dancers."

"You aren't? Why not?"

Ramsay shrugged. "After we got the one club, there didn't seem to be any more interest."

"Really? That's not what I heard."

Ramsay raised his eyebrows at me but didn't get a chance to press the point. A rasp of denim to my left caught my attention. I looked up to find Bob approaching. He looked better in daylight. His eyes gained color, a clear, light green. He'd ditched the overalls for regular jeans, his shirt was a fashionable burnt orange, and his shoes were closed-toe. There wasn't much to be done with that hair, but he'd tried. He'd tucked it into a ponytail. He smelled like laundry detergent.

He looked baffled at my presence as he bought a Coke from the lobby machine.

"Hi, Bob. Remember me? Cindy? These are my civilian clothes. Can we talk? Somewhere private?"

"Sure, um, sure," he said, and Ramsay, amused, pointed us toward a glassed-in conference room. It was furnished with one giant table with a neat hem of chairs. I closed the door behind us. Bob lowered himself into one of the chairs, glancing at the lobby like it was a lifeboat and he'd been imprisoned on deck.

"Remember we were talking about Luna? I found some stuff out. She wasn't killed in some random sex crime, I'm sure of it. And her murder had to do with her unionizing Naughtyland."

Bob was still glancing nervously out at the lobby through the glass wall of the conference room. I followed his gaze. A man bent over Ramsay's desk, spinning a file across it. He straightened. He was maybe thirty with a sandy thicket of hair, long sideburns and a goatee the size of a quarter. He laughed with Ramsay then looked our way, eyed me, then winked suggestively at Bob and pointed to his watch. I recognized him from his bad publicity photo and could feel the sweat of my nervousness. Sam Bowden, president.

"I haven't got much time," said Bob.

"Right. You're in a meeting. It's probably best if you just listen to this." I handed him a Walkman I'd found in Peter and Rainbow's van and I pressed play.

While Bob listened I watched Ramsay and his boss carry on their banter. Sam Bowden seemed to have mastered the shit-eating grin, which, no doubt, accounted for his success in life. He high-fived Ramsay and turned toward his office.

When I looked back at Bob a moment later, the recruiter looked like he'd been briefly pressure-cooked. He seemed sweatier and redder and his gaze was unfocused. The tape clicked off.

"Well?"

Bob removed the earphones. They lifted a halo across his hair. "Where did you get this?"

"I told you, it was Luna's. She had the goods on Grady and your boss. She had evidence of corruption and now she's dead. Doesn't that seem suspicious to you?"

He let the headset clatter to the table. "Union people don't take money. This isn't some political machine. We ensure decent wages and benefits to working people through collective bargaining. We promote social and economic justice."

"I don't need the spiel. I can read the brochure."

"I have to get back to my meeting." He rose unsteadily.

"Okay, chill. I just came down here to see if you knew who this Sam Bowden was, but I found him all by myself. Are you all right?"

He took a breath and left the conference room. He paused in front of his boss's door for a long moment before going in.

Hugh and I waited in a molded and corniced entryway for Angie Pritchett to undo her series of deadbolts. We were outdone by her new pad's Victorian frippery even in our party clothes.

"Nice old place," said Hugh. "San Francisco Stick style. Probably dates from the eighteen-nineties. This part of town was spared the earthquake and fire."

While Angie maneuvered through her nineteen-nineties security system, I took a step back and squinted up at the house. It was freshly painted in a polychromatic scheme that picked out its details. Vertical stripes of violet framed the doors and windows; lavender cutouts over-flowed from the outcrop of the definitively flat roof. The style was straitjacketed frivolity. The effect was beautiful.

Angie pulled me inside with a "Come in out of the cold." She gave us both down-home hugs that stretched the capacity of her salmon-trimmed-in-metallic-gold pantsuit. "And who have we here?"

I introduced Hugh. He must have struck her as non-threatening. She was removing his badly fitting tuxedo jacket for him, plucking it off his shoulders with the superglue strength of her new manicure—inch-long nails in a shade of coral.

She led us up the stairs to the third floor. "Let me take your coats and your purse, honey. I'll just put them in there on the bed. Forgive the place, I haven't had time to decorate! And we are smoking outside. On the fire escape in back. Make yourselves at home—there's wine, cheese in the kitchen. Introduce your man around!" We reached her landing and she went down the hall with our things.

We headed for the noisiest part of the flat, which is what San Franciscans call an apartment when it happens to be an entire floor of a subdivided Victorian. Bad jazz, a piney incense, and a buzz of conversation emanated from the front room. The room was pretty, glowing from candlelight, warmed up by the inlaid hardwood floors. Two bay windows trimmed in forest green and blue reflected the party. About fifteen people were drinking wine in various poses amid white candles on cast-iron candlesticks, the only furniture in the room. The opposite wall was papered in a busy floral with the same deep blues and greens of the windowpanes. The wallpaper wrapped around a narrow fireplace flashed with Italian tiles. I tried not to think of the room's aesthetic future once Angie found time to decorate.

I grabbed Hugh's hand and we joined a conversation circle, two women and one man standing by the fireplace. They were talking about wineries. Hugh was soon able to join in with information about the wine making process. I found the perfect excuse to leave them and went to get a glass of wine.

Once freed and with Hugh taken care of I went down the hall in search of Angie.

I found her in the kitchen, crushed up against a counter by the party's kitchen crowd. She was spooning white semisolids from a food processor into a cut-glass bowl. "He's cute, your date. Where'd you find him?"

"On my couch. He's my roommate. Listen, I called because of that tape you gave me."

"I heard her murder investigation has been dropped. Did you hear? Did they catch whoever did it? I'd sleep better at night with one less criminal to worry about. Try the dip and see if there's too much French Onion Mix in there." Angie was arranging Ritz crackers in a fallen domino spiral around a cutting board.

I dunked a Ritz into the white curds and ate. "It's great. They didn't solve the case, just let it close. Couldn't find any evidence or suspects."

She was wiping her hands on a kitchen towel. "Typical, huh? Well like I said, that neighborhood is going to the dogs. And good riddance. That's what this party's all about. Don't you just love Noe Valley? You can't imagine the kind of rent I'm paying here. Are you and your friend meeting some nice people?" Angie had tossed the towel onto the counter and was wiping it down, a task made slow by the fingernails.

"Yeah, great. You know, I have a theory about why Luna was killed. Did she ever mention to you that she was a union organizer?"

"Union organizer. Like in the stockyards? The Steelworkers, that was my dad's union. But it all went bust twenty years ago now. Fat lot of good that union did him. They couldn't even strike while the plants closed down all around them. Union had them by the balls. You want to take this out there?" She handed me the cutting board, with the cut-glass bowl now inserted amongst the crackers.

"Okay, but I want you to hear this tape."

Angie had turned to speak to another guest who was asking about the crime rate in the neighborhood. I left. I didn't see any place to put the tray of crackers in the living room, so I set it on the tiles in front of the fireplace. Hugh looked content. His conversation circle had expanded with a third female wine drinker. I went in search of my jacket and purse.

Angie was still trapped in the kitchen when I returned. She was smiling rigidly at her guest, two fingers spread above her wineglass as if ready to pluck a cigarette out of thin air. I suggested that we go have a smoke. She thought that would be a wonderful idea and excused herself. The fire escape landing was as densely packed as the deck of a sinking ship. A haze above the smokers rivaled the fog.

We jostled for a spot against the railing facing the tiny back garden, a square of green grass edged with blooming rose bushes. The night smelled like spilled wine.

"I owe you one. Stacy is such a bore. We work together." Angie took a huge deprived drag off a Virginia Slim.

I affixed the headphones of Peter and Rainbow's Walkman over Angie's hair-do and pressed play. She fluffed her hair around the unflattering accessory until the headset was buried in yam-colored layers.

"What's this?" She yelled.

"This was on the tape she gave you. But hidden." I yelled back. "Do

172

you recognize any of the voices?"

"These are union guys?"

"One of them is."

"Listen to these guys. They sound just like Dad's cronies, all those years ago. Why would Luna have been working for them?" The end of Angie's cigarette came dangerously close to igniting a cardigan that draped the shoulder of a close-packed guest. Then she raised it to take a puff. Her coral nails glowed translucent in the flare of the tip.

"She was organizing workers. An idealist, I guess."

"Idealist." Angie blew out a line of smoke. "In dad's day, it was a matter of survival, not some pie-in-the-sky notion. What union was she in?"

"International Brotherhood. They represent health care workers, office cleaners, and exotic dancers."

Angie laughed. "Exotic dancers. Well, I never. Is that considered one of the trade these days?"

I heard the thunk of the tape ending. Since Angie had talked through the entire taped conversation, I made her listen to it again. Silently. She listened while flicking ashes all over an unfortunately placed rosebush.

"You know, one of them does sound familiar."

"Which one?"

"This Sam person. Yes, I remember him saying: 'I'll go as soon as my business here is done, and you can get back to your *Dallas* reruns.'" She'd lowered her voice to impersonate the tenor. "He's the guy Luna was having pizza with that night. I'm sure of it."

Angie couldn't give me a detailed description of him. He'd been sexy, she said. When I pressed her, she added he'd been dashing. Hair color? Height?—Tall and dark. Build? Age?—Oh, young. One of those ageless types who could have been anywhere from twenty-five to forty-five. She seemed to be dreamily giving answers to *Cosmo's* 'Find Your Ideal Type' questionnaire rather than describing a suspect.

I dragged Hugh away from the decidedly tipsy trio of wine-drinking girls at well past one in the morning. Hugh seldom drank himself, but seemed excited by the prospect of going wine-tasting in the Napa Valley with the three of them. Apparently they'd invited him to do so the following weekend. He talked about it in the cab all the way to Sixteenth Street when I told him to shut up. He seemed hurt. I felt bad afterwards. He'd been good enough to go with me and he'd had fun and I hadn't, and I was being childish. But I was too grumpy to apologize.

At home, I followed Hugh into the kitchen. A swig of Coke would give me strength.

I found a half-empty open can in the refrigerator door. It was as flat as lemonade, without that esophagus-popping kick that made it the real thing. I took a few swallows anyway. Hugh was leaning against the stove, slumped in his tuxedo jacket, looking at the puppies—all asleep in a pile and not too interesting. Yohimbe was gone, either on a walk or in a desperate bid for freedom. Hugh's hands were shoved into the pockets of the pants of the tuxedo ensemble. The shiny stripe down the side flapped against his black-shined shoe like a breaking wave. Hugh wiggled his foot when upset.

"I'm sorry I snapped at you. I don't know what came over me. Hard day, you know. Thanks for coming with me."

After a moment Hugh nodded. "You changed the subject."

"What subject? You weren't saying anything. It even seemed for a minute like you weren't speaking to me."

"The subject was wine-tasting in Napa."

"Right. Have fun." I threw the empty can for recycling into a paper grocery bag pasted to the floor with the sludge that served for the recycling.

"You want to come?"

"I'm not much of a drinker. What, you want to go with a harem? I saw those three girls checking you out. What's your secret?" Hugh blushed and so I continued to tease him. A clatter up the stairs announced the arrival of Peter, Rainbow, and Yohimbe who burst through the swinging door, the dog's tongue lolling happily and our human houseguests pink-cheeked and energized from their walk in the cold. The mats of hair on their heads must have done a lot to prevent heat loss. They hugged me, often their way of greeting, and they hugged Hugh who belatedly patted their backs though he remained stiffly leaning against the stove. His face was even redder when they had finished and left for a night of sound sleeping in their van.

"Guess I'll be going to bed," he said.

"Good night, sweet prince," I said. We seemed to be friends again. I headed towards my bedroom quietly, not wanting to disturb my sleeping roommates. The door to Zan and Vivian's room was open. They weren't in their futon. Their digital clock glowed two-ten. Viv must have dragged her girlfriend out for an all-nighter, which wasn't necessarily Zan's style. Zan was kind of long-suffering that way. She couldn't say no to the light of her life.

Chapter Seventeen

I was deep into a nightmare about Conor announcing the birth of our quintuplets and serving take-out pizza to a picnic table full of every other man I'd broken up with messily when Geoffrey's bad breath woke me up. Alcohol fumes slapped against my face as he rocked me back and forth through his airstream. My eyes slowly focused on his enormous silver and black Kiss belt buckle, shined for his night on the town, zooming close-up then distant. The ornament appeared to pull him off-balance in his current state. Eventually it filled my visual field and then he fell over me. Our ribcages crossed swords. Futons aren't known for their give.

"Thank god you're awake." His voice was muffled in the quilt.

"I'm not. For god's sake, go sleep in your own bed." I kicked at him.

"Thank god you're awake."

"You said that. Why?" Geoffrey's face smashed against the quilt and he seemed to fall asleep. "Uh-uh. Get off me. You're not sleeping here."

The effort of wiggling out from under him woke me up further. By the time Zan came into my room I was alert. But I couldn't see her clearly until she flipped on the light switch and my eyes had a moment to adjust.

"Zan? What happened?" The first thing I noticed was that her blue jeans and green hooded sweatshirt were dirty, smeared black like they'd been run over by muddy tires. One frazzled blond braid unraveled down her chest. Red scrapes laddered one of her pale cheeks. Above them her blue eyes were wide but calm.

"Viv got held up."

"She what?"

"She's in bed. She's not saying much."

Not a good sign for Vivian. "Is she okay?"

"Her face has some bruises and she'll probably have a black eye, but nothing major. She's more freaked out than anything."

"Shit." I tossed the quilt off myself and onto Geoffrey.

"I'm going to go check on her." Zan left.

Vivian had a comforter drawn up to her eyes as she watched me enter her bedroom. Two dark lines had formed on either side of her nose, outlining bone. Her eyes were bloodshot in a way that made the whole of the white look pink, rather than veined with a red spiderweb. It looked like her skull had been jarred under her skin and resettled a bit down the faultline.

"God," I said. Zan gave me a look and excused herself to wash up.

"I'll be fine. Don't avenge me or anything. I'm going to look awful for a while, that's all."

"Oh, Viv. What happened?"

"This guy in a ski mask jumped us."

"Both of you?"

"Well, he shoved Zan against the wall and stuck a pistol in her crotch. That kept her still while he worked me over. Nothing much more to tell."

"Did he take your money?"

"I gave it to him first thing. I had about fifty cents."

"Did he take anything off Zan?"

"No."

"Queer bashing?"

"Looks like it."

"Were you in the Castro?" The nearby district was a mecca not only for gays but also for hoodlums looking for random gays to attack.

"Market and Haight."

"What were you doing down there?"

"Don't get preachy. Why shouldn't we be there? This is our city, too. Why shouldn't we be wherever we want? Don't tell me you're joining the conspiracy to keep women home and afraid of the big bad city. I'm not living that way. We went out."

Zan came back in, hair loose and brushed clean.

"Okay. Forget I asked. Need anything? Tea?"

"That'd be nice," said Zan. She sat on the futon. I left them facing away from each other and silent.

Mechanically, I filled the kettle, waited for the whoosh of the gas burner to ignite and put the kettle on the stove. Since I'd moved to the city almost every male acquaintance of mine had been attacked on the street. Hugh's muggers had stolen his bicycle and karate-chopped his glasses off. Geoffrey had been surrounded by three men in the Tenderloin and frisked, an event he recounted at parties with fake titillation and real terror. I'd come to the conclusion that despite the hype, nighttime city streets were more dangerous for men than for women. But maybe, I realized, that was because men travelled them more.

Zan joined me in the kitchen when the kettle started to whimper. I was arranging a pot, two teacups, and a honey bear on the cutting board I was using for a tray.

"It's okay, I can take it to you," I said.

Zan shook her head. "There's something Viv wouldn't want you to know."

I looked at her. The teakettle was rattling and billowing steam and about to shriek.

"It's about where we were tonight."

"Go on." I picked up the teakettle.

"We went to Naughtyland."

I dropped the teakettle back onto the burner and it screamed as a burst of steam was forced out. "What? You're kidding. Why? That place is a hotbed of homophobia. Some customer could have thought— I realize this is ironic, but someone who saw you there could have decided that you and Viv were perverts that needed to be taught a lesson. Someone could have followed you from there and beat you up."

"It wasn't my idea. Viv wanted to introduce me to one of the girls or something. She just wanted to go back. Can you turn that thing off?"

"I can't fucking believe this! She gives me such hell about working there in the first place... What happened to all that participating in the male gaze, or whatever it was, crap? Is she going to be there every time I work, feeling up the girls?" Zan reached in front of me to turn off the burner.

"Come on. Her thinking evolved beyond that a long time ago. You know, I'm not saying this to get you mad at her. I just thought you should know. She got kind of loud and was asking questions about the union."

"You're joking."

"No. There's more."

"God. She was talking about the union? Loudly? Christ."

Zan grabbed my hand. We were exactly the same height. "Look at me," she said, but all I could look at was the abrasion from her left eye socket to her jaw with a sheen like melted sugar on a sticky bun. "The guy who held us up whispered something to me. Are you listening?"

"Yes. Yes. What do you mean, whispered something?"

"It was a message. For you. 'Tell your roommate not to try to bring a union into Naughtyland.'"

"What?"

"He told me that, okay? Viv doesn't know that part. She was going through her pockets at the time. I decided not to upset her."

"Shit. It was fucking Lance. Zan, I'm sorry."

"Don't blame yourself. Listen, I'm suggesting you watch out from now on for your own safety. You don't always seem to think of that. I don't think Vivian will be going back there after this, so you don't have to worry about us anymore." She plucked the kettle off the burner and the steam settled down to a low train whistle.

Zan's hand shook as she poured the tea. Her lip wobbled and the scratches on her face brightened. I swallowed the rest of my tirade. Vivian had been indiscreet, but I'd save the furor for Lance. I suddenly felt bad about verbally illustrating Vivian feeling up strippers to her girl-friend.

"Like I said, she won't be going back." Zan took the tea tray and left the room.

I followed Zan a moment later. Vivian was completely covered by her favorite blanket, a purple velour lifted from a hotel chain, and Zan was on the edge of the futon sipping tea.

I said, "I think I know who your attacker was. Was he heavyset, brown hair?"

"Forget it. You're not avenging me! Stop acting like a redneck!"

"Well, he had a ski mask on," Zan said.

"Viv, did you recognize him as one of the bouncers? Did you, Zan?"

"You told her where we went?" Viv looked accusingly at Zan.

"I thought she should know, okay?"

"Oh, Christ, I'll never hear the end of it. Go to sleep, Aubrey. We can fight some more tomorrow."

I couldn't sleep—and not only because Geoffrey was hogging my bed. I put Luna's cassette tape and a hundred and twenty dollars in my jacket pocket. It seemed prudent to follow Sugar's advice and stash the tape off the premises. I shivered in the fog until a cab met me on Market Street. I took it to Naughtyland.

The crowd was so thick in the lobby that I had to wait outside for several minutes while Kevin gently frisked each individual. It was three-thirty in the morning, the closing weekend rush when Naughtyland stayed open until four-thirty. Lance was nowhere in sight.

"You working?" asked a white man with a crumbled face who'd stopped his late-night shuffle down Jones Street to stare at me, the sole woman in the spillover. His clothes looked like he'd crawled into them from below. They strained downward. "How much to see you naked?"

"You can't afford it!" scoffed the young man in front of me. Then, to his companion, "I'm not letting that fucking fag bouncer touch me. See all that makeup on his face? What is he, a fucking vampire?"

"Quit staring at her, sleazeball," his friend added, addressing the loiterer, presumably in my defense. "I know it sucks, but you have to let him frisk you, dude, or we won't get in."

"Dude, I'm not letting him touch my crotch. If he does, he's toast."

Our onlooker stared at my tits until Kevin came outside and told him he couldn't be chilling there, time to move on, my friend.

"Fucking homeless," said the first young man, as he pushed into Naughtyland.

I paid Kevin and entered. Plantagena was in the lithotomy position on the edge of the stage. The spiked heel of her tiny silver shoes pierced the shoulders of the plaid flannel fastened to a fake beer that sat before her. Plantagena returned her customer's expressionless stare with a smile. After a moment, she extricated her shoes from the cloth of his shirt and flipped over in time to the music "Love is a Battlefield" by Pat Benatar. She crawled towards another zombie-like customer, one of the thirty or so men gathered next to the stage.

Lance was backstage, rustling around in his starched version of a Blackshirt uniform to refill a dispenser with one of those rolls of brown nonabsorbent paper that school bathrooms are stocked with. He clanged the holder shut as I walked past. Funny how Mose Junior had denied him a shift-long view of the show, but Lance could still wander backstage. And apparently take breaks whenever necessary to follow and assault people. Several women were undressing at their lockers, and the bouncer's eyes oscillated from his janitorial tasks to their bare bodies like those of a teary soap opera actress pleading with a lover.

Before his eyes swept back in my direction, I buried the tape in the tangle of underwear in my locker. I said, "Looking for your next victim?"

"Maybe I'm looking at her now."

I took the threat and Micki and Moana as witnesses to it upstairs to Mose Junior's office. I threatened to sue, though I had no idea if verbal threats were lawsuit material, and my boss flapped around like a netted heron. Micki said her cousin's boyfriend was looking for work, reliable, ex-Marine, very intimidating. No good. No boyfriends. Mose Junior must have been thinking the front window would completely disintegrate if it got shot again. But it's my cousin's boyfriend, she don't even work here. No boyfriends. Let me talk to Aisling alone.

The two women left, holding hands to help each other down the stairs in their high heels.

"Close the door."

I did, and stood and waited. Mose had both hands in his thatch of black hair. The cigarette in his mouth needed tapping. He twitched. An inch of ash fell onto the photo cube of his family and broke apart with a little puff.

"Lance is not getting fired."

"What? He's been sexually harassing all of us ever since he started here. He threatened me with violence! He beat up my roommates, two women who were here earlier tonight. He's the one who assaulted Luna, he admitted it! There's lots of intimidating people in this town. This one is bruising your moneymakers. Are you afraid of him or something? This doesn't make any sense."

"You think I like it? I move him to the lobby. The way he stares at you girls. I know about lawsuits. Sexual harassment. What can I do? I move him away from the stage."

"He's still backstage. He's still in front of the stage whenever he can find a bar glass to wipe as an excuse. What do you mean, what can you do? You're the boss. You can fire him."

"It is complicated." The Marlboro was down to the filter. He looked at it as he ground it out.

"How so?"

"I have boss too you know, and he would not like for me to fire Lance."

"I know about your boss. Why not?"

My boss lifted his hands. "He tells me to keep him. What can I do. Not my department. You think I like a class-action?"

"Grady tells you you can't fire Lance."

"Yes."

"Does he tell you why?" I knew why. A resident thug keeping a fist in the face of any organizing effort—Grady's business insurance.

Mose Junior shrugged in answer to my question. "I don't know. He don't tell me why."

"Could it be that Lance is not only keeping the customers in line, but also keeping the dancers in line?"

Mose Junior held up his hands.

When I returned to the floor, the music had been cranked up to a last-chance level and Prince's falsetto was almost painful. I should be able to yell at Lance without being overheard. He examined me as I walked toward him. He was stationed near the bar, behind the tables reserved for the dancers. He could survey the whole club from there, which is why it was our spot for hunting for customers.

"No luck getting me fired? Too bad." He watched Temptress massage the pole with her tits. His fingers slowly tapped his shined belt buckle. He didn't bother to look at me once I was next to him, leaning against the back wall.

"You seem to have friends in high places. And I thought you didn't have any friends."

"Who needs friends when you got connections? Think I'd work this job for what they're paying that chump Kevin?"

"So Grady pays you more?"

"Yeah. Cash bonuses and insider stock advice. Internet stocks are the future. I'll be a millionaire. Then don't worry, honey, I won't be looking up your skirt any more. I'll be living in Hawaii."

"He pays you enough to invest with?"

"I'm worth it to him. Can't make enough by just working for a wage." Lance grinned. "Even if you're good at what you do."

"You attacked Zan and Vivian, my roommates."

"What, those dykes? They couldn't keep their mouths shut. At least that black-haired one couldn't. Kept screaming about how this place should be unionized. I eighty-sixed them. Some of the girls linked them to you. Don't blame them though, the other girls. They just wanted to make sure you kept your rowdy friends out of here. Bad for business, scaring off men." He watched Temptress lift one of her long legs and run her red high heel straight up the pole until she was standing in a split. Her g-string disappeared.

"You knew about the union when Jossie told you she thought Luna was Vice?"

Lance just sneered.

"And so that's why you beat up Luna?"

"Grady wouldn't go after Vice. He's not going to contradict the cops. Union, though, no harm in discouraging it. Outsiders coming in here messing with Grady's business."

"Did you kill Luna, too?"

Lance shook his head. "No. He doesn't pay me enough for that."

Our conversation petered out, but the music and the coaxing and the whoopin' and hollerin' in the club kept right on going, much too loudly. The Prince song had run right into Berlin's "Sex." I watched Lance. He watched Temptress. The black of Lance's outfit combined with the odd lighting in the club made his face and neck seem especially white. A quarter could have bounced off of his hair. His eyes were still, strafed by the swirling spotlights. They were large brown eyes, with long lashes.

Temptress was completely naked, lock-kneed, sway-backed, and shaking her long blonde hair into the crack of her ass.

I believed Lance. He was a creep, but he didn't seem to be a liar. He'd coolly admitted his assaults. Perhaps Grady really wasn't interested in killing.

"Some of us have got to work," he said, and went behind the bar to wipe a clean glass. His view of the stage was better from there.

So Lance would be the next man to get filthy rich off naked women.

I lay on the living room couch but I couldn't get to sleep for worrying. Somewhere along the line, I realized, I'd come to think of Luna as a friend. I'd learned so much about her, met her father and her oldest friend, admired her struggles, pieced together her motivations.

If Grady hadn't killed Luna personally, he'd put out the order. If he hadn't ordered Lance to do it, then who? Sam Bowden—was he the killer? He wasn't heavyset like Lance but young and agile enough to climb down from the deck. But Angie heard him leave by the front stairs. Only to steal back later?

Why did I worry? Whoever wanted that tape and killed Luna for it was going to come to me. I just had to be patient.

I was in the middle of a dream in which Grady was naked and shackled to a wall. He paid me to carve a tattoo into his upper thigh but the butter knife just wasn't working when I woke up. Sunlight clawed my face.

Geoffrey was asleep on my futon in the same jackknifed position I had left him. He didn't move when I turned on the light. The sparkly red leather jacket that brought back memories of my night as a hooker rumpled toward his head, baring the small of his back above his

501s. His skin was tanned. He must have taken time out of his crowded collage-making schedule to go to Baker Beach. Short golden hairs pointed downward and toward his spine. I was surprised no one had taken Eighties boy home last night. Geoffrey's sex life was normally varied enough in its cast of characters and range of activities to keep all of his roommates vicariously thrilled. At least he wouldn't have to worry about what he looked like in the morning. Not that he did anyway. I moved closer to make sure he was still breathing, and in answer his leather jacket crinkled up and down. I got dressed and turned out the light for him as I left.

Vivian and Zan's door was still closed. They'd probably sleep late, but I wanted to do something nice for them, like making them breakfast, with a flower on the tray. I put in two orders for huevos rancheros and a chorizo omelet for me downstairs at El QuakeO. A flower seller partially blocked the sidewalk a few feet south of our front door with his seasonal wares, which meant he was there year-round. In the fall he might have only top-heavy sunflowers flopping over his white ten-gallon buckets, but the springtime had expanded his inventory. I chose a thick-stemmed flower, its neon-orange blossom flat and big as my open hand.

Doña Rosa smiled at me over her stainless steel hotel pans of beans and rice that steamed at her all day long. She called the flower by a Spanish name as she clapped the omelet onto the counter. "Beautiful. That for your man upstairs?" She winked at me. I winked back.

While she assembled the stacks of eggs and tostadas and sauce I watched the Sunday morning burble of Church Street. The street's namesake was a neighbor, separated from our apartment and El QuakeO only by Your Mideast Deli, whose thick army-green awnings dimmed not only the store but significant square yardage of the sidewalk. The church had come before the neighborhood but was flanked by newer buildings and assaulted in spirit by aggressive commercial activity. It didn't matter, the church hadn't had a congregation in decades.

Doña Rosa swaddled two thick Styrofoam containers of huevos rancheros in a plastic bag. I took them upstairs just in time to answer the ringing phone.

"Ms. Lyle?" The voice sparkled like a celebrity's teeth.

"Yeah?"

"Ms. Lyle? Are you there?"

"Yes?" The voice was familiar. Even considering my harried night, it seemed early. Too early in the morning for a business call. "Who is this? Murray?"

"No. It's someone with a proposition for you."

The earpiece of the phone was halfway to its cradle before I raised it again to my ear. The man's voice sounded familiar, in a way that I couldn't place. "Do I know you?"

"In a way."

Suddenly, I did know him. It was the tenor from Luna's tape. It was Bowden himself.

"Who are you? What's your connection with Grady? What do you know about Luna's death?"

"Look, let's discuss this in person. Tell you what, let me take you to lunch. You like Vietnamese?"

"The people or the food?"

"How about The Palais. It's the best in town. Let's say, noon? You'll be there?"

"Sorry. I'm not big on blind dates with potential assassins. Who is this?"

He hung up.

At ten-thirty, the doorbell buzzed. I was in the kitchen, frozen in front of a mug of Earl Grey, keeping Hugh company while he washed the top layer of dishes in the sink.

Geoffrey flicked a hand through his hair. "I'll get it."

"Expecting someone?" Hugh asked.

"You never can tell when your prince will come. Didn't your mothers tell you that?"

"Pizza before noon?" He came back a minute later with a white cardboard pizza box, a shiny paper menu curling off the top. With exaggerated delicacy, he put the steaming grease-stained square in the middle of our small kitchen table. "Who ordered this? And will you be having wine with it?"

None of us had ordered a pizza. None of us even knew pizzas were made so early in the day.

"Well someone must have ordered it. Unless that cute bicycle messenger just wanted an excuse to see me in my morning state." Geoffrey raised his eyebrows at us.

"A mistake to our profit." Hugh dried his hands and flipped open the box. Sausage and mushroom vapors drove the last reminder of fourteen dogs from the room. "This isn't vegetarian," he complained.

"What do you expect? Not everyone in this town has y'all's eating

184

disorder. Looks like it's all mine," I said. Geoffrey grunted to imitate a pig and slowly pushed the pizza closer and closer to my face. I laughed until I gagged. "Too early for me."

"I'll take it down to Pat D. He's having a slow day for donations." He whisked it off the table and did a twirl. "Just wafting around that good smell."

"Dead pig."

"You've forgotten what you're missing."

Zan and Vivian came into the kitchen while he was gone. I rushed to get them their breakfasts. Zan's face looked sore but less raw, but Vivian's injuries appeared more dramatic than they had just after the attack. Navy blue lines had outlined her skull, but now Viv's right eye was completely ringed with mud-colored bruises, the socket considerably swollen. She had to tilt her head back slightly in order to see under her thickened eyelid.

Geoffrey came back, and he and Hugh and I fussed over them. No one mentioned the reason they were hurt, probably in deference to me. It was all my fault. I felt horribly guilty.

The doorbell rang once again. Geoffrey descended. Better him than me, I thought, feeling the toll of work on my aging thighs and knees. They seemed to hurt less if I kept them straight. Standing was less painful than sitting. A moment later Geoffrey clapped open the swinging door to the kitchen and handed me an envelope.

"Pat D. says 'Thanks' and that he found this taped under the pizza menu on the box. Looks like lunch was special delivery for you, Ms. Lyle."

"You're kidding. From who?"

"One of your many admirers, I'm sure." While I was tearing open the envelope, Geoffrey kept talking, "Don't worry, Hugh. She'll notice you one day." There was a rustling on my right as Hugh fled, the kitchen door stirring a sausage-scented breeze as it flapped shut behind him.

"What did you have to do that for?" Zan asked, looking at me. "What is it?"

Neither Geoffrey nor Vivian was paying any attention to her. They were both looking at my face. I struggled to regain control while I laid the note and the check on the kitchen table. The torn envelope fluttered to the floor.

The check was substantial enough to put Momma, Mellissa, and my entire acquaintance into used Hondas. It was drawn on the account of Local Sixteen, signed by Samuel Bowden.

Chapter Eighteen

"What is it, Aubrey?" Zan asked. Geoffrey and Vivian wasted no time on speech, but each leaned across the table to grab the papers laid in front of me.

"I don't believe it." Geoffrey's quicker hands had gotten to the check first. He shrieked and passed it to Zan, who looked at the small scrap of corporate blue, speechless, while Geoffrey continued. "That is one satisfied customer. You'll never have to work in this town again. What did you do to him, Aubrey? This time I do want details. Ooh, what's the note say?"

Vivian had been studying it, reading its one line over and over. She read it out loud.

"*'Is this a satisfactory price for the tape? Call me.'* It's signed 'Samuel Bowden' Letterhead, Local Sixteen of the International Brotherhood of Service Workers International."

"What did you do to him?"

"Who is this guy?"

"What does this note mean?"

I said, "It means Luna was betrayed by her own side."

Ramsay answered perkily on the first ring. He transferred me immediately, with no indication that he knew his boss had just sent me a check equivalent to a few years of salary for a woman with a liberal arts degree. Bowden answered, his tone cool.

Ramsay hadn't informed him it was me on the line, he said. A moment to get us off speakerphone. Had I gotten his note?

"You're president of the union. President of the union, taking bribes to keep strippers from joining your organization. Mind explaining exactly what is going on?"

"The rest of the union members weren't too happy about having sex workers in the ranks anyway. Here I thought I was bringing notoriety to our Local, if not prosperity. A new outlook. Just goes to show the conservatism of most people. Why don't you bring that tape over here and put it in my hand and I'll call the bank and authorize that check?"

"How do you know about the tape? How do you even know who I am?"

"Bob told me. In answer to both your questions."

"Did you try to buy it from Luna, too? Is that what you were doing at her house that night, besides killing her?"

"I went there for the tape, but I didn't kill Luna. I think it would be best for my career if a tape of myself accepting bribes didn't go public."

"She wouldn't sell it to you. She was no sell-out."

"Look, don't be so quick to judge. Believe me, the bribe thing was complicated. What choice did I have? Grady owns everything in town. We represent health care workers. He owns the hospital. We represent the custodians who clean office buildings. The buildings are Grady's. We represent San Francisco's hotel staff, the cooks and the housekeepers. Guess who owns a share in most of the hotels? It's hard to argue against his insistence that we leave his strip clubs alone. He could have made things a lot harder for us than he did."

"Right. He's a real softie. He probably makes more cash from those clubs than from the rest of his holdings put together."

"I doubt it. He seems to think the future of pornography is in the Internet. Maybe the clubs are a tax shelter, I don't know. I had no choice. I didn't want to get mixed up in this union corruption stuff. It's so retro. But I took the bribe because I had to and gave all the money to Azote."

"Your contact at ground level, or whatever? She was all too happy to turn in her former friend, who's now dead."

"Look, the whole thing turned into a mess. I just want that tape."

"What makes you think I have what you want?"

"Bob told me you did. As soon as you played the tape for him he came into my office and told me all about it. He never was good at subtlety."

"Where is Bob?"

"I'm afraid he was too earnest. That's our Bob. He was going to come forth with some information that he told me he heard on your tape."

"So he's—?"

"Taken care of. It's getting distasteful. Which is why I want to end this. Take the money. Let me destroy the tape. What do you want with it?"

As much as money meant to me, and as hard as I believed that the only thing wrong with tainted money was 'taint enough of it, I didn't consider Bowden's offer again. "Luna was killed for it. It proves you or Grady was responsible. At least I can expose her murderers."

"It doesn't prove Grady or I killed her."

"She caught you both in a bribe. You have reputations and jobs to protect. What was her life to you?"

"Calm down. All I want's the tape. I know where you live and where you work, and I'll hassle you until I get it. Not because I'm guilty of murder, though. I'm only guilty of taking bribes."

"Well I'm not." I closed my eyes and let another image deflate and buzz into space like a popped balloon. It was an old frame house in the East Bay flatlands, large enough so that Geoffrey and I could shave at the same time, with a yard for the puppies and my name on the deed.

"Take the money. I'll take the tape. Simple. You'll never get an offer like this again."

"That's where you're wrong, Bowden. I get a chance to tell condescending creeps to stick their offers up their assholes more often than you might imagine."

Once again the line was silent. Even the eavesdroppers in the kitchen were quiet.

"I'm sorry you wouldn't make a deal." Bowden hung up.

Geoffrey was even sorrier. He's the only one of my roommates who, after hearing the details of my phone conversation with Bowden, remained uncomprehending.

"You're passing up all that money and for what?" He rolled his eyes, looked at me again and sighed. I was clearly hopeless. "Will you all excuse me? I'm going to have a fit of pique." Geoffrey left the kitchen, returning a moment later to fill a paint-spattered jar with water from the tap. "Don't talk to me. I'm still having it," he said. He stomped out of the room without spilling a drop.

"It's just money." Peter looked genuinely puzzled.

Maybe Geoffrey had a point. I picked my cuticles and looked at the check. It sat untouched in the middle of the kitchen table. Maybe I was being foolish. I picked it up and put it on top of the refrigerator.

I made myself take deep, calming breaths and took a walk around the block. I scarcely felt the tentative morning sun, which gave more light than heat and promised a typical cerulean backdrop to the day. San Francisco's weather was like Muzak: mild, cheerful, repetitive. The winter months sounded a minor chord of rain.

At least the tape was in a safe place. I was at the corner of Church and Duboce, half a block from home, when someone spoke into my ear.

"Come with me." The voice was male. I'm not edgy normally, but the events of the morning had me spooked. I could see my front door. The traffic light flashed walk. I sprinted toward home.

I was slowed by the bottleneck of pedestrian traffic caused by the flowermonger. With a dodge to the right, I wedge-heeled through the white plastic tubs of gaudy spring blooms, soaking my flares limp against my ankles with warm slosh. A bucket of mixed bouquets spilled, and several passers-by and the vendor yelped. I called sorry as I clomped homeward.

I slammed the key into the round lock of the outside grille.

"Someone's looking for you," Pat D. spoke softly.

"Shit." The bolt slid, I tore the door open and sprang inside. I whirled around as I clanged it shut behind me, safe. My stalker caught up.

He wasn't Sam Bowden. He turned out to be someone I vaguely recognized. He must have been a customer, I thought. Just the thing to add to my troubles, being stalked by a customer. Perfect. He was tall, white, his brown hair plowed with gel. His shirt and suit jacket lay over each other as crisply as a sheet set. Matching dark pants broke perfectly over the insteps of a pair of shoes, real shoes, not tennis shoes, not crumbly workboots. The shoes were shined until they glowed. Even his schoolboy glasses sparkled. Naughtyland had a broad clientele, but truthfully, few people this well turned out were begriming themselves against its plastic chairs. But where else could I know him from?

"You're supposed to come with me," he said. "Get ready." He stood like an actor, arms arranged against his sides. His tone suggested his wishes were most often complied with.

"Oh really? And you are?" Suddenly I was much in demand.

"Azote sent me," he said.

I instinctively moved a step back. I imagined him in his underwear. Then I got it. He'd been the man in the flowered panty set.

"Don't go, give me a minute," I said. He nodded and took a step back. There was no way I was going up to Azote's alone. "I'll be back in one minute. Don't leave."

I ran back through the inner door and up the stairs. I didn't know who would be awake, but whoever was up was coming with me. Not only for the ride.

Geoffrey was reclined on the living room couch, a forearm draped dramatically over his eyes. The jar of water was on the floor next to him. Panting from my sprint up the stairs, I ran over to him and shook his elbow. His hair was wet from taking a shower and he'd changed out of his party clothes into 501s and a tight fitting ribbed undershirt that he'd dyed baby blue to bring out his eyes. He groaned with the movement.

"Geoffrey, I need to borrow you. Won't take long. Where are your shoes?" I said.

"Are we going to the bank? That's the best place to deposit that check."

"No. Our ride's waiting. Come on." I managed to elevate his shoulders a few inches off the couch. He slumped out of my grasp.

"I'm about to whine. What is your hurry? I told you I was having a fit. If we're not going to the bank with that check, I'm not going."

"We're going to a dungeon. Where are your shoes?"

"A dungeon? Whose?"

"I don't have time to explain."

"Explain while I put on my shoes."

I briefly described my previous encounter with Azote.

Geoffrey listened quietly until I was finished. After a pause, he removed his hand from his mouth. "You have got to be kidding me. Not a backless maid's dress."

"Is that all you have to say?"

"She does sound a bit intimidating."

"Just a bit."

"I'm ready." Geoffrey skipped down the stairs.

Flowered underwear man hadn't left.

"My friend," I grabbed Geoffrey's hand. "He's coming with us."

"She won't like that."

Geoffrey looked offended. Before he could offer a retort I squeezed his hand and addressed our escort myself. "Come on, you wouldn't want to disappoint her, would you? I get the feeling she doesn't deal with disappointment real well." We all hesitated.

"He goes or I don't," I finally said.

Geoffrey looked amused, then disgusted, then briefly like he was about to faint. "Just a touch too much tequila last night, I'll be fine." He smiled winningly at me and at our escort in turn.

We followed the man to his late-model Mercedes.

Billy Boy apparently didn't get Sundays off either. He answered the door in his usual custom-made uniform, accented this time with a purple feather duster wielded in his right hand like a sidearm. The color of the duster matched the bruises on his hairy knees. Miniskirts didn't flatter him. He looked at Geoffrey and me expressionlessly. Without a word of greeting, he whirled, revealing his split seam, and began the stately walk that served as a summons toward the living room doorway.

Geoffrey poked me and was trying to share a facial expression, most likely of glee, but I ignored him. I pulled him across the threshold and toward Azote's chamber. The novelty of Billy Boy had worn off for me during my previous visit. Our greeter had shoulder-massage duty today. He was already at his post by the time Geoffrey and I entered the room. At that moment our driver appeared through the doorway on the left. The suit was off. He wore matching panties and training bra in a blue floweret design. He couldn't have changed that quickly, I thought. He must have had them on underneath. And he was chesty enough to graduate to a bigger size, a congratulatory moment for any girl.

"Is he your slave?" Azote, reclined against the armrest of the sofa, indicated Geoffrey.

I didn't have to reply since Geoffrey tittered with laughter. Slaves don't laugh without their mistress's permission.

"He'll have to wait in another room. You know our conversations are private."

"Considering three people overheard them last time, I guess I didn't realize privacy was a priority."

"My slaves are completely trustworthy."

"Actually, I brought my friend here as a bodyguard."

Geoffrey clutched my forearm and opened his mouth to protest.

"Well, we'll put him where he'll be able to hear you scream." She kicked at our driver, who had moved to paint one of her toenails a sweet shell pink. "Nealy, take him back to quarters." Nealy capped the bottle of nail polish and padded up to Geoffrey.

"How thrilling. What do you suppose goes on in quarters?" My bodyguard whispered to me before he eagerly followed Nealy through the doorway to our left, the one the sushi had come through on my previous visit. Great.

"Get her a pillow."

Billy Boy repeated the ritual of moving and plumping several huge floor pillows at a crawl. Azote sat up on the couch. Her jeans were ripped at the knees and up the thighs as though they'd been clawed into those ladders of white strings. She wore a black leotard which showed the ripples of her abs. Her hair was kebobed into its bun by a sharp curve of silver tipped with a gold handle, an artifact that looked like the throwing-weapon of some elite class of ninja. The metal arc was long enough to glint from behind both sides of her head when she sat up.

Billy Boy pulled me down onto the two pre-plumped brocaded pillows.

"Get us something to eat, that's a good boy. And take something to her friend."

He bowed and left us.

I straightened my legs with a wince at the cracking joints. Despite the pillows' depth, I could find no sitting position that didn't involve knee pain.

"What's up?" I asked, as if I saw her all the time without being kidnapped for the purpose.

"I think you know."

"How did you find me?"

"Bob told me where you lived."

"Bob?"

"Yes. Don't worry, he didn't want to. I had to coerce him just a little."

I winced. I could imagine what a little coercing from Azote would entail.

"How do you know Bob? Is he okay?"

"Don't worry about Bob. You have something I want." She touched a hand to the ninja sword in her bun.

"What might that be?"

Billy Boy and Nealy reentered, each carrying a small black lacquer tray. Nealy set his in front of Azote on the floor. Pink pieces of sushi lolled on rolls of sticky rice like excised tongues of small animals. Billy Boy set a steaming bowl of soup in front of me. Tendrils of steam beckoned me over to smell the lovely beef broth. Azote told the men they were sloppy and dirty and to go wash their hands, then addressed me as they left.

"A certain tape." Azote deftly filled her mouth with a neat bundle of sushi from between the points of slippery red lacquer chopsticks.

"Tape?"

"Yes." Azote drew the silver talon out of her hair. She wove the metal ornament through two tears in her jeans, securing it into place with a flex of her taut pecan-colored thighs. She shook her hair loose then used both hands to refashion her bun.

Did Sam Bowden or Bob tell her about the tape? "I don't know what you mean."

"No?"

"No." I tried to keep my voice steady.

She sat back, skewered her hair, and looked at me. I tried to keep up my part of the stare volley. "Funny. Bob told me you played a tape for him."

"Bob told you?"

"He didn't want to. But don't worry, he's safe and sound in my dungeon. Though he might be a little cold and hungry by now. I'll let him go as soon as you give me that tape." Billy Boy and Nealy padded up to her, single-file like recess was over, and showed her their hands and fingernails.

"The tape's yours."

"Good. Where do you have it?"

"It's at work."

"I'll have Sam come to collect it from you tonight."

"Wonderful. You're doing all this for him?" I didn't let on I'd refused his offer of money not long ago. If this was Plan B, Sam Bowden must've telephoned her as soon as he hung up with me. But Nealy had arrived awfully fast for the timing to be right. Something made me think she was acting independently and that they hadn't communicated yet, that she had no idea he had already offered me money.

"He'll be doing me the favor."

"And you'll let Bob go?"

"As soon as I have the tape in my hand."

"What if Luna made other copies of the tape?"

Azote took a bite of sushi. "Don't think so. I don't think Sugar knew what she was doing for Luna." She set down her chopsticks.

"Sugar?" If I'd taken her up on the offer of food, I would have choked on it.

"White-girl whore. Friend of Luna's. She's the one who recorded it." Azote's painted lips closed around chopsticks and a pink, eviscerated shrimp.

"Okay, let's compare notes." Geoffrey stepped playfully in front of my feet as I slogged uphill to Fillmore Street for our unceremonious electric-bus departure from grand Pacific Heights. "Did she put you in that cage? I hope you had a more exciting time than I did. Not that I was up for much excitement, with this hangover. Can you slow down?"

I stopped while Geoffrey caught his breath. He was the one dancing around. The incline wasn't very steep on this block. The hanging signs of a psychologist and a doctor whose offices we had just passed swung only slightly off the vertical. The neighborhood was full of doctor's offices. The rich certainly seemed to need lots of mental and medical help. Geoffrey went on gushing about Azote's set-up.

"You're out of shape." I was barely listening to Geoffrey. Sugar had made the tape? She'd been the 'sugar' that Grady bought the Coke for while she was away from the table? If that was true, why hadn't she told me? Did that mean anything? And poor Bob, imprisoned in Azote's dungeon. I remembered his shy panic. That tape wasn't worth any more suffering.

"You're a hard taskmaster. Maybe she's giving you lessons?"

"Right. Thanks for looking out for me in what could have been a dangerous situation. Why do you think I brought you along?"

"So sensitive. Nothing happened. You could have briefed me before we went, you know, instead of yanking me out with false promises of sexual delights." Geoffrey put his hands on his hips, imitating me.

"Oh, forget it. Can you walk yet? Tell me what happened."

"Well, I was taken away by that man with the sagging behind. He's really not the type for backless and I told him so as soon as we got to the kitchen."

"He took you to the kitchen?"

"Yes, it seemed an appropriate enough destination considering his outfit. A beautiful kitchen, by the way. Ceiling hanger—one of those rectangular things—copper pans, skylights, built-in wok."

"No Crock Pot. No bleeding victim." I was worried about poor Bob.

"None in evidence. But shut up, I'm telling you what happened." He gave my side a light backhanded slap. "He told me I should sit at a large table that I can only call rustic in style, dark wood, rather medieval, and he asked me if I wanted a bowl of soup."

"How exciting. Beef?"

"God, no. Vegetarian. With coconut milk, vaguely Thai. It was delicious. The cook served it to me."

"Was he wearing only a diaper?"

Geoffrey looked at me sadly. "Unfortunately, no. He was wearing a chef's outfit, hat and everything. And what a chatty Cathy! I couldn't enjoy it in peace. Marvelous cook, though. I told him to serve you something greasy and full of red meat, that you'd never eat that exotic sushi he was assembling due to your lack of culinary adventurousness. If the leftovers can be slopped to the pigs, you'll love it. Did you like the soup?"

"Too good for the pigs. So the guys talked to you?"

"Sure. The cook guy is a CEO in some corporation in the Financial District. I didn't recognize the name. The other guys blathered on about venture capital. Nealy is short for Cornelius. Can you believe it? The outfits are the only things they have going for them. Those and what's her name. Some dungeon. The soup did wonders for my hangover. But you haven't told me about your encounter. I hope it was juicier. Does she want to hire you? Is she contracting out? No offense, but you're not the dominatrix type. Not that you don't have your hard edges."

"Nope. She wants my last clue to Luna's murderer. She's torturing someone until she gets it. I've decided to give it to her."

"It seems best to give her what she wants." We reached an intersection. These were inevitably graded into windy plateaus. We stopped to admire the view to the north. Sun-bleached buildings scattered in a dice-roll down the hill, stopped by the rugged blue arm of the Golden Gate's narrow channel. The dark water was only a stripe before headlands big as icebergs chased it down.

I would just give her the tape. I'd come close to finding Luna's killer, but Bowden was right. The tape was evidence of bribery, not murder. And I couldn't let someone else be killed for it. Not Bob. Not me.

Finally, Geoffrey said, "Bus," and we went to meet it. "What I really couldn't believe about all that, though," he said, as we boarded the crowded Twenty-two, "is how much those guys are paying her."

"They talked about that?" I jostled into the crowd in the aisle, looking in vain for a handhold. I settled for Geoffrey's sleeve as the bus lurched forward. "Sorry. How much?"

"Five hundred a week! I suppose she is the only positive thing in their lives." Geoffrey obligingly tucked my hand under his armpit and looked thoughtfully out the window at the mansions rolling by. After the inevitable bucking start, electric buses are a smooth ride, and an astonishingly quiet one.

"You're kidding," I said, not because I shared his opinion that Azote's services were no bargain. I had no blue book for domination services, but five hundred seemed far too little for a week of personal attention. I did my mental calculations. One thousand five a week from the Billys and Nealy. She couldn't be making that much in her claustrophobic booth at the Cher Cherie, maybe another five a week at the most. Grady's money must have made the bulk of the payments on the half-million dollar mansion and the limitless supply of sushi. "Did they mention if she has any other clients?" The bus made a sudden stop and I bit into the lip I had been unconsciously chewing. I blotted off a drop of blood.

"You okay? No, I think they're it. There were only three chairs around the table in the kitchen, anyway. And," he leaned over to whisper into my ear, which attracted the attention of an elderly lady who looked at us eagerly from the front reserved seats, "only three sets of shackles bolted to the wall by the stove!" He pulled away. "She's running a three horse stable, if you ask me. Señora, you are a voyeuse," he coyly addressed the elderly woman. She looked away with an impish smile, unacquainted with the word or simply disappointed by our chaste relationship.

I pictured Bob's leg hairs singeing off slowly like thousands of tiny sparklers by the stove in Azote's kitchen. I bit my lip again. Geoffrey noticed my self-inflicted injury and told me to stop being neurotic.

Chapter Nineteen

I got to Naughtyland early that evening, hoping Sam Bowden was already there to pick up the tape so I could stop worrying. The young executive's slender form was not one of the lone hunched figures, surgically attached to their beer mugs, that sat behind shadows of tables and at the horseshoe of the stage. Maybe by the time I got undressed and freshened my lipstick, he would have shown up. He'd be here, I thought, nervously chewing my lip. He'd be here and I could give him the damned tape.

I shoved myself between Plantagena and Temptress for access to a few square inches of the mirror backstage. Mine was one of twenty reflected faces darkening lips, plucking hairs and applying mascara. About half the women managed to talk without jeopardizing their make-up application. Cameron was smoothing expensive white cream over her neck and down into the dramatic cleavage netted by her clingy silver dress. It was a trick I'd taught her. Shiny cleavage makes your tits look bigger.

I was applying a sparkly coat of Carbon Ore on my right eyelid when I felt a searing pain just above my elbow. My hand jerked and the Carbon Ore striped green highlights through my eyebrow as a whiff of burnt flesh added itself to the scents of floral perfumes and sweaty girls in the dressing room. I screamed.

"Sorry!" said Temptress, from behind her bouncy soda-can-sized sausage curls. "God, you're edgy." She tonged another hunk of fine blonde hair with her thick curling iron, wrapped it in a spiral with a few quick expert twists before looking at me in the mirror. "You okay?"

"I'll live." Annoyed, I left the fray to stick my elbow, now decorated with a hot rectangle of red, under the cold water tap. It promised to be a crappy night.

I tossed my shirt and pants into my locker and traded my clogs for a pair of platform heels upholstered in black velveteen. I didn't bother to change into more festive underwear, and went out on the floor in the black sheer bra and red t-back panties that I'd put on that morning. You couldn't go wrong in the sex industry wearing black, white, or red. Bad girl, good girl, bad girl: the simple binary of titillation.

The shift was changing and no other dancers drifted among the customers to add color and movement to the dreary interior of the club. Generic jazz music was playing. Even the stage was empty. The spotlights that were normally a wide-array bombardment were dimmed and aimed at the stage seeking life, their gaudy colors blending into a muted white.

Sam Bowden still wasn't there.

I sat at a table near the bar where I could watch the door.

After a moment a small-built man in a business suit approached me. I really wasn't in the mood, but I gave him a lapdance. The only thing worse than giving a ligament-cracking lapdance to a man of some girth is giving one to a man half your size. I could barely find the guy. My bumps and grinds hit him somewhere around his sternum. Nevertheless, he bought three dances.

When I emerged from the cubicle with the apparently satisfied small man, Temptress was progressing down the tongue of the stage with a series of high kicks that would have put a kung fu master to shame. And kung fu masters didn't do them in four-inch heels. Each kick set her long curls bouncing. At the sight of her blonde sausage curls my burned elbow started to throb.

I explored the floor, pushing through what was getting to be a good-sized crowd, since a bachelor party—a score of boys far too irresponsible to marry—had shown up. They bayed at Temptress. Though they had the vocal enthusiasm of high-school cheerleaders at the playoffs, the men of these titty-bar cheerleading squads never spent much money on us dancers.

A cool hand fastened around my thigh.

"Hello," said the tenor voice of Sam Bowden.

"You made it. Or should I say you made it back?" He was tall, and I found myself addressing his chest. Bowden's workouts were evident through his clothing. He wore a black leather peacoat over a pale shirt and a tie that matched the shirt exactly. The monochrome look was trendy that season. His hair was a sandy pile, boyish and unruly as his grin. He stroked a sideburn with the back of his hand.

"Oh, I've never been here before. Never been in any of Grady's sex emporia. They seem like…" Sam looked around at the gunky mirrors, the filthy tables, the women clothed by wraps of string, the bachelor party lurching at the stage. He yelled over the Journey song because he had to. "…fine working environments."

"Right. Have a drink."

"No thanks."

"It's not a choice. Two-drink minimum. The bar's over there. I'll go get what you came for. By the way, I'm giving you this tape to free Bob, not for your check."

"I'll pass that along to Azote."

"You pass along a lot of things to her. Bribes, tapes. What do you get in return? No, don't bother answering that. She does your dirty work for you. Well, I don't want your money."

He just smiled. "Don't be coy. Everyone wants money. I'll call my bank and authorize it right now. You just run along and get that tape."

I left him pulling out his cell phone from his jacket.

The dressing room was empty. The new girls who didn't know better were working the bachelors. Their attentions to the party crowd cut down on the competition for the other customers, so the experienced dancers, who knew that men in packs are more concerned with maintaining their place in the hierarchy than they are in pairing off with some woman, were working everyone else.

No one was backstage to hear my screeches when I poked through my locker, then ransacked it, then gutted it, throwing the tangle of high heels, underwire bras, and six-dollar-a-pair panties to the locker room floor. The tape was gone.

I hid out in the locker room as long as I could. Who would have taken the tape? Nobody liked 'Eighties' music anymore. Only one person had known where it was, and what it was—Sugar had instructed me to make my locker the hiding-place.

I called home.

"Hugh! Get up off that couch. You've got to do me a huge favor."

"Again?"

I explained that a tape important to my longevity was missing and that I was sure that it was in the possession of a certain masseuse. He had to go to Missy Massage and get Sugar and/or her stolen goods over to Naughtyland before I was the next victim of a crime wave.

"Where's Missy Massage?"

"I don't know, in the Tenderloin somewhere. You'll have to look it up. Will you do it?"

"Of course I will."

"Quickly, Hugh. Be careful. One person's been killed for that tape already."

"I'm out the door."

I paced the dressing room and planned to remain there until Sugar and Hugh showed up or Sam Bowden figured out where I was. Then Plantagena bounced backstage naked—the glitter she'd rolled onto her body sparking with sweat—clutching the maid's apron she always wore for her final song to her breasts.

"You know you're up next?"

"Tell me, did you see a strange woman come in here today?" If Sugar had paid a stage fee, she could have easily gotten past the bouncers by saying she was new, or they just hadn't met yet, or she was there to audition.

"No. God, stop acting so crazy. I see strange women in here every day. I'm looking at a strange woman right now."

"Something got stolen from my locker—"

"How much? Cameron had eight hundred stolen the other day. It's all these new girls."

"Not money, a tape."

"I don't know anything about it. Get up on stage, girl. That's your song."

"Shit." I'd forgotten I had a job to do. The first chords of my Lyle Lovett song vibrated the sound system. The music went on without a break, mercilessly pumped out by a jukebox backstage, and we had to be ready to meet our songs.

I ran onstage wearing the bra and panties I had on, rather than treating the bachelors to my complicated cowboy outfit. By my third song Sam Bowden had jostled his way to the stage. When I reached to collect his ten-dollar tip at the end of my set, he pinned my hand to the bill with his.

"I can come backstage, you know," he said. "I've figured out where it is."

He was being ironic. A big neon sign over the curtained doorway that led to our locker room read, 'Ladies Only! Lounge' in pink cursive,

I decided I'd rather not break the news that his tape was missing backstage, where there was a chance we'd be alone.

"Be right out," I said, in the same tone I was using to thank the bachelors for their offerings. At the insistence of the several dancers draped over them, they'd pooled their resources and come up with four one-dollar bills to chuck onto the stage.

I threw my tips into a small scrap heap in my locker and heaved the rest of my crap on top of it and slammed the door. Luckily, my shoes had never come off, so I didn't have to negotiate getting into another pair.

I found Sam seated at one of the back tables. Cameron was dangling over him. Her slippery bosom collected a firelight glow.

"I'd like to speak with her, please," Bowden said.

Cameron glared at me as she straightened and stepped away. As far as she was concerned, I'd just horned in on her twenty bucks.

"The tape's missing," I said.

"What?"

"But I know who has it, and she's on her way."

"I thought we were going to be done with this thing."

"We are. She'll be here soon and you'll have it." I said with false confidence. I had no idea if Sugar would be at work, and I didn't know how to reach her otherwise. How long would it take Hugh to find Missy Massage, work up the courage to go in and ask for one of the girls, and, if she were there, convince Sugar she had to hand over a tape that she'd gone to some trouble, for some reason, to steal? What was she planning to do with it? Why hadn't she told me she'd been the one to tape it?

"I'm tired of this." Sam roughed up a sideburn with his knuckles. "I just want it to be over."

"The tape's coming."

"Tonight."

"Yes, I promise."

"Well," Sam stood, "I'm not hanging around with this bunch of morons to wait for it. These men, I mean."

"How am I supposed to—"

A movement from his hip was a wave of dismissal. "You'll find out."

Great.

I was too nervous to actually work that night. The only money I made was from customers who came up to me and asked for dances themselves. This didn't happen often enough to meet the cost of living, at least not for me. By midnight I had made eighty dollars over the stage fee and about ten phone calls home. I got no answer each time. Even Zan must have been out.

I was backstage on the payphone listening to the familiar ring of the apartment's phone repeat itself mockingly when the music in the club stopped. A primitive bachelor roar followed.

I hung up the phone after counting three more rings and went to investigate. It wasn't a power outage. The lights were still discoing around the club. Something onstage had attracted the crowd. Naughtyland was brimming with customers at that hour, all of them at that moment holding still and straining toward the stage, like dogs on point. Even their drinks were tilted stageward.

"And I'm here to audition!" The voice projected from the runway. It was startling to hear a voice clearly in that place where music always deafened. More startling to hear a woman's, loud and confident. More startling to hear it come from the stage. No one ever talked from up there, and what I heard wasn't just words but a proclamation.

"My name is Azote!" The voice finished and the roar resumed. Eartha Kitt once again made a growl out of the close-packed, recycled air.

A moment later Azote had shimmied to the top of the pole and I could see her. Her torso was cinched with a series of black belts. She had on nothing else, except for a spit-polished pair of black stilettos with slivers for heels. The slivers glinted like needles. Azote removed the wide belt that had bound her breasts and used it to fasten herself to the pole. She did a few twirls and then, from somewhere on her person, extracted a whip. In one motion she righted herself from an upside-down spin and flicked the whip over the heads of the bachelors. The lash electrified the hair of the few of them who didn't petrify it with gel or smother it under a baseball cap.

The crack came a second later, a boom like a fighterplane sucking a desert sky, a frightening, final sound as though she'd broken the backs of the molecules the whip had disturbed. She was already aiming another strike, and with an easy flick of her wrist the whip wrapped a coil down the pole and retreated, quick as a snake's sniffing tongue.

I felt the whip seize my own body in a boa constrictor hug. The feeling was my imagination but, after all, she'd brought it for me.

By the end of the Eartha Kitt song one of the bachelors was clamped to the pole with four of Azote's belts. She'd arranged two of them to squeeze his nipples, one strapped just above his areolas, one just below. One belt blindfolded him and the last cuffed his hands behind his back. Once she'd gotten him secured she undid the man's jeans and shucked them halfway down. He couldn't do anything about it. His companions loved it.

"Now I need a girl volunteer. You." She pointed to me. Before I knew it, her legion of fans had nudged me toward the stage, working together like cilia. I was heaved onto the runway by many hands.

"Hi, Azote."

"Seems like you need a little encouragement to come up with that tape." As she spoke, she undid her captive. His friends jeered as he pulled up his pants. He was thenceforth lowest in the hierarchy, down there with the gamma males, perhaps never to recover ground.

"The tape's on its way. Why is that tape so important to you? It's Sam Bowden and Grady who are doing the bribing."

"What should I do to her, boys?" Azote handled me like exhibit A, a warm, small hand to my neck and another on my upper arm, showing me around to all sides of the runway.

They had lots of charming ideas but Azote went with her own plan. She began by belting my wrists together.

"You're going to get your tape. No need to go to all this trouble. Don't tell me you're just Sam's lackey. I held you in higher esteem than that."

"I'm nobody's lackey," she said, smiling for the crowd as she pulled the belt a notch tighter in a way that subtly and painfully rearranged my wrist bones, as though they were pebbles resettled by a wave. "I really don't need to kill you too. All I need's the tape back. The hard evidence. You might have heard it, you might have figured out the facts, but no one's going to believe the word of a whore. Trust me," she bent me back over one of her strong arms and drew her whip up slowly between my legs, "I know."

The whip traveled up my midline. I thought I heard the crowd swooning.

"So you killed Luna," I said.

"She would have exposed me. She got Grady, I was next."

"She got Grady?"

"She sent cops to his place. They just happened to find him with a male prostitute. Convenient timing, right? Luna knew who he'd be with. She was trying to ruin his chances for mayor."

"She sent cops to bust him and Jossie?"

"She gave them the tip-off."

"On the night she was killed?"

"And she would have found a way to humiliate Sam and me, too. When he called that night to tell me she wouldn't accept his generous offer I had to do something." Azote had coiled most of the length of the whip in her hand and dandled the end over my bare abdomen. "It was easy to jimmy open her balcony door. I meant to restrain her while I looked for the tape myself. But she wouldn't tell me where it was, so it ended badly for her."

I watched my abdomen flutter between recoils from the whip's stings and my uneven breaths. Red welts bloomed on my skin.

"Why would Luna want to expose you?"

"She figured out I was keeping Bowden posted on her whereabouts and that he told Grady to target her. Only I knew where she was going after the Cher Cherie. When the Femme Royale got closed almost as soon as she got there she was suspicious. She came here, laid low, didn't mention the union, but still got harassed. Only I knew where she was. Well, Bob and me. But that loser obviously wasn't the leak. He's not exactly crafty."

She spun me around and cracked her whip across my back. The crowd panted.

"Exposing me," Azote continued, "would have gotten me off her back. She could keep organizing. I'd be made a laughingstock. The press would love it. Organizer of sex workers exposed as corrupt. They've never taken me seriously, all along. And I demand to be taken seriously."

A second lash followed, stinging my back an inch below the first strike.

"I take you seriously," I said. The pain wasn't agonizing but it was lingering, like cat scratches rather than blows. Two lines under my shoulder blades thrummed. Then the lines of pain reached out and joined hands and my entire upper back simmered.

"This doesn't need to go on. Where's the tape?"

"The tape's on its way." But I was giving up hope of that. It had been hours since I'd talked to Hugh.

The next lash tingled the muscles of my shoulders. That wasn't too painful, but in the final shimmy of that stroke, the whip's fringed tip traced my recent burn, snatching off the burnt skin and clawing raw flesh.

In a rare moment of solidarity, both the Naughtyland patrons and I screamed.

I felt blood make three runnels that converged to drip off my elbow.

I shuddered and the crowd lunged. It wasn't much blood, but it made her audience ravenous. Azote stirred the whip over the perimeter of the stage to scatter the men back.

Whistles and catcalls rang over the song's fadeout. Several shades of bass and tenor yelled things like "You got the job" and "I'll hire you myself, baby."

"This is going to go on until I get that tape," it was a whisper, close to my ear, strangely intimate because everything was starting to feel far away. I could smell the wax of her lipstick.

"I'd love for you to have it, believe me. But it's not here."

"Then we're going wherever it is. Simple." She tugged the end of the belt at my wrist and my wrist bones ground together. She clipped a dog collar attached to a leash around my neck. She shrugged on a kimono that had been a puddle of black silk on the skanky surface of the stage. She led me by the leash, backwards. Her third song was just starting, but Azote whipped a space into the crowd at the stage and hopped off the runway into it, ignoring the Himalayas of dollar bills that had been left for her. None of the customers dared get too close to my captor, though they had no qualms about feeling me up. Several of them seized me with disregard for sensitive parts, pulled me off the stage, and set me upright in front of the dominatrix so I could walk facing forward. Someone even scraped through the runnels of blood on my arm with a rough touch that I hoped hadn't been a tongue.

Azote steered me, and customers hustled aside to let us pass to the door. I noticed them no more than usual, a blur of teeth from a leer, a sloshing non-alcoholic beer, an odor of pizza then one of bright cologne, a paunch, a loafer, suspenders, belts, all caught by the beams of light from overhead.

One person was left between me, Azote, and the door. Lance stood behind the till, his eyes toward the stage. His ban from the club's floor seemed to have gone entirely out of effect. I tried to make eye contact with him. Perhaps he'd overcome our mutual loathing enough to protect one of his charges.

It seemed a slim chance. And as we passed, Lance didn't look me in the eye. He only warned me that if I was leaving I'd better pay Mose Junior extra for missing my final set. He told me my ride was outside, but hadn't been let in since he didn't meet the dress code. That was a joke. Naughtyland had no dress code.

Hugh honked furiously when we emerged under Naughtyland's marquee. He was in Peter and Rainbow's van halfway down the block. For the second time, I hit the streets of the Tenderloin wearing nothing more than skimpy underwear. Azote prodded me into the the cold, moist air, charged white by the buzzing signs and soured by misplaced waste. The night air soothed my whip-burns, chilled the rest of me, and congealed my raw wound. The sidewalk slapped the acrylic platform soles of my high heels, cheap shoes that cast my feet in the Barbie doll mold. I could feel the bones of my insteps drive toward my toes with every step.

I turned towards the van.

"That's my ride. He's brought your tape," I said, completely unconfident that it was so. For one thing, Sugar didn't appear to be in the van with Hugh. Geoffrey was, though, jouncing on the passenger's seat and waving furiously at us.

"Good." Azote steered me.

Hugh and Geoffrey followed our progress to the van's side door. The lenses of Hugh's glasses stretched and squeezed the flickering neon curves from the signs of the porn palaces on Jones Street. Geoffrey gaped. Sugar was not with them.

"You ladies work in there?" A young black man lounged against the van's side, trading hits off a joint with two buddies. "Because if you do, shoot, I'm on my way in."

"Open the door." A tug on the leash choked me. The door opened from the inside. Sugar proved to be on the other side of it, sitting with Yohimbe on the van's floor. Her face was moody with makeup. A beaded purse hung from a long strap off her shoulder. Her black coat bloomed around her like a vampire's.

"Do you have the tape?" I asked.

"I have it," Sugar said.

"Give it to her so she'll let me loose. You lied to me. You made that tape. Why did you steal it? And why didn't you three come in and give it to me in the club? We could have avoided all this." The leash and collar confined me to jerky movements as Azote directed me onto the bench seat.

"That was my fault," Sugar said, quickly. "That bouncer said something to Hugh about a dress code. It was bullshit. They just didn't want to let in an escorted woman. I kicked up a fuss and got us eighty-sixed."

"Don't just stare. Drive," said Azote.

"Where?" Hugh peeled out from the curb. The men who'd been leaning on the van shouted curses.

Geoffrey stared around at us girls, his eyes darting from Azote to Sugar to me. He was uncharacteristically quiet and, I assumed, on some sort of illegal drug. It was nighttime, after all.

"Head towards Market,"Azote commanded.

"Aubrey, are you okay?" Hugh asked, after we'd all had a moment to size each other up. He was speeding toward Market.

"I'll live." I sat rigidly since I'd discovered that reclining in the bench seat made my back feel like a lit broiler. Azote sat next to me, but her attention was on Sugar who stayed on the floor. Motion sickness, she explained.

"So you're Azote," Sugar said. "The great organizer."

"And you have my tape. Was it fun for you, fucking Grady and spying on him at the same time? Or is that the way you street whores always operate? Biting the hands that feed you?"

"Right, we're immoral. Some of us care more for our co-workers than for our johns. Luna set me up on that date. She told me to record any meetings my john might have. She figured out she'd been betrayed. She wouldn't tell me who it was that I was seeing, and I assumed it was a union boss. But Aubrey told me who Grady was, and I put it together. The thing went even deeper than just some union boss betraying Luna."

I remembered Jossie's accusation that Luna had been hitting up on her customer, Grady. So—she'd been making a date all right, but for Sugar.

"Surprised that a club owner wouldn't want a union going after his girls?" Azote sneered. "The only reason we got away with unionizing the Cher Cherie is that it's independently owned. Small family business. Grady and company own all the rest."

"No, it's no surprise that some CEO is going to be against unions. And I've always been cynical about union bosses. What is a surprise to me is that you, her colleague, turned Luna over to assassins."

"Sugar—" I started.

"Let me finish, Aubrey." Sugar turned to Azote. "Isn't that what they were paying you for, to be a spy? To let them know Luna's whereabouts?"

"Sugar, you've got—"

"No." She stopped me again. "Luna died for this tape. I might have recorded it for her, but I didn't hear it until today. She didn't tell me who it was she set me up with. She didn't tell me why. I didn't know Grady was the owner of Naughtyland. I didn't know she suspected him of paying off the union. But it's all here." Sugar patted her beaded purse. "A strip club owner, my dear john Grady, bribing a union boss.

And the union boss accepting the money gladly while admitting that you are his contact. Proving what I've known all along. The unions hate us whores. Not only will this tape get me all the recruits I need for a women-only union, the press is going to have a field day. One listen will be enough to disgust anyone."

"Turn here," said Azote, almost strangling me with a tug on the collar. Hugh gave one glance back at me, then swung the van onto Upper Market. The engine ground as the van strove for altitude. We were scaling Twin Peaks, the city's highest hills.

"It doesn't prove—" I began.

"Shut up. Hand over the tape." Azote flicked her whip for emphasis. Sugar dodged it, but its tip struck Hugh in the calf. It ripped a gash in his jeans.

"Youch," he said. Geoffrey shrieked.

"I'm thinking of never handing it over to anybody," said Sugar

"What?" I choked out to Hugh who dipped a hand to rub the scratch on his leg. He pulled his hand off quickly. It was smeared with a thin wash of blood.

The van sputtered and pulled to the left. Hugh's body slumped off the driver's bucket seat, the hands that should have been on the steering wheel fallen slack toward the floor. I'd seen similar poses assumed by persons on Valium. Bad move on Azote's part—how could she know that Hugh fainted at the sight of blood?

"Geoffrey, get the wheel," I screamed. He jumped up and reached over Hugh, grabbed the wheel and pulled frantically to the right. An oncoming driver's terrified face sped by the side window. Squeals and skids followed. Geoffrey got control of the van just before it crashed into a mural-painted retaining wall.

Sugar, in full rant, continued, unfazed by the near-accident. "Here you are a famous organizer—famous for being the first to organize sex workers. You're a figurehead, an inspiration. Only because people don't know the truth. In truth you're a traitor and a cynic. If you ever wanted to fight against oppression, you lost your idealism when the first camera focused on you and the first reporter listened."

We had reached a summit in the roadway. The dark shapes of Twin Peaks hung off to our right. The van's sweet hemp smell had turned acrid from grinding gears. Hugh had the plastic pallor of an action figure and the frozen passivity. Geoffrey seemed to be dozing off at the wheel. We rolled slowly through a red light.

Sugar and Azote didn't notice. Sugar was still seated on the floor facing the back, petting Yohimbe. "I know you don't want your corruption made known. As long as I keep this tape and keep it to myself, you'll help me. How about it, Azote? We work together. A woman-only union. With you as the figure-head, it will be a guaranteed success. In return, I don't tell anyone the truth about you. You'll be even more famous."

"Geoffrey!" I shouted. The van had lost momentum and was veering toward the shoulder—the shoulder of the oncoming lane. The shoulder that only a guardrail separated us from an overpopulated hillside that fell steeply toward the Castro. I jumped up but was strangled by the dog collar. "Let go of me! Damn it, Sugar, give her the tape."

Sugar pleaded with me. "Don't you see? She'll work with me as long as I have it. We'll establish what sex workers need—our own union. If she said the word, women would flock to her. She's legendary."

"Sugar, you don't understand. She—Geoffrey, wake up. Shit!" I grabbed at the dog collar, feeling the pricks of its pointy studs impale my palms. Azote must have let go of the leash because suddenly I was free to leap to the driver's seat. Yohimbe began a raucous barking.

"Don't argue with me, Aubrey. Luna was about to expose Bowden. Obviously he didn't want it to become public that he was taking bribes from a club owner to keep the strippers from unionizing. She wouldn't tell him where the tape was, so he killed her."

Though dressed only in decorative underwear, I was no longer feeling the cold. I hadn't driven a car in about four years, and I'd never been behind the wheel of an ancient behemoth such as the van. Rusting Chevettes had been more my style. I shoved Geoffrey aside and kicked Hugh's foot off the accelerator. I steered with one hand and touched Hugh's face with the other, cupping my palm over his nose to feel for breath. He was breathing—fast and shallow. Geoffrey had clattered into the windshield. It woke him up.

"I'm sorry, I'm on the weirdest combination of stuff right now. But Hugh said he needed me to help find your prostitute friend. I just couldn't turn him down. Where are we?"

"On Market, trying to stay on Market. Can you steer?" I unbuckled Hugh and pulled him out of the driver's seat. Azote had retrieved her end of the leash and I was choking. For a moment after, I couldn't speak. Geoffrey seemed willing to drive. I retreated to the bench seat and buckled myself in.

Azote was answering Sugar. "You're seeing the situation through your own bias. Using your logic, it could just as easily have been Grady who killed her. He was bribing a union not to organize his club."

"No. He's too powerful. He would never have to dirty his hands himself if he wanted someone dead. Half the people in this town are his lackeys. He even had some bouncer to keep everyone at Naughtyland in line."

Geoffrey got the van zinging down its proper lane at a fast, unsteady pace. The road curved around Twin Peaks. The other side of the hills was more suburban than urban. Wider lanes opened onto shopping centers. The van's engine seemed to mimic its driver, revving in and out of consciousness. I clenched the seat with both hands.

Tension cooked in the moment of silence.

Then, "You killed her!" Sugar said.

"You met Bowden," Azote said. "Surely you must have seen that he's too much of a wuss to actually kill anyone. It doesn't fit his progressive image of himself. Besides, it might soil his tie."

"Yes, Sugar! Azote's the killer. Give her the tape! She'll kill us too!" I found my voice.

"I don't even have to kill you. I'll just take the evidence, please. No one will believe the testimony of two whores."

"See, she'll let us go! Sugar!"

"They might, however, believe the testimony of two upstanding young men," Azote gestured at Hugh, passed out over the passenger seat, and Geoffrey, who looked dreamily out the window and pointed at the pretty houses that floated by. His head knocked into the glass and when it recoiled a filament of drool connected the window to his lower lip. "They've heard everything. They know everything. I'll have to kill them."

"What? No! They're both stupefied, look at them. Sugar, please give her the tape."

They were approaching a stoplight. It winked yellow, a polite metronome in the middle of a three-way intersection. Late-night motorists politely followed its instructions, black sedans and moss green compacts following each other to the right or left like bloodflow. Geoffrey wasn't slowing. Sugar didn't notice the intersection; she was looking at me

"You win. I'll give you the fucking tape."

The procession of pretty weekend cars that had been the cross traffic was gone. A giant red sport utility vehicle, towing a compact, charged the traffic light like a linebacker going for a sack.

I screamed. Thuds and cracks and shouts sounded like a rugby match behind me. I got kicked in the Achilles tendon. Yohimbe yelped, once. The van slowed and unguided, spun. At first the skid felt slower than it was. We seemed to move through sludge, as a frond of kelp follows waves. Then things accelerated. The side door opened. It let in cold air and the screech of brakes, followed by feminine screams, the blare of "Fly Like an Eagle" from someone's cracked car, and then—a gunshot. The bench seat beside me was empty—Sugar and Azote were gone, having been thrown from the van somewhere onto the street, along with Yohimbe.

I looked up into sodium lights, their poles looped with flapping plastic advertisements. We'd been stopped by one of the lightpoles at the entrance to a used car lot.

I could tell Hugh was alive by the R2D2 decal on his T-shirt. It shimmered with his breaths. I held his hand and watched the decal twinkle in rhythm with his breathing—green, yellow, red, green, yellow, red— in time to the stoplight, until the ambulances came.

Chapter Twenty

Only Geoffrey walked away from the accident. He never remembered any of it.

The ambulance guys treated my burn and whip marks, pasting the welts with a soothing salve and advising aloe in future for the burn, as I sat with Hugh on the way to the hospital. He'd come around before we got there and protested the expense of an ambulance. None of us had insurance. Once his wound was bandaged and there was no sight of fresh blood he was all right, sitting up on his gurney and chatting with a busy attendant about the four humours and the ancient practice of bleeding patients to balance them. With all his fainting at the sight of blood, he wouldn't have fared well in those days.

I went to admissions to check on Carina and Azote.

"This Azote got a last name?" The desk clerk asked.

I was sure she did and said so.

"Well you want to tell us about it because we don't file patients under their gang names."

"She's not a gangbanger—" I started to say, then gave up and asked about Carina Smyth. Carina had ended up in the same emergency room, SF General. I found her leaning against a Coke machine in the hall.

"You okay?"

She had abrasions on her face and was cradling her left arm. A streak of grease mortared a lock of her hair. The grease and her hair were the same deep black, the grease evident only from its iridescent shimmer. "I take it I don't look so good."

"You look like you'll have some bruises. Nothing broken?"

"I don't think so. Bruises, huh? Worse than broken bones in our line of work. Too visible." Sugar smiled weakly. "We can only afford to get hurt in places customers can't see."

I reached for her face and thumbed away a speck of black grease that marred her perfect cheekbone. "Liquid base is your answer. I have that on authority."

"Maybe I'll just take some time off. How's your friend Hugh?"

"He'll be fine."

"He's nice."

"I know. I can't find Azote, though, not without her real name."

Carina didn't speak for a moment. "I don't know. Azote got hit pretty hard."

"What? What happened?"

"After I shot—"

"You shot? That *was* a gunshot?"

She took a breath. "I had a gun. Just as a precaution. Hugh picked me up at work, right, and I always have a gun in my purse when I work. A tiny little one. I couldn't just leave it at Missy Massage. That's why we weren't let into Naughtyland. Because I was armed. Your bouncer, the first place he looked was my purse. When Azote attacked me—"

"You shot her!" We were whispering, but I couldn't make that sentence soft.

"No! It was in there with the tape! The gun and the tape were in my purse! I was getting the tape for Azote. I was just going to give it to her and end all this...and she saw the gun in there and we both went for it and then we fell out of the car and the thing went off! That's why the dog—"

"Yohimbe!" I'd completely forgotten about the slobbering, loyal German Shepherd.

"—got killed. I'm so sorry. The gun went off inside the purse. It disintegrated. Everything inside it disintegrated. You were spinning away and that red truck was trying to avoid the van and skidded right into Azote. Right into her. She...she got tossed a few yards. I don't know if she made it."

We were quiet for awhile. Corridor traffic flurried to the next emergency, faces drained of color by fluorescent lighting.

"She'd gone after the tape. I would have given it to her, I was giving it to her."

"It's okay. I know."

"She said she wouldn't kill us if she could just have it. She said without evidence, no one would believe the testimony of two whores."

"She was right."

"I know."

I didn't go to Azote's funeral. Her story made the paper.

"Champion of Sex Workers' Rights Dies in Car Crash." The headline dominated page one, above the fold. Underneath it was a photograph of Azote. Her straight black hair, its ends layered into points, skimmed her bare shoulder like a fan of needles. She had bangs in the photograph, a neat row tight as embroidery to her head, and her mouth and her eyebrows were slightly drawn in, as though the photographer had given her a suggestion and she was about to tell him what she thought of it. Her eyes were dredged in black liner and her lips in gloss but it wasn't enough to give an illusion. The heavy make-up only seemed ironic. Unlike a delicate flower, an obedient girl, or a love doll, Azote stared back.

Jennifer Lee, a twenty-six year old San Francisco woman known to union organizers and local sex workers as Azote, was killed late last night after being thrown out of a moving vehicle on Upper Market. She died instantly after being struck by a sport utility vehicle, according to police.

Treated and released were Hugh Devereaux of San Francisco, driver of the vehicle from which Lee was thrown, Aubrey Lyle of San Francisco, and Carina Smyth of Berkeley, for shock and minor injuries.

Lee became internationally known for her work as a labor organizer after she affiliated exotic dancers at San Francisco's Cher Cherie with the National Brotherhood of Service Workers International, Local 16. A pioneer in her field, Lee was the spearhead of the first campaign to unionize exotic dancers. Cher Cherie remains the only gentleman's club in the nation to offer union membership to its employees.

Lee, a native of San Francisco, was widely interviewed in recent years about her efforts to organize a group traditionally ignored by labor unions. A memorial service will be held tomorrow. Sam Bowden, President of Local Sixteen of the National Brotherhood of Service Workers International will give the eulogy. What follows is a reprint of an interview with Lee by Jorge Perez of the New York Times.

I didn't read the interview. The sidebar, in bold italics, read, *union organizer and part-time dominatrix Azote: a bad girl goes good.* I folded the paper and pushed it away on the kitchen table. I had a puppy in one hand and several more scrabbling at my feet since I was behind on the feeding schedule I'd taken charge of. The puppy, brindled, with a black face, paddled the air as I sucked up an eyedropper of formula for it from a Crockpot full of the stuff on the table.

Epilogue

Ten days later I had occasion to call up Sugar. A breathy young woman answered the phone at Missy Massage after half a ring.

Sugar was occupied, but didn't I want to talk to her? Her name was Candy and she was just as sweet.

I politely declined. Candy took my name and number. She'd have Sugar call me back.

It was the hottest part of the day. I lazily clicked the television channels around with the remote. Why did stupor-producing heat correspond with the time of day when nothing was on?

Hugh lay behind me, leg elevated onto the armrest. The cut from Azote's whip had been superficial but had left a scar, and Hugh favored the leg like an aging rheumatism sufferer. I bumped his feet back to make room to sit by the phone. He'd just fixed himself lunch, a stack of Pringles and a grilled cheese, and I was drinking his Coke when the phone rang. I left a Spanish soap opera on while I leaned over to get it.

"Hey," said Hugh. "I don't want to watch this program." He made clicking motions with his thumb, miming the action of the remote control that I still held in my hand. His other hand was full of puppy. With thirteen to raise, we were all full-time moms.

"Aubrey?"

"Sugar. How's business?" I handed Hugh the remote. He found a rerun of *I Love Lucy*. Ricky had Lucy cornered against their mantle and she had on the face that meant she was about to cry.

Just then Viv banged in from the kitchen, snatched the remote from Hugh and furiously punched the volume lower. She handed it back and left. She was studying for final exams and was even more intense than usual.

"Could be better. At least I'm not in jail every week. The massage parlors aren't as lucrative as the street. But it's kind of nice. They have a little altar here. It's covered in red cloth and fat little green Buddhas. They remind me of some of the customers." She laughed. "God love them. We light a lot of 'money release' candles."

"Did that check clear that I gave you?"

"Just today."

"Great." I'd thought of the perfect use for Bowden's money—funding the first sex-workers' union. "Don't spend it all in one place."

"Don't worry. Seed money for outreach. When my organization comes together, I'll put you on the board."

"I'd be honored. Anyway, good luck."

"Thanks. Listen, I think it's going to work out. I have a new partner. Experienced in union building."

"Who's that?"

"Bobby."

"Bob?"

"It was my idea. He has nothing else to do. He quit Local Sixteen, you know. He was totally traumatized by the corruption. He confronted Bowden about the bribery he'd heard on your tape, and know what Bowden told him?—that if he really wanted to experience worker solidarity he should help him get rid of the evidence! Of course Bob resigned his post then and there in moral indignation. Then Azote scared the shit out of him by locking him up in one of her cages and threatening him with god-knows-what until he gave her your address. Poor Bobby. The best part is that Bowden was so worried about what Bob might reveal that he wrote an internal memo and confessed to all the members of his union that he'd taken a bribe to keep sex workers out. Passed along a bribe, I think was how he put it."

"You're kidding. He must have consulted a spindoctor. What happened?"

"He confessed and he was absolved. He got a slap on the wrist. But in the meantime, the rank and file voted officially not to let in more sex workers. Since everyone in our business is corrupt, we tempt them to corruption, you see."

"No."

"That's their thinking."

"Unbelievable."

"Whatever. I knew it all along. That's why I'm working to create a union for sex workers only."

"Wait. How's Bob going to help you with that? What about Marx and organizing from within and being one of the workers you're organizing and all that stuff?"

Sugar laughed. "Bob's very dedicated to the labor movement, you know. He's proven he'll go to some lengths, shall we say, for the cause."

"What lengths?"

"He just started his new job at the Male Bag. He's now your fellow lapdancer." Sugar made a kissing noise and hung up.